Colleene,

THANK YOU FOR supporting my creative endeavor! Enjoy!

BRANDYWINE

THE CHICAGO TRILOGY

BRANDYWINE

THE CHICAGO TRILOGY

A WORK OF FICTION

BY

DON MISKEL

WITH ILLUSTRATIONS BY
BENJAMIN MACKEY

TRANSITION SQUARED PRESS

First Printing, 2019

ISBN# 978-1-951618-00-1
Written by Don Miskel
Cover Design by Benjamin Mackey

Publishing Imprint: Transition Squared Press
235 W Oakbrook Dr
Ann Arbor, MI 48103
TransitionSquaredPress@gmail.com
Printed in the United States of America

Publisher's Note
This is a work of fiction. Names, characters, places, and
incidents are the product of the author's imagination, or are
used ficticiously, as in the case of the city's landmarks and
police department. Any resemblance to actual persons, living
or dead, is entirely coincidental.
Beloved music is invoked by title and artist, without quoting
lyrics, and the author trusts that the reader will follow
Brandywine's lead and appreciate these fine tunes.
The novel is set in 2009~2010, Chicago, IL, USA.

For
Thelma Camilla
and
Carolyn Dolores,

two mentors who taught me that
The sky is only the beginning when you
fuel your rocket ship with imagination
to break gravity's pull
and go beyond limits.

"Blessed are the peacemakers:
for they shall be called the children of God."
- Matthew 5:9 -

"As one man can defeat ten men,
so can one thousand men defeat ten thousand.
However, you can become a master of
strategy by training alone with a sword,
so that you can understand the enemy's
stratagems, his strength and resources,
and come to appreciate how to apply strategy
to beat ten thousand enemies."
- The Book of Five Rings -

Contents

Contents page 2

Guide to Illustrations

Story I

Sulfuric

Triangulated on the suspect, my partner and I had reached a stalemate. Holding my pistol steady, the front sight appearing between the dovetailed rear, I was mirrored by Sergeant Perry on the other side of the classroom—and it dawned on me that I had never faced a situation quite like this before. Sure, back in Afghanistan, my life had often been threatened, from the air and from the roadside, from the enemy—and sometimes even from our own forces—as every troop knows, friendly fire is just as deadly as a criminal's bullets.

The perp didn't have a gun, but there was nothing friendly about him. This nimrod had chosen a completely different kind of weapon—a flask of acid. Dr. Maurice Bolduc clutched his wife Shauna against his concave chest with his left arm while his right held a flask of clear liquid inches from her horrified face.

"Don't move, slut," he hissed in a semi-effeminate voice. Had the situation been different, I would have laughed; he was clearly one of those egghead intellectual types. Without his current weapon of choice, he was about as threatening as. . .well, let's just say he couldn't bust a grape with a push-button sledgehammer. And, considering the beautiful woman he held captive, I guessed I'd hit upon the problem.

"Maurice, think about what you're doing," she cried, tears glistening on her cheeks. "You are over-reacting!" She twisted neck around to face him.

From my vantage point, I could see tears form in the unhappy husband's eyes as he locked gaze with his wife, and I recognized a look of love on his anguished face. A lump formed in my throat when he leaned forward just an inch or so and buried his nose in her voluptuous honey-colored hair.

Aw man, that's sad, I thought, never letting my gun waver.

"Ew, what are you doing?" she said, jerking her head away with a shudder.

Bolduc immediately straightened up, hurt showing on his face. "How could you? After all I've done for you?" he whined. "I still remember the first time I ever laid eyes on you. First day of class, back—what? Nearly ten years ago," he said, a faraway look in his eyes like he was seeing her again for the first time.

Mrs. Bolduc's futile attempts to escape made the acid jiggle and foam, setting off her screams. Listening to him, she stopped struggling and grew quiet.

"Remember, Shauna? You said it was love at first sight for you, too!"

She turned her face away from him and her long hair hung down, partially obscuring her beautiful face, while the professor maintained his hold on her. Using both my outstretched arms, I held steady, looking for my chance to intervene as the jilted husband turned down memory lane.

11

Bolduc was at least fifteen years her elder and they looked to be from entirely different worlds. I would later find out that he'd earned a PhD in biochemistry when he was just 22 years old—graduated from this very same university. While other folks that age were more concerned with dating and frat parties, he'd been handpicked to join the same department that he currently led, beginning as a lab rat.

I stress the "currently" part because, if Bolduc survived this incident to be led away in cuffs, surely these prestigious halls of higher learning would be handing him walking papers before morning. Which amped up the possibility of this turning into a suicide-by-cop scenario, and a messy one at that. Luckily, it was semester break, or we could have been dealing with an entire classroom full of on lookers and potential victims.

Love crimes beat hate crimes hands down for drama. People tend to suspect, fear, and loathe their significant others a lot more than they do the Nazi Party, the Crimson Jihad, or whatever other terrorist group is occupying the news headlines that week. History reveals a long and sordid catalog of folks doing some rather awful things while claiming love for their god, their country, an ideology, or another person. Jealousy comes as naturally as breathing, and every boy, young or not, wants to keep his toys exclusive to himself.

"I'm really sorry it had to come to this, Maurice," she said, letting a little softness creep into her voice.

"Then let's just go home, sweetheart. Forget the whole thing," he wheedled, though he continued to brandish the acid near her face. "Let these nice policemen get back to work…"

"You know it won't be like that," she said with an edge. My ears played ping-pong as the two quarreled.

Even though Shauna Bolduc's pretty, collagen-injected face was twisted into a mask of anticipated anguish, her husband's mug was etched much deeper with pain. I didn't have to wonder what this was all about. Awards, accolades, and fellowships do not a great lover make.

Maybe she was a gold-digging student, or she saw him as an academic idol. He took her home for private "study sessions" and, voila! They were soon married. His paycheck funded her tummy tuck, boob job, and anything else that might take her a step closer to perfection—for his benefit, or for hers? It was impossible to know. She wanted hubby's attention, but he was always off playing Lord of the Lab Rats, getting published in scientific journals, traveling the lecture circuit, and signing autographs for his thickly bespectacled fan base.

Meanwhile, wifey was burning up on a bed of lust.

Even when the good doctor was home, his passion was science rather than the art of painting on his wife's beautiful canvas. That could only go on for so long before she sought attention elsewhere. Yeah, I'd seen it a thousand times before.

"A man isn't meant to live alone," continued the professor, pulling his wife even closer.

"People get divorced every day—take it like the man you claim to be," she said, her tone void of compassion. I winced, in spite of myself.

Bolduc tilted the tube a fraction, to which Perry growled a command. Shauna flinched and her wild sobbing rose a few decibels.

"Give me one good reason," the professor shouted, seething, hair wild—he truly looked like the stereotypical mad scientist at that moment—"one reason why I shouldn't burn off this harlot's pretty little face!"

"I'll give you a reason," I said through clenched teeth, "my partner is surgical with that piece of steel—a decorated combat Marine. I've earned my ribbons and medals, too. Dr. Bolduc, we don't want to shoot you. So please, pretty please, gently place that container on the table next to you or this is going to get messy."

"Yeah," Perry's deep voice was calm, ". . . and we don't

want that."

There was no good cop/bad cop dynamic between my partner and me. We were both bad, offering no quarter for those who ran afoul to the point of putting other people's lives in danger. We weren't into coddling. They paid other people to do that.

"I want to talk to someone else," the professor countered. "Call your boss or a hostage negotiator."

"Already en route," Perry mumbled, his hands and eye steady on the target.

"Nothing much to negotiate, Professor," I chimed in. "We're here to stop you from making a huge mistake. It's not too late. You don't want to hurt this little lady. Whatever she's done, you two can talk, maybe work things out."

"No! I tried. I tried so hard," he wept, shuddering. "Anything she wanted, no matter how expensive or ridiculous, I provided it. Lavish gym memberships, shopping trips to the Magnificent Mile every week at least, and her with her daily kale smoothies. Anything she wanted," sobbed the hapless professor.

I wrinkled my nose at the thought of having to drink a kale smoothie every day.

"I cut back my work hours. Cancelled seminars. Passed on projects. Even went to counseling. She just doesn't . . ." Here his voice broke and I watched the flask tremble while he maintained his grip on the struggling woman, ". . . love me anymore," he finally choked out.

"You call that trying?" she sneered, and I marveled at her temerity under the circumstances. Then she made it a whole lot worse. "Don't fool yourself, Maurice. It was never about love. Just accept that we're over and go away."

"You'd like that, wouldn't you? Me just disappear so you could be with your busker boyfriend every night."

"He's not . . ." Shauna began but he cut her off.

"She's a whore," he snapped, addressing me. "Screwing all my colleagues wasn't good enough for her, she had to take it to the streets."

That was the extent of my kid glove approach. I looked him in the eye. "Do what we tell you to do and you can both come out of this alive."

The suspect's eyelids fluttered, realizing the gravity of the situation. "You know, if you shoot me," he commented, sounding quite confident all of a sudden, "by reflexive action, I'll end up dropping this acid on my whelp of a wife anyway. Do you want to live with the memory of watching her flesh burn down to her skull?"

I wasn't so proud to admit that I'd seen worse. I held my tongue in check and maintained professionalism.

Unspoken smart-ass retorts aside, Bolduc had a good point. The acid was a liquid medium and therefore, unpredictable as hell. A hollow point between the eyes would snap his head back and there was no guarantee what would happen. The force would carry him backward, causing the caustic fluid to splash on the counter and cabinets behind him. Maybe the tube would tilt those remaining few degrees, anointing his wife's head and face anyway. Or, even still, he might drop it, sending the splash our way. I wasn't interested in getting burned or disfigured.

Perry's cheek twitched, signaling that his irritation and impatience had reached an apex. That was about the point where folks went from alive and kicking one minute, to being zipped up in a body bag the next. The professor theorized everything from an intellectual angle; not realizing my partner wasn't that deep a thinker. Once Perry locked in on target, he couldn't care less which way the acid fell.

"Relax," I told Perry without looking in his direction. I heard him exhale, which offered a brief window in which to reason with the over-educated clown before putting a cap in his ass.

"Okay, Professor, you've got a point."

He smiled and nodded, confident in his perceived upper

hand. Over confident, actually, because he didn't know that his smug attitude meant nothing to men who'd made their bones dodging bullets in combat zones on other continents.

"We're at an impasse," Bolduc stated, as if he were teaching a lesson. Then, he called on me, "What do we do now, Detective?"

"Let's slow things down a tick," I said, lowering my sights and bringing the weapon, still pointed at him, to my waist. I could still discharge rounds just as effectively. Sarge never lowered his piece. The suspect was as good as dead if we willed it so.

I was an avid chess player and had no tolerance for the politics of war. I identified with the knight more than any other piece on the board. Like the Trojan horse, I could be overlooked and underestimated, a sudden perpendicular move often baffling my opponent.

A Navy man to the core, my standing order was to nullify the enemy, not to hold conversations, make promises, or concessions. That was why military officers and police hostage negotiators got paid the big bucks. When I'd returned home to work once again with Chicago's Finest, shedding the camouflage uniform for a suit-and-tie promotion in the Investigations Bureau, my basic thought process—acquired on the street and in the desert—remained the same. Though intricately carved and presented, my job was simple.

"Put down your weapons," Bolduc demanded.

"Nothin' doing," I heard from my periphery. "No can do, Doc."

"If you don't," the professor warned, his tone menacing. "I'll douse both you and her."

Mrs. Bolduc whimpered, "Please, Maurice!"

"Yes, please Maurice," I echoed sarcastically. I was getting tired of this dude.

He was unaffected. "Have you ever seen what sulfuric acid does to unprotected skin?" He leveled his eyes in my direction, glanced at Perry, then settled back on me, trying to engage and interest his audience. "In short order, there's an instantaneous dehydration of dermis and muscle tissue, burning beyond belief. The corrosive process is so severe that even water won't initially stop it."

He paused his dissertation, smiled, and turned his attention to his wife, who'd begun sobbing again. "And no amount of plastic surgery will fix that, my dear. Do you think the acid will eat through the silicone implants I paid for?" he taunted.

Though she may have played around, Shauna Bolduc didn't deserve this. Even if the dousing didn't kill her, it would leave her a circus freak for the rest of her life.

"Again, I urge you to put down your weapons, inspectors."

I said nothing, returning my firearm to eye level, lining up the front sight neatly with the rear one. Even with his wife close to him, my shot would hit him square between the cheek and nose. He might sling the acid, drop it, or fall back with it. By that time, I wouldn't care.

She cringed, watching me. He smiled.

I switched from Isosceles to a Modified Weaver stance, reducing my profile and giving Bolduc less of a target at which to throw his container of acid. *If it came to that.*

I took in air through my nose, exhaling through pursed lips, consciously slowing my breathing and heart rate. The steel was heavy in my hands, but my will to hold it on target superseded any discomfort I was beginning to feel. I hoped Maurice Bolduc had made his peace.

Shauna's eyes were still wide, desperate, and . . . beautiful. It occurred to me briefly why he'd made her his wife. She was stunningly pretty with flowing blonde hair. Her breasts were more than ample, and she had all the right bumps and curves.

Unfaithful or not, she didn't deserve to die or leave this room misshapen and scorched.

"Dr. Maurice Bolduc," I bellowed suddenly, the volume

surprising me, "Do not tilt that flask any further!"

Fortifying his stance, Perry mumbled "fuckin' milk toast."

"Place the liquid gently on the counter to your left, release your wife, and put your hands in the air!" I boomed. "I won't say it again."

Shauna had been quiet for a few moments, but my command seemed to embolden her. Laced with venom, her low voice may have carried enough weight to tip the scale as she relayed her feelings to her husband. Zoned onto my target, I only caught three key words: "never," "failure," and "impotent."

When she finished her invective, a complete hush fell over the room, the only sound being the hum of the air conditioner.

One massive sob escaped from the professor, and then his eyebrows dropped and his face hardened.

I had made my decision.

The professor looked me in the eye and winked.

The woman abruptly came flying toward me in slow motion. Her mouth was open in a scream I couldn't hear. Her husband had given her a solid shove in the back.

I sidestepped with the grace of a matador, my pistol reacquiring Bolduc at the sternum. *Ole!*

If he even looked like he was going to launch the acid in my direction, he would get two to the chest and one to the head before a drop could touch me.

Perry's finger was already in the trigger guard, applying pressure, but he never got off the shot.

Nor did I.

Bolduc opened his mouth wide, tilted the glass container, and poured the contents into his throat.

Audio exclusion or not, I heard his gurgling howl loud and clear; the wail emitted from a man with a disintegrating connection between his chin and his neck. His cheeks hollowed immediately, his nose and lips dissolving in an acrid cloud, melting his face and jaw.

He fell backward to the floor, writhing and kicking, the remaining fluid baptizing what was left of his head. As the substance ate through his Adam's apple and vocal cords, the screams devolved to a saturated hiss.

Perry got on the horn, instinctively demanding the dispatcher send an ambulance. I hadn't even thought to make the call, completely mesmerized at the horrific sight of the Incredible Melting Man.

The professor's body jerked reflexively for several minutes while we waited for the paramedics to make it up to the third deck. There was no way I was going to attempt first aid.

A putrid haze hung in the air. We had to step out of the room just to breathe.

A couple of firemen worked with Shauna Bolduc just outside the scene. They were careful to keep her attention away from what had been her husband. A reddened knot on her forehead grew into a goose egg, but it was a blessing. Not a single drop of acid had touched her pretty face. The wound would heal, and her mascara-streaked eyes would return to normal. And, though destined to be beautiful again, I wondered about the condition of her soul and the emotional scars she would carry forever.

"Sorry for your loss," I mumbled, all but avoiding her gaze, as I filed out after my partner. We had a memorandum of agreement with the university cops, so the investigation would belong to the city. Because Perry and I had been directly involved, the processing of the crime scene was turned over to Vargas and Mellon.

"Good one, Brandy," Vargas said, jabbing me in the side. Both investigators walked over to take a peek between the lab tables at the steaming remains of the doctor's final science project. Mellon turned as green as his name suggested; later, we'd have to give him shit for getting sick on the scene.

Captain Kodjoe showed up, asked a few questions, then told us to head back to the station for official statements and debriefing.

Loved those.

"Hey, at least we didn't fire off any rounds, Cap'n" Perry said, cheesing from behind that thick mustache of his. He looked like a washed-up porn star whose heyday had passed twenty years earlier.

Kodjoe frowned. "That's this time. Back to the office, you two."

"10-4," I replied, nudging the sergeant to roll without complaint.

* * *

A steady breeze came off Lake Michigan, but it wasn't cold. Felt good to be outside breathing fresh air.

We walked across the campus lawn in silence. I can't speak for my partner, but I was trying hard to "un-see"what we'd just witnessed. I'd watched plenty of people die but had never seen one disintegrate into a mess fit for a horror movie. Realizing the image was going to haunt me in nightmares, I swore to return to the VA Hospital for those PTSD sessions my therapist had suggested.

We reached our unmarked unit and began that dance we always did since first being assigned together. Each of us held keys in hand, heading toward the driver's seat, looking at the other with raised eyebrows. Our body language argument turned into a mishmash of "I'll drive - No, it's my turn- It's okay - I'm right here - Me, too."

I always relented without a fuss, and did so this time too, giving my senior partner a pass—which really meant— letting him choose the music.

Climbing into the passenger seat, I braced myself for the inevitable and waited for the likes of Hank Williams or Kenny Rogers to issue from the radio.

As we left the campus, passing the DuSable Museum, I was pleased to hear the introductory narration followed by the sparse guitar of John Lee Hooker's "It Serves Me Right to Suffer", *a Blues classic.*

I glanced over at Perry, but he made no move to change the channel. I let myself enjoy the song, though it may have been more appropriate for the broken-hearted professor, but then, maybe not. Love makes no sense, causing the most intelligent people to do the stupidest things.

"That work for you?" asked Sarge, waiting till after the last strum to click off the radio.

Rolling south on Lake Shore Drive, with the Museum of Science and Industry passing by in a blur on my right, I side-eyed my partner, wondering if this was heading toward some kind of a confrontation. Truth be told, I wasn't really sure where I stood with the veteran investigator, and now was as good a day as any to find out. By then, we'd been partners for three months, through the call to the university had been our most unique event to date.

I mentally reviewed my actions at the scene. Flawless, unless I was missing something. He couldn't have any gripes with my performance.

As a newly minted detective, I was automatically an outsider. I'd put in my years on the streets before being mobilized to Afghanistan, as was my obligation as a Navy Reservist. Maybe not everyone agreed with my promotion shortly after my return to the department, despite my specialized military training. Adding to that, with my father's historic struggles with alcohol, I wasn't all that interested in spending off-duty time knocking back beers with my fellow dicks at the local watering hole.

That put Perry and I in a strange place.

There was a definite disconnect. While I was raised in the inner city, he came up on a farm in rural Wisconsin; I was a squid and he was a jarhead; I liked the Bears and the Sox, while he rooted for the Packers and the Cubs...I could go on and on.

The crags in his leathery face and the played-out mustache told me he was a relic of a bygone era. Tall, gruff, and with a propensity to wear shit-kicker cowboy boots—even in the summer, he had almost as much time on the force as I had been alive. Everything in his demeanor was passingly cordial at best, if you counted the occasional grunt in response to a question. In the military, we would say Sarge was on his twilight tour—his last hurray before retirement. I tried to see it from his point. What the heck did he need with some snot-nosed junior partner at this juncture?

"Sure, I like it a lot," I said. "I respect the classic stuff." My father used to play Blues on Saturday nights, and John Lee Hooker was one of his favorites.

"Define classic," he growled, his bushy eyebrows already knitted on his prominent forehead. "Name some artists."

I had just begun to rattle off a short list that included Grandmaster Flash and Rakim but my partner was already shaking his head with a frown. I hadn't even gotten to Run DMC, a band he probably would have heard of.

"That ain't music," he stated with a dismissive wave of his hand. "We're not listening to that—*stuff*—while we ride."

I guessed the word he'd nearly used to refer to my choice of music was "shit," though he'd all but bitten off his tongue in order to *not* say it. I wanted to ask what kind of *shit* he listened to, but figured it would be counterproductive.

"Well, Sergeant," I said, barely able to control my temper. I fully understood how the chain of command worked but and I was not one for playing shy. I had gotten used to kicking in doors in hot zones, but I had also learned to work with just about anyone, no matter how obtuse. I took a deep breath. "What kind of music would you suggest that we might both enjoy?"

He named some artists, most of whom I'd heard and a handful I never had. The compromise came when I admitted that I'd grown up with my dad playing records by the Doobies and the Eagles. He wasn't expecting that.

"Favorite song by them?"

I assumed he meant the latter. "I guess it would be a toss-up between 'One of These Nights' and 'Take it Easy' for the Eagles; 'You Belong to Me' hands-down for the Doobies though."

Perry grinned at the second cut I named by the first group, probably because it had a strong country feel. I was waiting for him to protest that Michael McDonald had all but killed the Doobies' original sound—which was more akin to Blues—for something smoothed-out and closer to Soul. Surprisingly, Sarge shelved that argument for another time, but I'd be ready when he wanted to debate it.

"However," I added, "though he was a late addition to the group, I'd be a fool not to mention Timothy B. Schmit's lead vocals on 'I Can't Tell You Why.' Now, that song was so cool, it even got play on the R&B stations."

He nodded, gave a gravelly grunt, punched the radio knob and fiddled with it as he drove. I sighed and looked out the window at the passing city.

In a moment came the sultry sound of the saxophone, giving way to Bob Seger soulfully leading "Turn the Page."

"Alright, partner?" he asked.

"Hell yeah." I let down the window and savored the lilting notes along with the breeze as we took the long way back to the precinct. We'd found our classic channel, and maybe our common language. I nodded my head in time with the cadence of the drum, considering that maybe partnering with Sarge wouldn't be as bad as I'd initially assumed.

The End

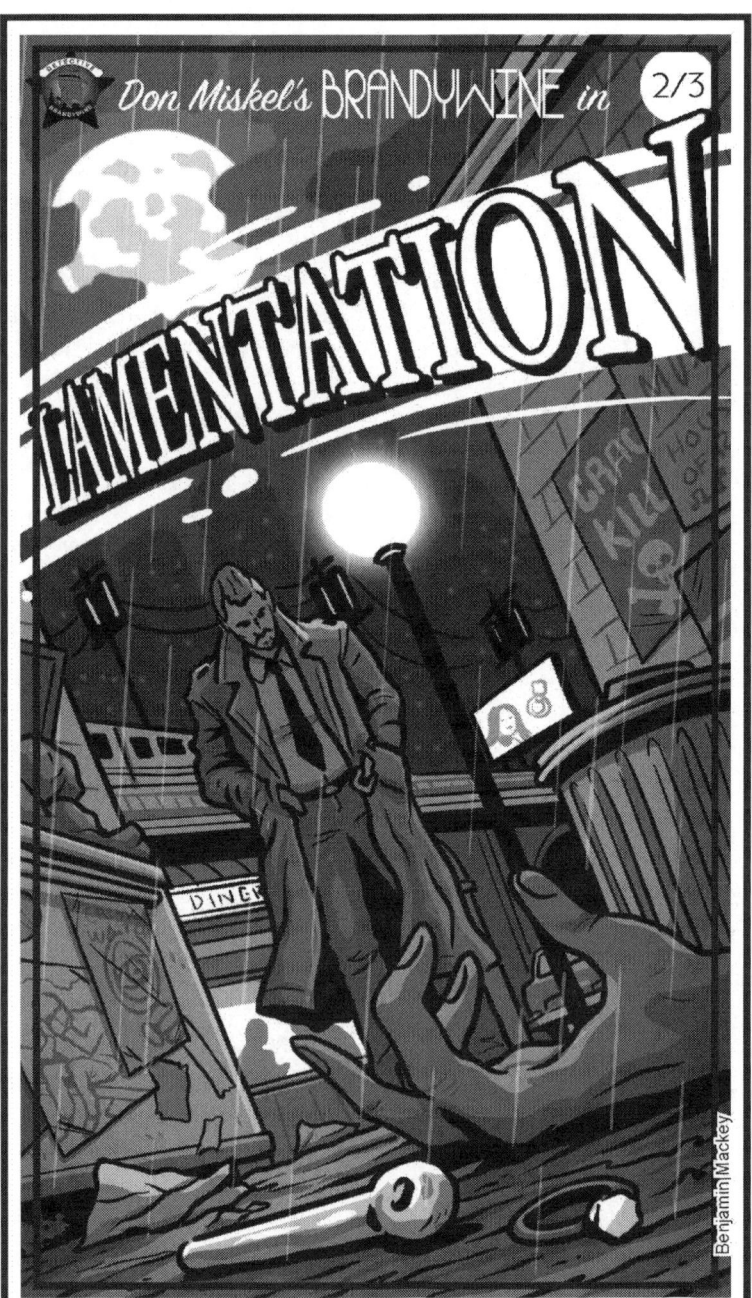

Story II

Lamentation

Chapter 1

The saddest were the young. A kid chases a ball and gets hit by a car—or a bullet. A toddler who never had a chance gets left in a van with the heat index scraping triple digits. A teen just trying to live makes the wrong friend.

And then there are the "unattended transitions" we have to prove—or disprove—as suicide. Summer was barely over and I had already seen far too much death.

No matter how callous the average detective might seem to the casual observer, only a cold-hearted bastard could fail to be moved by the pileup of corpses. I never allowed myself to get used to it—not in the war zone overseas;

and not in the one much closer to home—the streets of my hometown. It was an epidemic of lost youth—which might sound romantic when uttered by a coffee house poet, except for the sobering reality that the subjects were all dead.

It was true what they said about the murder rate correlating with the rise and fall in temperature. Every winter, a deep freeze held the city in its frigid grip from Christmas till after the Chicago River ran green for St. Pat's. It was the only time the body count seemed to let up a little, though the dead weren't above lurking under the winter snow and ice, postponing their discovery till the thaw.

When the concrete jungle warmed and the flowers blossomed through cracks in the sidewalk, the Grim Reaper shook the dust off his robe and got back to business—and baby, during the hottest days of the year, business was a-boomin'. Now, as school had started, and the mercury begun to descend, we would hopefully see a decrease in brokenhearted mothers wailing over children caught in the wrong place at the wrong time.

My stomach churned a bit when we got the call. While taking time to finish up his hoagie, Perry assured me that the feeling would eventually pass. "Nothing short of Armageddon stops lunch," he mumbled, breadcrumbs sprinkled throughout his mustache.

I wanted to rush to the scene of the crime—a holdover urge from my prior assignment to Patrol Division—as if a speedy arrival could reverse what awaited us. But I was no longer a first responder; my captain already gave me *that* speech when I first reported to Investigations a few months back. Our job was to pick up the pieces and assemble them into some understandable order that would support us nabbing the culprits.

"Gonna finish that?" Sarge asked. He'd already killed off his own sandwich and laid his kosher pickle to rest, but that obviously wasn't enough.

My poor Italian beef, with only a single bite taken, sat neglected, sidling up to a small hill of kettle-cooked chips. Despite my lost appetite, I wasn't ready to give it up. Canting my head with a frown, I gave Perry a ridiculous look. "I'll just bag it and eat it later, if you don't mind, kind sir."

The elder investigator shrugged his broad shoulders and wiped his mouth with his napkin. As massive and barrel-chested as he was, he suddenly seemed a deflated little kid who'd been told to stand in the corner.

"Oh," he said, just shy of sucking his teeth. He took a final swig from his root beer can, crumpled it in one huge paw, stifled a belch, and stood up. "I guess we'd better bounce, then."

A notorious street gang, which went by the moniker "The Devoted and Quoted Players" (or DQP for short), was making its mark on the South Side. The call concerned a skirmish between the DQP and members of a rival set—most likely the Sherman Park Hustlers—at the 55th Street Dan Ryan station. It was a busy transit hub, with a bus stop on the street above, and a train running right down the middle of the expressway below. Plenty of traffic meant the potential for multiple victims.

A young mother had sustained injury while trying to protect her infant during the clash of the two gangs. The death toll was two: one by gunfire and another from a beat-down when the victim had tried to run. I was proud to hear that several citizens had overwhelmed the gunman—a DQP called Grimy—and held him down until the first police units arrived.

Raymond Gibbons, aka "Roach," would be listed as a victim, and in many ways he was, though everything about him, from his tats to his rap sheet, said he'd been banging for years. His orange t-shirt was soaked in blood. He'd caught a round in the sternum. Had the bullet been a smaller caliber, he may have stood a chance. However, the .45 slug was large enough and traveled just slow enough to deliver the equivalent of a point-blank mule kick. Though the coroner's office had the final say, I figured he was a goner as soon as the lead cracked his chest plate.

Though clad in the attire of a DQP, Theodore Shelton, the second of the deceased, reminded me more of a schoolboy than a street hoodlum. Lacking proper guidance, so many young men of color made the mistake of believing all that thug-life bullshit portrayed by their homeboys and the media. The teen had fallen in with the wrong crowd and paid the price. There were no tattoos on his arms, his exposed legs or his hairless chest—bared in a futile attempt at CPR. The baby-faced prospect had been kicked and pummeled to death. The Hustlers' preference for steel-toed boots meant that the trauma to the victim's head was particularly gruesome. With EMTs unsuccessful at reviving young Shelton's bruised and broken body, he was unceremoniously loaded into the wagon along with the dead member of the rival gang.

Amazing how these two warriors from rival tribes could be quietly carted off together without so much as a peep between them. Their days of yelling threats, throwing gang signs, and battling over turf were gone forever.

I felt a heavy mitt clasp my shoulder. It was my partner. "You okay?"

"This stuff always bugs me, man."

"You'll harden to it enough to do the job but don't get too used to it. 'Cause then it'll warp your outlook and you'll end up a jaded curmudgeon like the old man," he said, apparently referring to himself.

I watched the meat truck pull off with the two bagged bodies. An ambulance had already taken the wounded mom to a nearby hospital for treatment. I sighed. "How do you wanna break this up, Sarge?"

"I'll take the Hustlers and you take the Players."

"And the witnesses?"

"I'll get the folks who were at ground zero; you take the peripherals."

"10-4," I told him and headed toward the train station entrance, while he focused on the immediate area of the bus stop. Witnesses are key, particularly when the crime takes place in broad daylight. I collected several names and numbers but was drawn to a teenager who sat sobbing on the curb. Had he been in the same spot when the melee broke out, he would have had the best vantage point to see everything that went down. I introduced myself and prepared to take a quick statement.

"You're understandably upset by what you saw," I said.

The young man, whom I would come to know as Carlos Davis, Jr., surprised me by saying he knew both DQP members personally. There was nothing about his clothing or manner that denoted gang affiliation. He was just a kid from the community who happened to be heading for the train. I would run his information, as was standard practice, but I knew that not every neighborhood kid was a thug.

Later, going over what we'd collected before heading back to the car, I asked Perry if the families of the deceased had been notified.

"Nope," he said, stifling a yawn.

"Sleepy?"

"Yep. For me, that usually follows eating a lot of red meat. I should be somewhere digesting instead of messin' around with cadavers and witnesses." He paused, stretching. A sly grin came to his face. "Speaking of food, what about that sandwich you didn't finish?"

Perry had seen some rather heinous crime scenes over the years. Like most hardened cops, he'd worked out a way to lighten the mood with comedic quips.

"Sarge, if you even think about touching my Italian beef, the paramedics will be treating you for a bite injury!"

"Brother, don't even joke about that shit," he said with a laugh. On our way to the car, he told me about the huge hassle he went through following an incident when both a man *and his dog* actually did bite him. Of course, he made sure to over-exaggerate the gore, giggling while explaining the horror of receiving a series of rabies shots to the stomach.

Chapter 2

Theodore Shelton lived only a few blocks from the bus stop where his fate was sealed. Unlike on TV shows, we did not draw white chalk outlines around corpses. It would have been difficult anyway, as the victim had met his demise on the nearby grassy boulevard. From what we could gather, he was run down by three Hustlers.

Being kicked and stomped to death was a terrible way to go. I had to inform his folks without divulging too many painful details. Though I could have made the notification by phone, inviting his parents down to the morgue to identify the body, it was so impersonal. I felt compelled to go "old school" and break the sad news face-to-face.

The apartment was located on the top floor of a three-story walk-up. Perry trailed behind, determined for me to take point. Sounds of life emanated from each domicile, with people conversing and televisions droning. A dog was barking, followed by a woman's hollered demand that someone "take that mutt for a walk".

My partner took up position on the landing between the second and third floors so the person opening the door could see him beyond me. Typically, when serving a high-risk warrant, we would have weapons drawn, and be sure to stand to the side of the door. Tactically, windows, doorways, and staircases were considered fatal funnels of fire. What I'd learned in the military was reiterated in my police training. Though there shouldn't have been any danger, I habitually stepped to the right of the door and bladed my body, making myself a smaller target.

I leaned into the recessed doorway, taking a moment to listen. A familiar tune came from deep inside the house, a woman's muffled voice sang along, accompanied by the sound of squeaking floorboards. She was dancing to the music, oblivious to the news I bore. I tapped politely on the door, trying to place where I'd heard that music before, even as she was turning it down.

"Use your key, Theo," the lady inside yelled.

I cleared my throat and loudly stated, "Police, ma'am. May we have a word?"

The creaking of floorboards grew louder, announcing her approach. One lock turned, followed by another, before the door came open. Two things greeted me: the sumptuous aroma of dinner on the stove, and the ample-sized, brown-skinned woman of indeterminate age who'd cooked it. She tossed a towel over her shoulder and stood akimbo. "How may I help you?"

"Madam, my name is Detective Brandywine . . ." Though her expression was weary, her eyes were lovely.

She'd probably been a real looker several years and a few pounds ago. She rolled her eyes and her lips down-turned. "What's he done, now?" she asked.

"Ma'am?" I was thrown off.

"You need to hurry up. I have food on the stove."

"May we come in," Perry asked from the staircase. I had fumbled the ball and he saw a way to keep it in play.

"Please do," she said hurriedly, stepping away from the entrance, and rushing back toward the kitchen.

There was no reason to suspect that she would come back with a steak knife in hand but I remained alert, as I was trained to do. Perry stood behind me in the foyer, and pushed the door closed for the sake of privacy. I could smell collard greens and the unmistakable scent of crusty cornbread wafting through the air. Glancing about the room, I noticed a slightly faded photo of a younger version of the woman with two young children in her arms. There was also the requisite image of Christ opening his robe to reveal his thorn-pricked heart. It hung a few feet above a desk with an open Bible. I recalled a similar setup from my own childhood.

"Sorry for being rude, officers," she said, tossing the towel over her shoulder again, and wiping her hands on the apron she wore over a blue flowered house dress. "I'm in the middle of making dinner for my son. I hope to God Theo hasn't gotten into any trouble."

"Mrs…"

"Miss Shelton. Valerie Shelton," she corrected. "You can call me Val."

"Valerie," I said somberly, "We have some bad news."

Everything that had been beautiful about Valerie Shelton drained from her face in that moment. Her eyebrows lifted before the question had the chance to cross her lips. "Noooo," she said, shaking her head. Her eyes grew glassy and red. When she tried to talk, her throat was full of mucus. "Good Lord, nooooo!"

While Perry was a veteran when it came to this grim duty, I was so busy watching her facial expressions, that I failed to notice when her knees suddenly buckled.

"Brandy!"

I responded, instantaneously grabbing her arm before she could collapse. In a smooth movement, I directed her to the living room sofa. The heartbroken mother's face was upturned and suddenly relaxed, her wailing stopped with her losing consciousness.

"Val," I said, patting her hand. "Valerie." She didn't budge. I grabbed her wrist and found her pulse.

"Is anyone else here?" Perry bellowed. When nobody responded, he said he was going to the kitchen to take the food off the eyes of the stove. I hadn't even thought about that, but it made perfect sense. After the news we'd brought, she would likely forget all about dinner, allowing the contents of the pots and pans to burn until the place caught fire.

My partner emerged from the back of the house with a tumbler of water, which is something else I wouldn't have considered.

She came to with a gasp and sat up, looking about the room at Perry and me, probably wishing she'd only had a bad dream.

"Who...what?"

On my knee next to the sofa, I removed my hand from her radial pulse. I rose enough to sit on an ottoman, while maintaining eye contact. "Theodore is gone, ma'am. I'm so sorry."

Valerie doubled over, crossing her arms, trying to embrace and comfort herself. She rocked and cried so intensely, I thought she'd pass out again from shortness of breath, but she didn't. We were silent, allowing her to grieve.

"He was just here this morning," she said, looking desperately from me to Perry and back. She was hoping she could reason with us, as if we, the heralds of death, had the power to turn back the clock. I looked down, feeling helpless.

My partner asked if we could call someone for her, but she shook her head.

"Was Theodore involved in the neighborhood gang?" Perry asked softly. He handed her the water.

She took a sip and nodded. "I-I told him to stop trying to be street tough. That wasn't Theo. He was a sweet boy! He was *my* boy," she exclaimed, and then her eyes narrowed at Perry. "Why would you ask me something like that?!!"

She launched the tumbler across the room. Her wrath was directed at my partner, who didn't flinch as the cup flew over his right shoulder, splashing water onto his shirt. That's when I noticed that he'd chosen a plastic cup instead of a glass. Baptizing him thus, the vessel bounced impotently off the adjacent wall.

Despite his gruff, cantankerous manner, I was learning

all sorts of things from my partner that I wouldn't find in a book. "Ma'am," he said evenly, "We need you to calm down. It's a standard question because Theodore was the victim of what appears to be gang violence."

She burst into tears again, telling us her oldest son was already doing a bid for getting involved with the DQP. With their father absent from their lives, she could do little to keep her boys out of trouble. "I thought taking them to church would keep them out of those damn streets," she exclaimed.

The timbre of her voice was laced with the realization of betrayal. She'd loved her God and had done everything she knew to keep her family on the straight-and-narrow, but it didn't work. With no husband, an incarcerated older son, and her baby murdered, she lost hope. The wounded ululation was the sound of her heart rending.

Her head was turned, and she was sobbing softly when I stooped to place my business card on her coffee table.

Her hands rubbed up and down the backs of her arms. I wished I could hold her but it wasn't my place. I wanted to assure her that everything would be all right but I couldn't lie to her. She didn't even react when I whispered that she would have to come down to the coroner's officer to positively identify Theodore's body. I apologized again and we let ourselves out. I felt like shit lumbering away from her apartment and back down the stairs.

"Glad I didn't send you in there by your lonesome," Perry said when we were sitting in the cruiser.

"So am I. Thanks."

Chapter 3

Some people meditate. Some self-medicate. I work out. It gives me a chance to gather and prioritize random thoughts. It allows me time to ponder life and death, faith and the lack thereof. Sometimes it helps me forget.

I figured that producing some sweat equity would clear my head so maybe I could sleep that night. Though I typically make full use of my health club membership, I didn't much feel like being around anyone after the horrors of the day, especially that last heartbreaking task.

The door to the precinct's tiny exercise room squeaked on its hinges, a harbinger to the dust-covered, all-but-forgotten setup inside. Rumor had it the mismatched gaggle of dented, dinged, and damaged equipment was all cast off from other city departments. Half-rusted and needing repairs, most of it probably should have been carted out and set next to the dumpster for bulky item pick-up. A boxy, defunct television hung from a bracket overhead; it qualified as the most high-tech accoutrement in the space.

Perusing the dankness, I identified the basics of what I'd need for my workout: an elliptical machine, a treadmill, and some free weights. A stationary bicycle would've made a nice alternative. There were two—one with a missing seat, making it a cruel ride indeed, and the other sporting a handwritten sign taped to its handlebars, declaring it was out of commission. And no, the seats weren't interchangeable.

Despite possessing all the charm and feng shui of a Gulag dungeon, the primary benefit to this spot was the isolation it offered. Most cops had enough sense to vacate the premises after their shifts. There was little chance of being disturbed here.

My ear buds were plugged into my phone, granting me access to a mix of songs to keep me pumped during my sessions. With my Old School Hip Hop, Classic Rock, R&B, and Funk favorites in rotation, I would be able to take my mind off the current investigation. Of all the music genres, I was a self-declared funkateer, preferring to hum along with the likes of the P-Funk All-Stars, James Brown, the Time, and the Elements—better known as Earth, Wind & Fire. However, that evening I was in no mood to try to mimic Maurice White's baritone or Phillip Bailey's soaring falsetto.

'No matter what the family says, this ain't yer fault,' I heard Sergeant Perry's voice echo from earlier when we'd climbed the pissy, malt-liquor-stained staircase to Valerie's house. I recalled how her apartment had seemed like a pristine oasis in comparison to the rest of the building and the neighborhood. She kept it tidy, trying to maintain a safe place for her family. But, somehow, the grime from the outside had crept in. I cranked the music, trying to drown out the despair I saw in her face when I brought the news that her baby was dead.

I focused on my playlist, Philippé Wynne's voice front-and-center in a playful tune entitled "Uncle Jam." Like a lightning bolt, my mind jumped to the Chicago connection. Wynne had come to fame performing with the Spinners, who'd achieved notoriety under the production and guidance of Gamble & Huff, a duo responsible for what was known as Philadelphia Soul. Many artists came to them to define their sound, including Teddy Pendergrass and the Windy City's own Lou Rawls.

Even on full tilt, my ear buds seemed to whisper, their

maximum volume overridden by my thoughts. It was one of Rawls's hits that Valerie had been playing while making dinner for a son who would never return home. As she crafted a culinary masterpiece, Lou's deep voice declared his woman would never find a love like his. I used to laugh at the song as a kid, considering the music sounded like something from a hotel lounge instead of topping the R&B charts of the time. Melancholy settled over me, adding unwelcome weight to my bench press.

Rawls had grown up in the Ida B. Wells Homes, a former, rather infamous housing project not far from where young, impressionable Theodore had lived. The singer had probably honed his singing chops and romantic skills in staircases that were similarly fouled with the stench of stale urine. Lou was fortunate to have made it out alive, establishing himself on an international stage.

I hadn't the foggiest notion of whether Theodore's hopes and dreams had transcended the trappings of his neighborhood. I only knew that his chance to escape had disappeared in a boulevard bum-rush.

"We aren't here to save the world," I heard Perry assuring me. Hearing the sound-bite ring in my head reminded me that we were enjoying our lunch when the call came in. While we joked about nothing, two young black boys had died in a senseless fray.

I recalled us leaving the Shelton apartment to return to our patrol car. As my foot touched the first step in our descent, Sarge placed his hand on my shoulder and reiterated, "Again, it ain't your fault."

Still in a daze when he'd said it, I now understood why: he knew I'd be replaying the event in my mind.

I hit the treadmill for a while, not bothering to set the timer. After a mile at full speed, I squinted at the sting of sweat dripping into my eyes. My mind fixated on the kill count and unnecessary violence in my city. Not for the first time, I thought about supporting or maybe even starting a community youth program in my old neighborhood, a

place where at-risk kids—that would be most of them—
could hang out instead of falling in with the gangs.

The Chicago Police Department was as needed as it was
despised, especially in the part of town arguably referred
to as "Chi-raq". I hated that term. Constant media reports
and rumors proliferated of officers applying Gestapo-style
tactics and shooting unarmed citizens who often looked
a lot like me. Then, there was its sordid past, boasting a
history of corruption going back well before Capone ran
the streets. Between the days of tommy guns and crack
wars, an illegal police raid rendered corpses of Fred
Hampton and Mark Clark, leaving a permanent stain on
the CPD.

I was harassed by cops myself when I was teen, but
then, I was also mugged by other teenagers and wannabe
gangsters from my own neighborhood. Trying to change
the image of Chicago's Finest while protecting the
residents from each other required one hell of a balancing
act. Made me something of a boy scout to try to pull off my
mission to change things, I guess.

By the time I finally ran out of steam, my muscles ached
and my lungs burned. My arms had turned to rubber and
another bench press attempt could've resulted in an injury.

The demons had not been exorcised, but I was too tired
to give them any heed. Soaked through and through, I
promised myself a hot bath with Epsom salts after getting
some fresh air.

* * *

A short drive later, I found myself sitting on a bench in
Washington Park. A welcome breeze blew in from Lake
Michigan, easing some of the day's heat. The sun was
setting and folks were trying to get in a final jog or dog
walk before the park officially closed.

I was propped up near one of the lagoons, the cattails
grown tall. With night approaching, hanging out so close
to the muddy shore probably wasn't the wisest choice;

mosquitoes and gnats were attracted to both the stagnant water and my post-workout stink. I sniffed under my arms and tried to convince myself I didn't smell like a plate of freshly diced onions.

A makeshift choir of horny crickets transmitted desperate mating calls as darkness rolled in. At least somebody is gonna get laid. The prospect of returning to my empty residence had me in no hurry to get back there.

"Damn," I said aloud in response to an audible stomach gurgle. I'd never retrieved my sandwich from the office fridge, and after my workout, I was starving.

"What's that," came a voice. I thought I was alone but somebody had sat down on the other end of the bench without me even noticing.

"Nothing," I said. He looked like one of the homeless people who would make their beds in the grass after the park closed. "I was just griping about . . ."

I paused, considering how rude it would be for me to make a fuss about my choice of cuisine to someone living out of doors. I studied him at a glance. He was a big, older white guy with long frizzy white locks and round wire rimmed glasses. I imagined birds nesting in his unkempt beard. Beneath his hirsute appearance was a welcoming face.

"Hope I'm not bothering you," he said, waving a hand from side to side.

I chuckled. "Not at all, sir. Everybody deserves to enjoy a good sunset."

"Yeah and a beautiful one it is. Too bad it doesn't set over the lake," he said, thumbing east of us, where the sky had already turned a shade of indigo. "Hey, you're not gonna arrest me for sleeping on this bench tonight, are you?" he asked bluntly.

"Huh?"

He grinned, waiting for an answer. "How do you know…"

"Just a good judge of character, I reckon," he remarked,

pointing at my sweat-stained tee.

Over my left pectoral was the faded image of a five-star badge. On my right were letters that read, "Windy City's Finest." I got the shirt right out of the academy, when I had participated in a charity Olympics against the Fire Department. We beat them in the tug-of-war but they'd taken the barbecue competition outright. Leave it to the smoke-eaters, whose daily concern was cooking their next meal.

"Oh, gotcha."

He shrugged his rounded shoulders, pushing his glasses up on his nose a bit. "Hey, what can I say? It's a gift."

"And one I obviously need to develop." With the badge and lettering faded from years of countless washings, no one had paid any mind to what I was wearing. I'd blended in with the rest of the civilians just living life. However, I knew that in certain parts of town, my old t-shirt could have drawn the wrong kind of attention.

"Brandywine," I said, extending my hand politely.

"Mmm hmm," he hummed, shaking it firmly.

"And you are?"

"Just a face in the crowd making small talk. Most people wouldn't take any notice of someone like me."

"I notice everything."

"Except your shirt and the fact that I sat at the other end of your bench."

I grinned. "Well, except for that, of course."

"Don't wanna be rude," he said, "but I don't believe in just giving my name out for no reason."

"Is someone looking for you?"

"Yeah," he said with a smirk. "I'm a hit-man on the lam, spending my days upping my cultural quotient perusing the exhibits at DuSable Museum and my nights taking turns around this sprawling, 372-acre garden." He paused and chuckled. "No, seriously, nobody's looking for me, Officer Brandywine."

"Detective, actually," I said before I could stop myself.

The sides of his mouth turned up and I got a good view of his stained teeth. Flashing a genuine-looking smile, he crinkled his eyes.

"Ahhh—this gets more interesting as we go along.

Okay, let's make a deal: if we bump into each other again, I'll tell you my name and a detail about myself."

"Works for me, sir."

He nodded, probably glad that I wasn't trying to prod or poke. Hell, I did that for living, already.

"May I ask you a question?"

"Prefacing one question with another," he mumbled. "As long as you don't ask something condescending like, 'how did you wind up living out-of-doors?'".

"No, nothing of the sort," I assured.

"Because that kind of question can be broached in another conversation, after we get to know each other better." He leaned over a bit and whispered with a wink, "I don't kiss on the first date!"

The unexpected humor in his remark caught me completely off guard, causing me to stifle a sudden laugh. When he began giggling, I knew it was okay to let loose. We both doubled over and my eyes got wet with the effort.

It was the best I'd felt all day.

When we had composed ourselves, I got around to my query: "Since this is our first date," —I said those two words while making air quotes—"do you mind if I buy you dinner?"

"You're not feeling sorry for me, are you, Detective Brandywine?"

"Hells no," I said with a chuckle, "I'm just being nice, man. After a very long day, I'm too lazy to cook and don't want to eat alone. Besides, those vendors look like they could use some of our business." I thumbed toward the food trucks parked on Cottage Grove Avenue. "Though I should be eating something healthy, I really have the taste for a hot dog piled high with onions, tomato, and that neon-green relish we love so much around here. I won't

42

feel so guilty if I have a co-conspirator. Want one, too? I'll throw in a pop to sweeten the deal. Whaddaya say?"

"Don't drink soda, unless I have no choice," he said. "I will take an Italian lemonade with that dog, if you're offering. Drag it through the garden, minus the sport peppers, with an extra dash of celery salt, please."

"Spoken like a true connoisseur with an appetite. Coming right up."

A dining experience is always better when shared with friends. Though we'd just met and I had yet to know his name, my new acquaintance had friend potential. We sat in comfortable silence, savoring each bite, every sip, and the sounds of fading laughter as parents headed home with their kids.

When I stood to leave, he gave me a two-fingered salute from his bushy eyebrow. "Until again we meet," he said.

"We shall see. Sleep well," I responded. I didn't ask if he wanted a few bucks because that wasn't the reason he'd spurred up the conversation in the first place.

"With such an awesome dinner in my substantial gut, you're damn straight I'll rest well! Thank you for the meal and the company, Detective. Get some rest."

I grinned. As of late, my sleep had been fleeting, at best. I knew two things, though: I was glad our meeting had brought some much-needed laughter and I had the strangest feeling it was the beginning of something, though *what*, I wouldn't hazard a guess.

Chapter 4

I awoke the next morning feeling like I'd laid down in front of a steamroller parade. Though I know better, I had skipped stretching after my workout—though it would have been worse had I not taken a hot bath before bed.

I popped a couple of ibuprofen and drank a big glass of water. Though my Navy years had conditioned me to early reveilles, I was still averse to taking any professional responsibility before noon. Since making detective, my workdays typically began in the afternoon, considering the nefarious elements of our society tend to operate in the shadows. It was a nice perk, though sometimes duty called early. Like today.

Alphonso Grimes, who witnesses claim pulled the trigger, leaving Raymond "Roach" Gibbons a martyr for a vacant cause, was my first appointment of the day. With his only ally out of the picture, Grimes had been tackled and held down by bystanders till the CTA security team arrived at the scene, and minutes later he was taken into custody by CPD. He was briefly held at the precinct before being transferred to the Cook County Jail on 26th & California, where I sat waiting in a spartan interview room containing three chairs and a table.

To have caused such mayhem, Grimes wasn't a very big guy at all. But then, the same could be said of Napoleon Bonaparte. The suspect was delivered to the drab room by a hulked-out deputy whose name tag identified him as

Matthews. A chain around the prisoner's skinny waist ran through sets of cuffs for his hands and feet. The arrestee gave his grudging cooperation as the jailer secured him to the table.

They could have skipped the restraints for all I cared, though my firearm and pocketknife had been checked upon my arrival per standard procedure. As bad as the little dude thought he was, I would mop the room with his sawed-off ass—without my gun or knife—if he got out of line.

Prior to the murder charge, the miscreant's rap sheet consisted of trips to juvenile detention centers for petty theft and a laundry list of assault charges. Though considered an affiliate of DQP as per his last arrest, Alphonso Grimes had obviously gone full bore. With their blood-in, blood-out policy, the killing of a rival cemented him a spot in the gang. With his track record for strong-arm robbery and intimidation, Grimy's graduation to the big leagues was inevitable. The good thing was, now that his eighteenth birthday had come and gone, he was no longer a minor. I didn't have to wait for a parent or guardian, just his lawyer, who was oddly absent.

Muscle Head Matthews (probably not the name his parents gave him) had no neck; his noggin was welded to his broad shoulders. He resembled a cross between a Frazetta painting and a comic book strongman, having to turn his upper torso each time he changed direction. Though his slow, telegraphed movements would be a disadvantage during an actual fight, his bulk strength would likely be a boon. With his massive size, looking like he was about to burst out of his skin, anyone in their right mind would not be faulted for crossing the street to avoid him. The deputy shifted himself toward the door to perch outside.

He would have remained inside, posting up in the corner, had I asked him to stay. Oh, Grimes would have loved that—it would have made me come off as nervous. That punk didn't worry me. My exercise regimen maintained my nearly flat stomach, allowed me to eat whatever I wanted, and ensured I remained quick on my feet. Though nowhere near as bulky as the uniformed Viking standing on the other side of the door, I was formidable.

The fact that I don't have huge biceps and veins popping out all over could be why Grimes thought it was okay to test me. I didn't strike the imposing figure of his escort, but I held an easy 10" vertical advantage and outweighed little Alphonso by at least a good 50 pounds of lean muscle. Small dudes with shifty eyes were not to be underestimated but neither were detectives who didn't allow badges and guns to give them false bravado.

Though Grimes looked like he could scrap, I figured it was his firearm that gave him the nerve to treat a public bus stop like a drug corner. Officers seized several rocks prepped for sale from a plastic baggie in the young banger's pocket. I saw the whole thing as either an initiation tactic or him trying to build notoriety. The problem was that he'd brought young Theodore along for the fateful ride.

His burner's serial numbers were partially marred by acid but I could guarantee the weapon was linked to several other crimes. That pistol and the corpse of the Sherman Park Hustler it left in its wake granted Grimes an immediate rep as a stone-cold killer, which was probably what led him to ply his trade in such a public venue in the first place.

The Hustlers operated out of the neighborhood surrounding the eponymous park anchored on 55th & Racine. As a show of power, they'd begun using the 55 Garfield bus to travel east, right into DQP territory. A run-in between rival sets was inevitable. Grimy's outright challenge to their blatant disrespect built his street cred, so he was feeling himself.

"Whachoo want, mang," he asked with a sneer.

He flexed his entry-level jail-house physique, which was meant to accentuate the appearance of upper body strength while neglecting the lower. The goal was to make the shoulders broad, with muscular arms, and a cinched waist. After he'd had some months to perfect building his lats, his back would resemble a cobra's hood. He was new to hard time but had a good starter kit going.

"Nothing, until your lawyer arrives," I said without batting an eye.

He was sizing me up, balling up his lips, trying to make an impression. We were locked in a staring contest and he felt he might win.

"Nice choice of footwear," he said, dipping his eyes but not blinking. It was a way for him to maintain his quest for dominance. "Didn't know they let y'all rock sneaks with suits."

I just smiled, proud of my high-tops, and happy when people noticed them. I was trying a new brand called Cigar Conglomerate. Though I didn't smoke, I dug their designs. I'd worn a gray canvas pair that day, which went well with the dark herringbone pattern of my slacks.

"Yah, I really like them. And it's a black-owned business to boot. Want their website?" I said, though we both knew he'd be wearing standard-issue jail attire for a long time to come. My inquiry was rhetorical, meant to pass the time till his lawyer arrived.

He ignored it anyway.

"I know that if we weren't in this room, you'd be wantin' to break one of those off in ol' Grimy's ass, right?"

I sighed.

"That's what y'all are good at doing," he continued, "beating up on brothers, thinking we all crooks and killers!"

Funny, because the witness statements and evidence pointed a rather accusatory finger to the fact that he was both.

"You like running your mouth, don't ya?" I asked.

He grinned, using it as an excuse to moisten his eyes with a quick flutter of the lids, locking back in a moment later. "Sure do. Shit, I can chew the fat all day without tellin' you a damn thing that I don't want you to know. Yeah, you might think you got some dumb street kid, but..."

"Don't say another word," demanded his attorney, stepping into the room, his red hair pulled back in a frizzy ponytail. The disheveled lawyer looked as if he'd received notice of the case only a few minutes before. I knew the public defender from my trips to court and other interrogations. His suits always looked like he'd slept in them, ties were crooked and shoes were unpolished—but he wasn't the schlub he appeared to be. Challenged fashion sense aside, Public Defendant Mark Avery, like Grimes, was not to be underestimated.

"Sorry I'm late," he said, unloading a bunch of files onto the table. "Have you advised my client of his rights?"

"No need of it yet. We were just making small talk while waiting on you."

Avery fumbled about with his paperwork, whispering something into his client's ear, to which the accused shook his head repeatedly. I marveled at the unlikely duo, one looking like a chipmunk and the other—an alley rat.

Rodents with different agendas.

After assuring the counselor there was no need to issue a cleansing warning, I advised Alphonso of his rights and began. Our previous conversation and staring competition had just been warm-up, like foreplay before the fuckery.

Though it had been awhile since I'd played, I well understood and loved the game of chess and I operated my investigation with a chess-like mentality. I would keep them dazzled with my bishops and rooks, so my knights could swoop in for the L-shaped kill. I did want a confession of his involvement in the whole fiasco—something his sense of braggadocio demanded he take credit for—but what interested me more was finding out where he'd obtained the weapon, as well as his admission that he'd carried out the murder under orders of the DQP.

I easily got the first. Much to the chagrin of Avery, Grimy had willingly given up the goods.

"Is he dead?"

"Who's that," I asked, as if I hadn't the foggiest notion.

"That Hustler I bucked down. What was his name, something like Centipede or Fruit Fly? Oh yeah, it was Water Bug, wasn't it?"

Avery leaned over, admonishing his client in a whispered yell that he should shut his mouth on the matter. Grimes didn't give a damn, since he had a reputation to build.

"What do you mean by 'bucked'?"

"Well, I didn't have a shotty available," he said, referring to the weapon he wished he would've had loaded with double-odd buckshot. It took little marksmanship and had the tendency of making casualties of innocent bystanders, so I was also glad he hadn't used a shotgun.

"Too hard to conceal. When I say I bucked him, it's a euphemism to ask if I killed his punk ass," he stated proudly.

"What are you trying to do?" the red haired man demanded, jumping out of his seat, sending files falling to the floor. Though he was used to representing gang bangers, he obviously hadn't had many who were so willing to 'fess up to their crimes.

"Don't worry 'bout me, counselor. Hell, I'm just telling the dick something he already knows. They got the evidence, the snitches, and probably even raw footage!"

Avery slammed his fist onto the metal table. It was bolted to the floor so it couldn't be used as a weapon. "Detective, a moment please while I confer with my client!"

Their voices became louder as I excused myself from the room. As the argument ensued, I leaned against the wall opposite Matthews. "How goes it, brother," I asked the walking side of beef.

"It's all good," he squeaked, sounding more mezzo soprano than second tenor. I nearly bit a hole through my lip and had to feign a coughing fit to hide my laughter. The bulky corrections officer was built up like an action figure but vocalized like he'd been sucking on a helium balloon. I imagined his nuts had shrunken to the size of raisins.

Being facetious, I asked, "How much time you spend in the gym, man?"

He grinned, glad I'd noticed his physique (as if anyone could miss it) but too daft to realize I just wanted to amuse myself by hearing him talk some more. His blue eyes brightened and his hands became expressive of the soliloquy about his 4-hour regimen, his diet, the raw eggs he drank, and all the supplements he took. Like Grimy, he was willing to chirp about one thing but not reveal the source of the other. He used every opportunity to preen, pose, and smack his fist into his hand, going on and on about his routine, while persistently avoiding any mention of Vitamin S—*as in steroids.*

That was for his doctor to worry about. At the moment, my plate was full with two bodies in the morgue and a suspect who loved running his mouth.

I shook hands with the deputy (which was like sticking my paw into a vice) when I was summoned back into the interrogation room. The large man with the girlish voice was smiling, like he was satisfied that he'd made a new friend.

Avery stood up as I cleared the doorway. "My client wishes to invoke his right to silence."

"You sure, Grimy?" I asked, feigning ignorance. "We were just getting along so fine."

The lawyer's face went from passively pale to an angry red. He'd figured out what I was getting around to asking and had obviously advised his client against answering. I wasn't sure why it would even matter to the round-faced professional, whose home was probably in some well-appointed community far away from the inner city. Maybe he was altruistic. Or maybe he had another reason. Either way, for all my smart-assery, there was nothing I could do once the suspect agreed to shut down.

Grimes sat staring straight ahead, avoiding my gaze. I could only guess that his public defender told him that pointing a finger at the DQP organization could get him raped and shanked in the shower. Whatever it was, after his previous propensity for talking shit, the young man was quiet and thoughtful.

"Is there anything else?" Avery asked, his intense, green eyes fixed on my face.

"Well, I guess not. Hey, Grimy," I said, again using his nom de guerre. I took my pinky and thumb, wiggled it next to my ear and told him, "Call me if you change your mind."

"That's quite enough, Detective," the lawyer warned.

With that, I stepped out, patted my pal Matthews on the shoulder, and headed to the desk to reclaim my weapons.

Two of Perry's suspects—the ones who'd stomped Theo to death—were also being held at the county lockup. My partner would squeeze them until he got the name of the third—the one who got away.

Perry and I were in for a long day and, with us chasing down separate leads, there would be no time to fuss over what we would have for lunch. I considered texting him that if he made it back to the office before me, he could have the rest of my sandwich—but I didn't. No point pulling his focus away from the case.

Chapter 5

Next up was an appointment I could actually look forward to: speaking with Carlos Davis, Jr, minus security checks and annoying attorneys. I got him on the line and he invited me to his house. I offered that we could meet at the precinct, thinking that I didn't want his neighbors to recognize me as a cop and label him a snitch.

"Hold on," he said. "My father would like to speak to you."

"Hello," the older man greeted almost cantankerously.

Good afternoon, sir."

"You can feel free to come by to talk to Junior. I need to get ready for work, so I don't have time to post up in your office."

"My concern, Mr. Davis, is retaliation from . . ."

"That's no problem," he said, cutting me off. "We don't believe in that 'snitches-get-stitches' bullshit 'round here. I'm raising this young man to stand up for what's right, regardless. So, you can come on through."

Without another word, he handed the phone off to his son. I told him I'd be there within the hour.

* * *

"Afternoon, Detective. Come on in," the young man told me.

The apartment was nowhere near a palace, but I felt like royalty after my morning at the jail. The scent of pine and other clean smells wafted through the home. The floor had been swept and swabbed. Obviously Junior and his dad Carlos Senior were not simply trying to impress; they had a regimen.

The teen bore a look of sadness in his eyes, but his handshake was firm. His father's grip was steely, and I felt I was in the company of straight dealers. A glance around the front room revealed a threadbare sofa, which was sunken in the middle, and did not match the carpet or the drapes. There were no cute little animal figurines or knickknacks that might have earmarked a woman's touch.

I was offered a seat at the dining room table and something cold to drink.

"We've got pop, lemonade, juice, and water," the dad said. "Junior will get you a glass and show you to the fridge. After that, you're on your own. Now, excuse me. I've got to get dressed and go pretty soon. Take your time and get all the information you need."

I rose, but Carlos Senior made a motion for me to remain seated. He nodded, shook my hand, and disappeared into his bedroom.

"Mind if I record this and take notes," I asked.

"Not at all, sir."

"Don't have to call me sir," I assured him.

He stated his name, other identifying information and, with little prompting, began breaking down what he had seen the day before. He talked about heading downtown with his girlfriend, his buddy, and his friend's younger sister. "When we got to the bus stop, we had a choice of taking either the Dan Ryan, or the old el up toward Washington Park. We decided on the Ryan."

"What did you see before going down to the train?"

"Grimy and Theo were standing a few yards from the stop, up to no good."

"How so?"

"Slangin' and bangin'," he said, using the terminology for selling drugs. "They recently fell in with the DQP—

Grimy is just a hard head and Theo wants—*wanted* to be just like him."

He stopped talking and looked down at his hands on the tabletop. I could see he was upset from losing his friend and I gave him a moment to compose himself.

"You okay?" I asked, taking a sip of water, pointing at his glass as a suggestion for him to do the same.

"Yeah," he said, clearing his throat. "Guess I'll be alright. I used to hang out with those guys until not too long ago."

"What happened?"

"Well, a few months back, we were chilling on the corner."

"The same spot as yesterday?"

"No, up the street, near the gas station," he said, thumbing back toward 55th Street. "Anyway, there was this old white lady …"

"She live around here?"

He frowned. "Heck no!"

"Junior," came his father's slightly muffled voice from the other room, a warning in the tone. He'd clearly been listening to our conversation.

The boy straightened up and corrected his previous statement, which had apparently been too near to cursing: "No sir, she had Michigan plates on her car."

"Go on," I prompted.

"She was passing through, on her way to Iowa I believe. Her car was almost out of gas when she pulled off the highway to get some."

Junior relayed that Grimes wanted them to rob the elderly lady—Miss Margaret, he called her. However, Junior chose otherwise, which meant filling her tank and sending her on her way, *un-accosted*.

"How did your friends feel about that?"

He sat up straighter, taking in air to inflate his chest. "Let me put it to you this way, Detective Brandywine: we stopped being friends that day."

I nodded my approval and couldn't help but grin.

According to some media portrayal, only knuckleheads, thugs, and bangers came out of the city's more rough- and-tumble neighborhoods. But nothing could be further from the truth. There were upstanding men like Carlos Senior, raising young gentlemen like his progeny in what seemed to be just rubble.

"I'm not sure if anyone has told you, but that was a brave thing you did, Carlos. It's a brave thing you're doing now."

The youth smiled and blinked twice. There was a little wetness in his eyes, from his friend's demise for sure, but maybe some from pride. *Nothing wrong with a little self confidence.*

After securing the information important to my case, I stayed and talked with Junior, drinking lemonade—and then when that ran out, water again. Early on, Carlos Senior had walked through on his way out to an extra shift and shushed us not to bother getting up. I knew he had to be hoping this attention from the police was a good thing. I guess that partly relied on me, or maybe more than partly. I felt a certain weight on my shoulders along those lines.

At my urging, Carlos Junior pondered his future aloud. "I love reading," he declared, "I'm working through the classics," he said, holding up library editions of *Moby Dick* and *Things Fall Apart*. He said he wanted to start learning martial arts, and eventually confessed how much he missed his mom.

I had wanted to ask about his mother. I assumed she was dead but saw no photos of her on display. Though my own mother transitioned after I was grown, I could identify with the teen's sense of emptiness. He kept talking, next about his hopes for college, so I let him go on, actively listening, while the shadows lengthened.

When I finished my water and collected my notes, I stood and gave him my card, encouraging him to hold onto my number. Pending his dad's approval, he could call me anytime, official business or not.

I stepped out of the apartment into the early evening air

and took a deep breath.

"Now there," I said to myself, unlocking the door to my vehicle, "is a good kid."

Driving home, I thought about Carlos Jr. and other young people like him who just wanted to grow up and have a normal life. Though there were organizations here and there that offered an "out" for those trapped in the inner city, it wasn't enough, not by any measure. Once again, I considered if I would have a role to play in the change.

Chapter 6

I spent the next few hours at my desk, inputting data, reviewing files, and connecting dots. My cherished Italian beef wasn't quite as good coming out of the microwave as that first bite when it was fresh, but I was grateful for it. I was surprised Perry hadn't shown up, since he seemed to almost live at the precinct. I yawned, said goodnight to the stiffs coming in for the graveyard shift, and headed my tired butt home.

Less than three hours later, I awoke to the phone ringing.

Calls in the middle of the night meant one of *four* things. Since my mother was gone, my family consisted of only my sister and me; she and I weren't on speaking terms, so I knew it wasn't her. The second would have to be a catastrophe just shy of 9/11 with all hell breaking loose and serious backup required. Of course, a third possibility was a booty call.

My consciousness slowly rose to the surface and I let myself consider that possibility. A midnight invitation to a bit of freaky-deaky and the reduction of somebody's headboard into chopped firewood made me smile. It would be even more relaxing than the extended shower I'd enjoyed when I got home earlier. Though long overdue for a romp of that sort, the fact that I was between relationships meant a south-pointing probability that hovered just north of zero.

I lay there for a moment, staring at the ceiling before squinting at the glow of the nightstand clock. My state of hibernation having hit so suddenly, I was in no mood to be dragged out of my slumber. More out of spite than anything else, I let the phone protest once more before answering.

"Yeah," I growled, forgoing formalities. No need to be polite when someone was ringing in the small hours. "Whatcha got?"

A woman sobbed, giving my nickname an extra syllable, whining *"Br-aan-dy!"*

Like a switch had been flipped, my heart rate jumped into overdrive. Even bleary-eyed and dull-minded at such an ungodly time of the night, my awareness immediately went to the location of my weapon. It was a holdover from too many days spent in hot zones. My heart banged out a jazz drummer's staccato as my body prepared for fight-or-flight. I sat up and squinted, scanning the room, listening for active threats.

Lucky me—not there, not then. No trigger-happy insurgent, and no boogeyman with his thumb on a detonator. I took a deep breath, soaked in my surroundings, and recognized my location. I was home. Though there was always the chance that I might trip over a pile of dirty clothes that hadn't quite made it to the hamper, home was a place of relative safety, with no flying bullets or IED explosions.

My therapist at the VA Hospital had gone over an exercise enough times for me to know what to do when these episodes began. Even in diminished lighting conditions, I picked out a point of familiarity. It began with a framed poster of a bullfighter that hung opposite my bed. I had purchased it in Spain and had it framed at a shop in Hyde Park. Next, I noticed my closet door, which was slightly ajar. Nothing but suits, a couple pairs of jeans, and my collection of sneakers (mainly high-tops) inside.

Then my eyes rested on the glowing numbers of my alarm clock, which was the last point of triangulation. "Home," I sighed.

"Wh-what," the lady on the phone asked frantically.

Bringing myself down from a potential episode, I had forgotten I was holding the phone to my mouth.

The caller sounded high-strung and, with her voice hitting an upper register, I couldn't make out who she was. My head floating around in a sleep fog didn't help any. Years before, I had learned to never call a lady by another woman's name, so first I needed to level down the intensity.

"What's going on," I asked, calming my tone, hoping she would follow suit.

"It's *me*," she said, clearly expecting me to readily recognize her. The voice was familiar but one I hadn't heard in a long, long time. "Vickie," she added, dispelling any need for further divination.

Now, that name rang a bell; in fact, it set off a series of explosions brighter than the summer fireworks by Buckingham Fountain. The voice of Victoria Millikan, nee Robicheaux, hadn't graced my ear in a month of Sundays. She'd gotten hitched in a small ceremony not long after our breakup. She actually had the nerve to send me a wedding invitation, which had been upsetting for me. I wondered what she expected and spent considerable time worrying about what to do until I realized I could simply send a card in my stead. It was with a sense of finality that I had signed, stamped and mailed that card.

And I'd practically forgotten about her—until a couple of months ago, when the texts started coming. The first few messages were friendly, before turning more than a bit flirtatious. Twice I reached out but my calls went straight to voice-mail. Her communications strongly hinted that all was not right in marital wonderland. Part of me wanted to give in to her more coquettish messages, while my mature side decided to remain cool and aloof. Hell, no matter how excited I might be at the idea of seeing her again, she had made her decision. Now, out of nowhere, she chose to disturb the best night of sleep I'd had in a long time.

As military reservists, we'd each been recalled to active duty and served in a mobile security team based out of Bahrain. We were sent to some rather hairy spots along the Arabian Peninsula. Memories, images, and bits of information ran through my head like an express train barreling past stops.

My tone immediately softened. Like it or not, she had that effect on me. "Hey, Vickie. What's wrong?"

"Can we talk?"

It occurred to me that, though I was available throughout the day, she'd waited till the ass hour of the morning to pose that question. It brought to mind the *fourth* reason why someone would call so late: to catch me off-guard.

Not a morning person, my brain didn't operate even close to full function until I'd had a workout and a good breakfast. Vickie was probably trying to catch me in a vulnerable state so I would agree to something ridiculous—a request for a loan, or maybe something worse.

I got out of the bed and stretched, allowing blood to flow from head to toe. I needed to brace myself, just in case. "Sure thing," I yawned and rubbed my chin, noticing that my goatee could use a trim. "I'm awake and this'd better be good. Now, talk."

"In person," she demanded.

I glanced again at the digital timepiece, a glaring reminder that I had barely entered my REM cycle. My head swam with images: a boy's sprawled body, his tearful friend sitting on the curb, Professor Bolduc's gruesome suicide, and his unfaithful wife.

I reeled myself back into the present. Vickie was on the other end of the line, awaiting a response. "Where would you like to meet?"

"Um, give me your address and I'll come over," she said, as I thought she might.

Hells no! I shook my head several times, thanking my lucky stars that I'd moved to this new pad since we'd broken up.

"Damn, I'm Hungry," I said flatly.

"I could use a bite to eat too but you don't have to be rude, Brandy," she admonished.

"No," I said. "That's the name of the spot: the Damn, I'm Hungry Eatery. It's an all-nighter on the Near North Side."

I told her where it was located and ten minutes later, I was steering my Chevy onto the Outer Drive. I don't like flying blind, but she wouldn't divulge anything more to me on the phone. I didn't know what I was walking into.

Rarely do I carry off-duty, though I usually leave a holdout piece in my glove compartment. I'd been working plainclothes for a minute, and having my piece on my side put me in a different frame of mind. I made an exception this time, concealing the pancake holster under my untucked shirt. The department-issued weapon was good beneath a suit jacket but, outside of work, I preferred the slimmer profile of my 1911. With the magazine single-stacked with .45 rounds, there was little chance of it printing against my clothes. Plus, the knockdown power of the larger, slower round gave me a certain sense of comfort. "When in doubt," I recalled Perry saying, "whip it out!" Though corny and rife with double entendre, my partner had a good point.

"I was thinking of someplace cozier," Vickie had suggested before I hung up. I knew she was talking about a dark, express-herself-over-drinks-and-get-things-twisted-between-us kind of hole in the wall.

She clearly thought I'd lost what was left of my natural mind.

I wasn't in the mood for adult beverages or candlelit corners that could be misconstrued as romantic. We needed someplace brightly lit and populated by sane and sober folks. The more above board, the better. History had already proven that the two of us couldn't behave when left to our own devices.

Driving north with my upper head in charge, the lower

began to throw a tantrum. Like a petulant child, my resolve and several inches stiffened. My feral side yelled at the concept of me probing the depths of her id. The logic of me steering clear and running away so fast I kicked my own ass suddenly seemed tainted. I was figuratively howling at the moon, wanting the two of us to mate and to be left panting like a couple of shameless mutts.

Nope, I kicked back. I wouldn't allow Vickie that kind of pull anymore. I wasn't down for any of her games.

With no traffic, I reached our rendezvous point in less than 20 minutes. Though other shops in the almost-posh community had mostly closed, the Damn, I'm Hungry Eatery remained a beacon of hope for insomniacs with an appetite. Rumor was, it *never* closed, not even for major holidays. A favorite of the late-night crowd, the diner got its name from an eponymous Smooth Jazz tune. The amusing thing was that the sign advertising the place simply read "DINER." It was kind of an inside joke, since the city fathers must have shied away from the restaurant's actual moniker posted in huge letters for all to see. The studio musicians, beat cops, taxi drivers, and the hopelessly sleepless who frequented the place swore by the cuisine. Besides their Alaskan waffle (a buttered bit of Belgian delight piled high with ice cream, whipped cream, and fresh fruit—I promised myself I would NOT order it), the menu boasted a full complement of hearty home-cooked offerings—it was a cut above your typical greasy spoon.

I parked in a nearby lot and ambled the sidewalk toward the restaurant. Approaching the warmly lit place at three in the morning, I was glad to see it was still there. The Windy City had done its best to reclaim and gentrify the area that had once been more notorious for its proximity to Cabrini-Green Homes than for big business. As the Gold Coast expanded north, the location of the public housing project with its near views of the lake had made it hot property. Apartments in the neighborhood were gutted, upgraded, and deemed condos, while Cabrini itself was completely demolished, with only its entrance sign surviving. Two decades before, it had been a battlefield for the likes of the Disciples and the Vice Lords over drug turf. Now, the war was fought between real estate companies and large corporate stores vying for clientele.

Despite the ongoing overhaul, a certain, unsavory cast of characters remained that the city couldn't weed out. Vagrants, junkies, and those engaged in nocturnal street trade hung around the fringes like cockroaches. They skittered about in dark doorways and under the el train tracks, waiting for opportunities to panhandle or pounce.

Wearing my pistol probably hadn't been such a bad idea, after all.

My femme fatale was already there when I arrived, posted up in a booth away from the panoramic windows that overlooked the street. She rose when she saw me enter and leaned in to embrace. Her face was fuller from some added weight. It was good to see her.

"Good morning," I said, and tried to give her the church-lady hug—not allowing her breasts to press against me— but she didn't let that deter her. Her honey-colored hair had been thrown together in a quick style. She held me like she never wanted to let go. Her familiar scent almost swayed me. If I hadn't pushed her gently back, we would have just stood there holding one another, causing a scene.

We sat down and I dismissed the passion in her greeting, concentrating instead on the menu. "You order yet?"

"Yes," she replied, looking at me intently. Something unspoken lurked just beneath the surface.

The blood in my veins froze and blocks of ice encased my feet. *Had we gotten pregnant the last time we...?* The unexpectedness of the thought threw me. At one time, that was exactly what I'd wanted, but things had vastly changed since then. My guts churned as I wondered if her puffier cheeks were postpartum.

Sensing my sudden apprehension, she encouraged me to

relax. "No babies, Brandywine. No babies."

I breathed a sigh of relief. That kind of drama—and responsibility—was the last thing I needed right then.

The waitress came around, looking as if she was three-quarters of the way through a double shift. Her name tag, pinned at a slight angle on her otherwise pristine uniform, identified her as Aileen. She looked worn for wear, the bags under her eyes carrying suitcases of their own. In a droll but friendly voice she asked, "What can I get you, hon?"

I perused the menu, licking my chops at the idea of that ice-cream-covered waffle with three strips of crispy bacon. I reminded myself that it had been several hours since I'd wolfed down my much-coveted Italian beef sandwich. But as much as I would've loved to partake, my waist didn't need to be taking on the Alaskan in the middle of the night.

"Hot tea, ma'am," I ordered, delivering a healthy slap to my pleasure-seeking id. "With lemon." My stomach growled its complaint.

Vickie's eyes were swollen, the rims and whites reddened from what must have been one extended crying session after another. She stared beyond me and looked like she was about to start boo-hooing again.

"Hey," I said softly, drawing her attention, splaying my fingers with my hands flat on the table. "You called me out of my coffin at o-dark-thirty. Was it just for the indulgence of my company? Or is it something more?" Part of me (not a part I was proud of) wished greatly to join in that indulgence.

She forced a smile. "Under any other circumstance, that would be just what I'd need."

She worked her hands together, rubbing over her fingers in a quick, nervous gesture before dropping the left into her lap and grasping my hand across the table with her right. Her Creole skin was soft as the French vanilla ice cream I wanted on that Alaskan waffle, her eyes and hair the color of agave nectar...

I snapped out of it, reminding myself that neither the waffle nor the woman was good for me. I wasn't there to flirt, reminisce, or play footsie under the table—no matter how tempting the notion. I pulled back faster than intended, yanking away as if glowing embers tipped her fingers.

Startled, her eyes widened. "Everything okay?"

Aileen sauntered back into the frame, presenting a bagel and a bowl of mixed fruit for my former lover. She placed a small, steaming pot on the table next to my cup and saucer, lemon wedges on the side.

"Be needing anything else?" the waitress asked, her voice hoarse, and the desire for a nap etched in her worn face.

"Nothing for now, ma'am," I remarked. "Thanks."

I felt a pang in my heart for our server, her frazzled brunette hair netted and pulled back into a bun that had begun to unravel. Aileen probably had teenagers that would be waking up for school in the next couple of hours when she got home. Lord knows, with money so tight, when someone called out sick at work, some folks had no choice but to take the extra shift.

My mother punished herself in a similar fashion, dragging her perpetual exhaustion from one job to the next to keep a roof over our heads. On weekdays, she woke Tammy and me with ginger kisses instead of an alarm clock. Breakfast was whatever she'd brought from the diner where she worked the graveyard; which typically meant day-old pastries, but we were grateful. We started our day as Mama was bringing pause to hers. Once we were up, she would curl up into the corner of the faded sofa, too tired to take off her uniform and without enough time to lie in her bed. Half-asleep, she would remind us to brush our teeth, read the Proverb of the day, and button up our coats before leaving for school. Mama would drift a little while longer, then get on her feet, hit the shower and go to her full-time day job.

My eyes were affixed on Aileen.

"He's gone, Brandy," Vickie said, popping my fragile, reminiscent bubble.

I peered at her, puzzled for a moment. "Who?"

"*Nigel*," she intoned, as if putting emphasis on her husband's name would give it gravity and meaning to me.

It didn't.

Rather than responding, I took a sip from the teacup and got the tip of my tongue scalded. I grimaced and focused on the diminishing pain. It was a good distraction from Vickie's unfolding melodrama.

"Where'd he go?" I asked, not even bothering to feign a passing concern.

Her eyes watered but she wouldn't allow herself to weep again—not yet, anyway. She wiped away the tears with the back of her hand and composed herself. "Ever cry so hard your head hurt?"

I gave my beverage another go. This time, the gods of the tea leaf were a bit more merciful, allowing me sip without inflicting third-degree burns.

I pondered her question. Even upon seeing my beloved mother laid out in a casket, I hadn't shed a single tear at her funeral. Tammy was all over the place and angry at me for being so stoic. Hell, even if I had blubbered like a baby, I would never give the woman sitting across from me now the satisfaction of knowing that.

"Nope," I stated flatly.

She sniffled a bit, ignoring my answer. "Well, I've been crying over this man."

I considered pointing out that she'd never bawled over me, but then, I'd never given her anything to cry about.

I wanted to empathize but couldn't. Wanted to tell her that I'd spotted Nigel Millikan for the piece of crap he was when I first saw his paper-thin smile sprawled across her social media accounts. Wanted to say I told you so . . . but I didn't.

"What do you want from me, Vickie? I know you didn't

bring me out here in the middle of the night so you could boo hoo on my shoulder like I'm one of your girlfriends or something."

"Find him for me, Brandy," she half-pleaded, half-demanded.

I was already shaking my head, about to tell her I couldn't take private cases when her voice grew sharp and jagged, like shattered glass. "Please!" she cried out.

The background hubbub of the short order cook, customer chatter, and a worn-out server named Aileen suddenly stopped. Just like that, everyone was wide-eyed, warily expecting the spillover of an unresolved domestic dispute to jump off into the restaurant. The group of nocturnal misfits, hopeless zombies, and mid-shift workers only ogled for a moment, but it was a moment too long.

I shushed her.

After a beat, Vickie repeated herself, calmer and more controlled this time: "Please." She couldn't hold the tears in check; they erupted from her golden-green eyes. The patrons and staff had gone back to what they were doing, and we faded into the wallpaper. She ignored her food, streams carving rivers down her cheeks. "Please," she repeated almost inaudibly, a bubble of snot inflating and deflating with each sob, threatening to evaporate any vestige of attraction I still felt for her.

I was conflicted. Seeing her that vulnerable, not caring that she looked uncool, caused my heart to want to bond with hers.

I dismissed grainy, black-and-white images of the two of us moving slowly, skin to skin. I was on top of her, my hands cradling her head. I'd peered into her soul and got caught up. The walls of the restaurant disappeared and we were back in the military, stealing away for R&R at the Grand Oasis Hotel in Dubai. I'd slid the clerk my credit card before he'd even told me how many dirhams the room would cost.

I lost myself there, my body moving in time with hers in

the middle of the desert. I thought she'd lost herself in that sea of sand, too . . .

Two days.

Two days of subsisting off room service, without a stitch of clothing, never leaving our rented suite. I thought we'd understood each other beyond words. When it came time to head back to Bahrain, we agreed to chalk it up to a fluke. But every time we stole away into Manama, we found ourselves tumbling between sheets.

A year later, with both of our orders up, we demobilized at Naval Station Great Lakes, Chicago being hometown to each of us. Though we hadn't met until we were a world away from home, the naive and romantic little boy in me figured that overseas magic would jump the pond and we would be together forever. I was wrong.

I took a swig from my mug, the reality of my surroundings coming back into view. The land of flying carpets and gold souks was gone, and I was left to stare at Vickie's barely nibbled bagel. I inhaled, blocked the entrance to Memory Lane, and concentrated on the present.

While part of me wanted to reach out and hold my ex-lover, another part of me wanted to shell out money to cover the bill and Aileen's tip, turn on my heels, and get ghost while I could. I should've chosen the latter. Instead, I told her through clenched teeth, "From what I can gather about his time away, your husband's probably an addict."

Though stating the obvious, it was as if I had faked her out before surprising her with a sucker punch to the gut. Her countenance shifted, eyes still raining, but now angry. "You're pissed because I loved Nigel and not you!"

I pretended not to notice her slight. "When was the last time you saw him?" I asked, all professional-like, which got her to calm down and talk. I listened closely, recording every detail, working things out like an equation in my head. Sarge joked that when I went into that mode, I was like a human abacus.

Nigel had disappeared three days before. What made me suspect he was chasing a pipe and not another woman was that he'd done it before, according to her.

Most cheating men tried not to be so obvious about their absences. Being gone for days in a row typically meant the subject had lost track of time during a binge of some sort. Missing time led to being fired from work, which, as intoxicating as another woman could be, wasn't how men usually functioned.

I sent a text to the mid-shift watch commander so he could relay the information and check the citywide sources. I put feelers out to the county lockup, as well as the precinct cages. The last check I did was with the city morgue, in search of a John Doe matching his description.

Nada. Nathan. Nothing.

I stood up, pulled my wallet, placed two crisp bills on the table, and told Aileen to keep the change. There would be enough left over to make the weary waitress's eyes pop. Like buying my as-yet-unnamed homeless friend dinner in Washington Park, it felt great to make good people smile.

I glared at Vickie, who remained seated, staring up at me with some weird look. She was not on my happy list like the waitress or my park-dwelling friend. My former lover's drama wasn't worth my energy and I was angry at being sucked in.

"I'm leaving," I said without emotion, and walked out of the cafe.

Chapter 7

Vickie sprung to life and followed me into the parking lot. The night air was noticeably cooler. We stood there with me perusing North Halsted Street to make up for the momentary loss of words.

"I'm going to have to go look for him myself," I told her. I had no clue of where to start but it sounded good.

"I'll come with you."

"No," I said tersely. "You're gonna get into your car and take your ass home. I'll contact you if and when I find something."

"I'm pregnant, Brandywine."

The words sprung from her mouth without provocation, striking me across the face like a solid pimp-slap. My jaw dropped, ruining my poker face. She'd just told me, not a half-hour before, that there were no babies. She just meant none of *my* babies.

My legs were buzzing with electricity, partially from the caffeine but more from adrenaline. I wanted to take off but Vickie's words were like railroad spikes, nailing me to that spot.

"What?" I asked rhetorically.

"I said, I'm…"

"I heard you twice the *first* time," I growled through clenched teeth, the soap opera nonsense getting to me.

She stood silently by her car door while my cognitive calculator went to work. That was why she had put on weight. It was why she was so emotional and why, as I was noticing then, her nose had spread slightly. Though I never excelled in Mr. Chew's class, I knew one thing with which even my condescending, smug-ass high school math teacher would agree: the child Vickie was carrying couldn't possibly be mine. That realization came with both a sigh of relief and a heart a bit more broken. It explained why she seemed so desperate to find the meth-fiend (or was crack his drug of choice?) sperm donor to her unborn child. Though she could have filed an official missing person report, she sidestepped that and tried to put me on the case, off the record.

I took a gander at her belly, the rounded shape of which was hidden under a jacket and an oversized blouse. Wanted to ask her how far along she was but it didn't really matter.

Grainy memories rendered on scratched film stock. . . images of multiple hotel visits, stolen kisses—and more, the mental pictures sharpening as they played out. Deep down, I'd hoped it would happen then. Wanted to initiate our own legacy between the clandestine walls to which we'd confided our secrets in a series of moans. I had wanted us to create an ongoing life. Wanted her to be the one to nurture my seed.

Instead, there I was, standing in a parking lot, wads of chewing gum stomped into filthy, flat disks on the pavement. My dream of a desert oasis faded to the reality of bums pissing in corners—then begging for pocket change with those same nasty hands.

I turned to the woman I once loved; the woman who took that love for a joke. I remembered how focused Vickie had been with an M4 rifle in her hands. I recalled her applying that same focus and skill when we were detailed to escort ships in and out of the Straits of Hormuz.

Her uniform was likely packed away in a dusty footlocker, along with ribbons and medals, all but forgotten. The woman she had become was a shadow of the one I'd known. The one I'd met and served with would have never allowed herself to hook into a degenerate with a habit.

"Nigel," I said, speaking his name for the first time.

I chuckled with bitter sarcasm. "How the hell do you get a pompous name like that and wind up strung out somewhere? Shit, he should be somewhere rocking a foo-foo smoking jacket, sipping champagne with his pinky up!" I turned my anger to her. "Instead, he's probably holed up in a tweaker pad, scratching sores into his skin, fending for his next hit. And you left me for *that*?!"

"You don't have the right to judge me," she snarled. Gone was the timidity and sadness. The red in her furious eyes was that of a mad dog, foaming at the mouth. "DO YOU HEAR ME?!" she screamed.

As had the restaurant patrons, people froze and stared. Like a herd of gazelles, they perused us. After a moment, determining there were no predators to prompt them into a dead run, they resumed their activities, searching for warmth—whether natural or chemical.

Then Vickie slapped me. Hard.

My first instinct was to draw back and cold cock her.

Had she been anyone else, I probably would have, though I had yet to hit a woman, ever. My face stung but it was far from the worst I'd ever felt.

She cursed me and spat onto my shoe. I stared in shock at the toe of my driving loafer; desecrating the white leather was a yellowish globule, so thick with mucous, it wouldn't even run off. I considered cleaning it with a swift, well-placed kick to the crack of her ass.

This was the type of drama I wanted to avoid.

I knew her temper all too well and, at one time, had found it endearing. Her mother had been a débutante from a respected New Orleans family. They boasted a bloodline that could be traced back to France. Her father was a multi-linguist, who would later teach his daughter the differences between Mandarin and Cantonese. However, when the young couple relocated to Chicago, sophisticated lineages did not necessarily translate to large paychecks, and the Robicheaux family moved in and out of some of the city's rougher neighborhoods. Though they pulled themselves up by their bootstraps and eventually purchased a home in an upper middle-class suburb, the experience of ghetto life never quite left their daughter.

Vickie's childhood had been a study in dichotomy, like a graffiti artist's version of an M.C. Escher illustration. Though she carried herself all prim and proper like a suburban-bred mallrat, the 'hood came right on out whenever she got upset.

This time, that fury was reserved especially for yours truly. She rolled her eyes and rotated her neck as if she had been raised where South Halsted Street made its way through Englewood. Spittle gathered at the corners of her mouth and flew from her lips.

I saw through her anger and asked what I really wanted to know: "How long you been on that pipe, girl?"

She grimaced, her face becoming a horrible, twisted Halloween mask. It held just like that, muscles locked in place, nose wrinkled, and teeth bared. She wanted to deny it, wanted to cuss it away. She figured if she'd gotten loud enough, kept me distracted by her antics, I wouldn't pick up on the telltale nuances. Her eyes were bloodshot from a smoking session, not just from crying. When I inhaled, I noticed the faint stench in her clothes. Upon the realization that her defenses had been circumvented, her features softened but she didn't answer.

"So, did he run off with your stash, your money, or both?"

Her eyes were puppy-dog sad again, but I was far beyond giving a damn. "W-we were going to smoke that last little bit, then kick for good," she whispered.

My eyes stung in an unfamiliar way. I hadn't shed a tear for my mother but now something shifted in me. Vickie continued trying to convince me but I only caught snatches and sound bites. Addicts always lied about their habits, attempting to gain sympathy from the people who cared most.

"...I only tried it so he could see how bad it...I just...and when we found out we were pregnant, we..."

I shook my head, trying to exorcise her voice from my ears. The Global War on Terrorism had been a nightmare come to life but it held nothing on the bad dream unfurling on this side of the pond.

"The baby," I choked out in someone else's wounded voice. "What about the life . . . *inside* you?"

"We were trying to stop," she protested weakly, believing her lie, hoping I'd do the same. That was part of her sales pitch. But I wasn't buying.

"Shut up," I croaked.

"Don't do this," she said, her face full of embarrassment. "Please...don't... *You*, of all people, have to believe..."

"Shut. Up."

"Brandy," she begged, arms outstretched.

"Where's your ring?"

"Huh?" she asked, looking dumbfounded.

"Mims and Smitty went on and on about the rock Nigel gave you when he proposed. They were at your engagement party, remember?"

Realization set in. Then irritation. Then her anger reignited. "You know what happened to the ring," she hissed.

I shook my head, not wanting to hear the words, though I knew the answer.

"I *smoked* it, motherfucker," she bellowed. "Happy?"

"Actually, no. I'm not happy."

That threw her for a loop, slowed her roll. Her eyes were bulbous, having expected me to gloat over the mess that was her life. However, I took no delight in seeing her do badly, even with another man.

"I'd much rather you and Nigel had a great relationship and a healthy baby. Hell, a whole *slew* of kids! I'd rather *that* than for y'all to be a couple of dope fiends!"

Vickie just stared, as if the wind had been knocked out of her.

She had dedicated her service to a country that trusted her with secrets, just as I'd put my life in her hands. I had trusted her with the life of our unborn daughter before she…

No.

It was a memory I couldn't replay: Vickie going to that clinic two years before…

"I *loved* you," I cried. Like a sickness, the words had sat at the pit and soured my stomach. They had to be purged.

"And you love me still," she yelled with arrogance and venom.

Her features darkened and I could see traces of an irrational fiend lurking beneath her skin. Without warning, she closed the gap between us, wrapped her arms around my neck, and forced her lips onto mine.

I shook myself free, pushing her back violently. "THE FUCK *OFF* OF ME!"

"If I told you to take me home with you…if we simply forgot about Nigel, you'd do it!"

She charged again but this time, I stiff-armed her. She was acting crazy enough, I couldn't let her get a hold of my gun.

She pushed forward, wiggling her tongue about like a disgusting pink slug, hoping to mate with mine from an arm's length. Using her defensive tactics training, Vickie turned slightly and, before I could stop her, she was back on me. This time she not only wrapped her hands around my waist, but also intertwined her legs with mine. She was determined to kiss me; I suppose she thought it would bring back the spell of the djinn.

Untangling from her was like trying to escape the clutches of a self-entitled octopus. Each time I parried; she discovered another place to attach. I was engulfed, stuck, and didn't like it.

I had never hit a woman before, not even in the line of

duty. There were other ways to gain compliance. I balled up a fist and dug my thumb into the pressure point in the hollow where her earlobe and jaw hinge met. The effect was instantaneous: she yelped and leaped away.

She backed up a few steps, hunched over and winded, but looked up at me in defiance.

"You'd marry me and raise this baby as your own," she panted. "Because you love me that much!"

I used to love her even more than that. But letting my infatuation with Vickie rule my life, after everything she'd done, would be like sucking on sugary sweets before bed every night. It would rot my soul.

"I'd get clean for you! Our baby could be treated! We could finish the life we started in the oasis!"

Hotel rooms full of treasure. Wishes granted with a rub of the lamp, or the caressing of flesh…

Her voice grew coquettish. "You could be with me whenever you wanted. I'd deny you nothing!"

For a moment, I stopped fighting what I knew to be my better judgment, relenting. I imagined the baby she carried was mine and told myself the child would never know if we never told. I put my arms around her, wanting to believe her promises to clean up and leave her husband.

"I'd make love to you every morning before you went to work."

I perked up at the thought.

"Every night, after dinner, you could have me for dessert."

An addict who didn't want to get clean couldn't be reasoned with. Her twisted logic could only make sense when I skewed my own. But as she continued to run her mouth, I realized she would say something to let her slip show. That came when she said, "You could pimp me out to your friends if you wanted…"

I snapped back to reality and saw the demon for what it was. I'd seen the same type of unclean spirit in my alcoholic father.

"*Hell you say*?!"

She cackled, the voice not quite her own. "You heard me, Mr. Policeman!"

I lifted my hands from her waist and pushed her away. I understood then that every text message she'd sent was a ploy to get into my good graces. If I was fool enough, she'd lie to have the stability of my paycheck while continuing to get high with her drug-addled husband.

She carried on like a woman possessed. "Think of how much money we could make! Definitely more than you do on a damn cop's salary!"

Good sense kicked me in the head like a mule. I stared in awe at the shell of the woman I had once adored. Looked at her and saw her image on antiquated film stock, rendered beautifully and classically in the theater of my mind. That ghost had been suspended in another world, one that had since dissipated and been turned on its ear.

There were so many things I wanted to say, questions I wanted to ask of her and of God.

But I couldn't.

I simply turned and walked away.

Had my life been a romance novel, it would have begun raining, and I would have left her as the downpour hid my tears. But there were no droplets falling from the sky or from my face.

I could feel her eyes boring into my back and heard her calling my name from what seemed to be a faraway precipice on the other side of the ocean. That's where we were: worlds apart.

"Don't you turn your back on me," I could hear her demand through a distant sounding tube, but her status and right to demand anything from me got whisked away like an autumn leaf in a lake-front breeze.

Vickie may have fooled me when she stole my heart and then ran off to wed another man, but I still knew some things about her ego. With the initial surprise of my wordless exit gone, she expected me to turn around to look at what she imagined I was losing. But I refused to give her that satisfaction. I relegated her to my periphery, which was the closest I'd ever let her come to me again.

I turned the ignition, and with a glance in the rear-view mirror, put my vehicle in gear and drove out of her life; her crazy, jacked-up life.

Coming away from the curb, I accidentally bumped a button on the steering wheel, which switched the radio to a preprogrammed R&B station with a Smooth Jazz format after midnight. The host was playing a mellow set for those who worked nights or insomniacs that had the misfortune to be up at such an ungodly hour. I was greeted with the opening strains of a song I hadn't heard in a while but I had to admit was perfect for the occasion: "This Masquerade." As was his signature, the masterful George Benson's ethereal voice complimented each note he plucked on his guitar.

The lyrics questioned the games played by two people on love's fringes. It was a song that described the failed relationship between my parents; by way of bitter inheritance, the song had somehow become mine.

I tried to ignore the shrinking and then blurring figure in my rear-view mirror. Vickie stood in the middle of the street, surely hoping I'd bust a U-turn and submit to her game. I focused instead on the road that would take me back south. If I hurried home, I could still sneak in a two-hour nap before it was time to get up. It promised to be another trying day.

The End

Story III

Thief of Hearts, Jack of Clubs

Rayford

Except for a tiny G-string, the muscular dancer lay naked on the massive bed, his injured foot parked atop a pile of pillows. A compression dressing girded his swollen ankle, while a melting bag of ice slumped nearby like an innocent bystander. The painful throbbing was getting worse and worse.

"Pathetic," Rayford Goodbody said, glaring at the traitorous appendage. He'd spoken it aloud, though no one else was in the house. Not since Friday.

From the red silk-covered bed, he idly watched the huge wall-mounted screen with the sound muted. It was a nature show with soaring views punctuated by birds of prey dropping out of the sky and swooping down on small unsuspecting mammals. Though dramatic, it could not distract him from the gnawing pain in his ankle—or his wounded heart. Sunday afternoon already; he'd been left behind all weekend, with barely a text the whole time. He felt so abandoned.

He thought back to Friday's brutal early-morning choreography session. It was the crew's last chance before hitting the road later that day on the first leg of a multi-city concert outing. He'd been so pumped. They'd always performed at their best as a couple—he and Janus—while on tour together. Three major and several minor trips in three years; they'd all been great. Lately, with things seeming to sour between them, Rayford knew it was the perfect time to hit the road. He had set it up as a personal challenge, outdoing himself with the creativity and drama of his choreography. He was giving this his all, to try to grab Janus' attention back from the interloper.

But he'd pushed himself too hard and had made a mistake, landing wrong and torquing his right ankle. With the weekend coming to a close, he had been strictly following doctor's orders for over 48 hours and couldn't believe it still hurt this bad.

"Absolutely no weight bearing" the physician had said, flipping through the x-rays.

The male nurse was really nice and had fixed him up with the elastic wrap and crutches and made sure he understood the discharge instructions. As Rayford listened to the young man's advice, he was touched at how kindly he spoke. His current relationship was so fraught, it was heartening to be spoken to as if he mattered. Tucking the paperwork and meds into his man purse for him, the nurse had called a cab, and then walked outside with him when it came. On an impulse, Rayford had given him half a hug before getting into the cab.

"Take care of yourself, man," the nurse had said, and shut the taxi door.

Rayford arrived at the South Drexel Avenue address to see the tour bus parked in the church lot next door, and a steady stream of worker bees going back and forth between the bus and the Victorian greystone. He'd crutched his way up the wide steps to the expansive porch and through the propped-open front door. It took a moment for his eyes to adjust to the dim light inside after the sunlit day outdoors.

Just when the injured choreographer had come alongside the huge Dogon tribal mask guarding the foyer, Janus had stepped out of the shadows. Rayford gave a little shriek and jumped back, nearly losing his balance on the crutches. Though he'd seen it dozens of times, the menacing mask's intense stare and bared teeth always rattled him, and his lover's vampiric emergence from the depths of the house was timed for the perfect scare. It was true, the dancer did have a flair for the overly dramatic, and he slid into hysterical giggles once he recovered from his fright. Though Janus snickered, he was apparently too distracted to find the situation all that amusing, so Rayford got serious and just told him what the doctor had said.

"Sure, fine," the DJ responded before he was completely distracted. "Hey, not that keyboard," he shouted to one of the roadies, cursed under his breath, then followed him down into the basement.

"I'll just go get packed," bleated Rayford, standing there by himself.

Straightaway, he hobbled across the smooth hardwood floor to the compact guest room where he kept a few of his things. Negotiating the tight space with his crutches, he packed a small bag while trying not to bump his tender foot—which hurt like the devil when it happened—and was harder to avoid than one might think. Obviously, he wouldn't be able to do any dancing, but certainly he was needed on the excursion as chief choreographer (not to mention the practical and emotional support he provided Janus).

But he couldn't get anyone to help him with his valise; his fellow dancers and the others on the road crew either looked down or got busy with some other task. He tried to carry it himself, but found that trying to get around with the injury while holding the bag, was a foolhardy and agonizing experience.

To his credit, Janus came to say goodbye, checking that his lover would have what he needed to survive for a few days. Realizing he was about to be left behind to convalesce, Rayford begged to go along, becoming rather emotional, in fact. But the DJ remained steadfast, citing doctor's orders. For the first time since they'd been together, Janus was going on the road without him—and it hurt.

Three o'clock sharp, Friday afternoon, Goodbody had stood at the living room window and watched the tour bus pull away, tears in his eyes. He fell onto the sofa, and let himself slide into a fit of self-pity, listing out all the disappointments of his young life. He even admitted aloud that his parents might have had a point when they'd opposed him leaving the dance academy just one semester before graduating. He almost had a bachelor's degree, but he'd let it go for love. That impulsive decision, made nearly three years ago, was on his mind more and more, and thinking about it made him feel even worse. Eventually, exhausted from his ordeal, he slept the daylight away.

Rayford awakened in pain to a dusky parlor. Gingerly, he got his body moving, and went in search of ice.

A prepaid debit card lay in the middle of the clean kitchen counter. *Janus does care.* That gave him the impetus to pause and evaluate his situation. Leaning on one crutch to fill a plastic bag from the ice maker, Rayford made the conscious decision to accept his reality and take control of his recovery—and thus his destiny. Though he prided himself with breaking rules and barriers, he would acquiesce to the doctor's orders. He would stay off the leg, keep the ankle elevated, compressed, and iced. Thus, the injury would heal faster so he could get back to work, join the tour—and Janus—that much sooner.

Maneuvering with the crutches, he surveyed the first floor of the early 1900s mansion, considering where he would hang out for the next couple of days. The original rooms on the main level, including the renovated kitchen, boasted towering ceilings, as well as pristinely restored hardwood floors polished to a satin gloss. Janus' home was a large gallery-like space, and the dancer found it easy to get around it with his crutches.

Sculptures, canvases, and other pieces of art displayed throughout the house brought a unique dimension to the century-old urban mansion. The ancients and the indigenous inspired the well-known DJ's eclectic palate. Greek theater masks and those of Australian aboriginal lineage adorned walls in Janus' office. Elsewhere on the first floor, colorful Haitian paintings hung next to framed, black-and-white charcoal sketches of nudes in various states of action and rest. Works of African art and Asian calligraphy extended up the L-shaped staircase toward the second floor.

Goodbody recalled with fond nostalgia that flirtatious evening now over three years ago, when Janus had taken him on a private tour of the house and introduced him to his procurements. Only 25 at the time, the young dancer had thrilled at being noticed by the decade-older star, and his feelings since then had only matured.

He passed through the dining room and into the front parlor where he'd napped on the sofa. There, several display cases held Janus' treasures and collections. In addition to an elaborate snow globe collection (which had grown by several since his first tour of the house), Rayford recalled that the DJ had proudly pointed to the replicated bust of Afro-Asiatic Queen Nefertiti, which he had picked up during a visit to Cairo. Strategically illuminated, she sat on an Ionian-styled pedestal and was quite impressive. But once Rayford had become a regular at the house, he came to know that there was only one important image within these walls.

He moved past the small guest room and the DJ's office, stopping at the bottom of the stairs that led to the upper floors. He looked up and sighed. The master bedroom would have made a comfortable and luxurious convalescence suite, but going up and down two flights of stairs for food deliveries and ice would be problematic. He turned toward the back of the house and stepped into the lovely sun room addition. This was one of the many upgrades made to the house during the nearly twelve decades since its first brick was laid. Charming, but not quite right for his needs.

Finally, he came to the home theater and slid open the large pocket door. Back before Rayford's time, Janus had merged a formal library and its adjoining study and created this soundproof screening room where guests could watch films—and do anything else that struck their fancy.

The floor was elevated a few inches. This is where the choreographer's nimbleness came in handy. Though it was nowhere near as graceful as a dance move, he swung his body through his crutches and stepped up on his good leg into the room.

Though referred to as a home theater, this room's most notorious nickname was "The Temple of Ecstasy," for all the debauchery that took place between the heavily insulated walls.

Rayford was no stranger. With the exception of the master bedroom, this was his favorite space in the house. He looked about the trappings and figured there were worse places to take a respite than a room with a huge screen and a fully stocked bar.

This room's walls also displayed artwork, though readily of a more explicit nature. Instead of tasteful nudes, there were woodcuts of human beings engaging in all sorts of acts of sexual congress. A blushing concubine happily serviced her lover from a silk swing, while two Indian gentlemen engaged in a ménage a trois with a smiling blue-skinned woman. Other illustrations were of a man buggering another, a bare-breasted harpy riding and simultaneously disemboweling an enraptured masochist, and a lady peeking intently through a keyhole with her legs cocked and hand up her frilly hoop skirt.

All the chaises, couches, and chairs were upholstered in crushed blue velvet, while the massive custom-made bed in the center of the room was covered in red silk. This was the hub, and, with spotlights directed onto the circular mattress, something of a stage. Guests on an elevated tier on three sides could easily observe the action.

The choreographer didn't care about the various couplings that'd taken place on the pillow-covered podium—he simply wanted a place to recuperate and watch videos. The room was kept in pristine condition, with its cushions steam-cleaned, and its surfaces polished after each soiree.

Goodbody would have preferred an uneventful evening at home with the man he loved, but there were concerts to be performed and money to be made—without him. Reality bites. For him, a video and pizza at home—alone— would have to do.

Before tucking himself in for the night, Rayford gathered all the pillows he could find (without going upstairs) and made a little mountain on the red silk sheets so that his foot would stay elevated and immobile while he slept. He got himself a fresh icepack and a bottle of water, plugged in his phone, and set the master remote where he could find it. He thought about getting a beer and decided against it, decided against a pain pill as well.

It was a restless night, due to the discomfort, but

Saturday was better. Rayford mostly stayed in bed, except when necessity called, and then he would hobble to the kitchen or the front door for food deliveries. Several times, he texted Janus his thoughts and feelings and hoped in vain for more than a perfunctory response.

Saturday was opening night, and Janus was slated to perform at the Fox Theatre in downtown Detroit. The forlorn choreographer was disappointed not to get a call or any response to his "Good luck! You'll do great!" text that he'd sent an hour before the entourage was set to take the stage. Janus was probably overwhelmed without Rayford there to run interference, he thought.

Sunday would be the second of two nights in Detroit, then the tour would move on to Milwaukee with an off-day before performing there on Tuesday. The dancer's spirits lifted as he dared to hope that Janus would pick him up when he passed through Chicago on his way to Wisconsin.

Sunday morning dawned with no new texts. Rayford thought about what he had given up when Janus had plucked him out of school early. He tried not to dwell on those futile thoughts, and instead, told himself to be strong, and to not send anything more to Janus until he'd gotten a response to his earlier messages.

Despite his intention, he couldn't help feeling hurt, bored, and lonely. He composed a message in his mind. Then, before he could stop himself, he'd acted on impulse and sent a long string of texts telling how he'd spent the weekend getting better so he could rejoin the tour right away. How he'd ignored the liquor cart. Wasn't taking pain pills. How he wanted to support the show as chief choreographer, and (being rather presumptive, he knew) as partner to the star.

As soon as he hit send, he began to regret doing so. But he'd meant every heartfelt word.

Janus still didn't respond.

Rayford fixated. Couldn't stop staring at the silent

phone. Finally he decided to watch a comedy, which helped a little. Then he took a nap.

* * *

Sunday afternoon, Rayford leaned on his crutches and stared into the fridge. He considered his options: half a leftover pizza, a few cartons of Chinese take-out, a bin of various fruits and vegetables, pickles . . . the "Home Alone" novelty had worn off and he was feeling a bit desperate.

With a sigh, he closed the refrigerator and looked at his phone again—for the millionth time.

He consulted the various delivery menus in the drawer.

Nothing sounded good. He opened the fridge again looking for a beer, and found it lacking.

But Rayford Goodbody needed relief. And he knew where to find it.

Making his way to the screening room, he ditched the crutches and hopped over to the liquor stash. After some careful deliberation, he chose an aged Kentucky bourbon. After slamming a couple of shots, he collapsed onto the huge bed, and fell into a deep sleep.

* * *

Awakening to painful throbbing, Rayford had no idea how long he'd been out but saw remnants of daylight spilling through the open door of the screening room from other parts of the house. Still Sunday, apparently.

He glared at the swollen appendage, atop the pile of pillows, the ineffectual, half-melted ice bag slumping nearby. For a while, he focused his attention on the nature photography that served as a screen saver. Images of gorgeous mountains and valleys faded into pictures of a forest canopy.

He found himself sucked into an imaginary quest, seeing the world through a hawk's eyes, scanning the grassy carpet below for signs of an unsuspecting meal. Switching his thoughts to that of the prey made him feel sad and vulnerable.

Without anything to occupy his mind, he couldn't help but concentrate on his ankle, which hurt all the worse.

Spotting his man purse on the opposite side of the bed, he smiled, remembering the pain pills tucked within.

He reached out and swam across the giant bed toward his goal, inadvertently bumping the remote control somewhere along the way. The giant screen on the near wall switched from the colorful drone shots to black-and-white split-screen views of the outside of the house. It took him a minute, but he saw that the views came from cameras mounted above the front and back doors and showed the entrances, porch, walk, and the scene beyond.

Goodbody laughed at the hilarity of the moment, and then frowned at the profundity. Janus, with all his bravado, living in such fear, to have cameras pointed at the house, presumably for protection. Heavy is the head that wears the crown. Better to be a lowly court jester.

When prescribing narcotics for the injured performer, the doctor had NOT suggested a whiskey chaser, but Rayford's aching heart pounded in time with his injury. Waiting for the pills to kick in, and knowing they would wear off too soon, he threw back another shot. The liquor spread fiery wings in his chest as it went down, washing away physical pain, but leaving a nagging worry.

Things between him and his lover were changing, and Rayford didn't like it. The "events" with her—three-person romps that were more a competition than a personal pleasure—had become more frequent; and he suspected they might even be meeting without him.

On impulse, he grabbed his cell phone and speed-dialed the DJ, knowing he would be getting ready to take the stage at the Fox.

Rayford was glad and a little surprised at the conciliatory tone in his lover's voice.

"How's your foot, Goodbody? You been getting some

rest?"

"Hurts like hell. I wish you were here," he whined.

"Stay there at my place, you'll be able to relax." His familiar baritone voice was comforting, though its tone was unfamiliar—it wasn't like Janus to empathize. Rayford lay on the sea of pillows and imagined his boyfriend sitting in his Detroit dressing room, coolly perusing his collection of stage shades, feelings safely locked inside.

Janus asked, as if he really cared, "Where are you spending your time? Which room?"

He flushed at the thought of Janus imagining him as he was doing the same. It felt good to be taken into consideration. His heart lightened, forgetting about his ignored texts as he babbled gleefully about the nest he'd set up for himself in the Temple.

Janus let him talk, and then said, "If you need anything, hit me up, and I'll have somebody take care of it—"

Rayford's mind and focused jealousy went directly to his rival. His mood capsized, giving way to his underlying insecurity. He didn't consider that Janus could have just as easily sent one of the security guys from the club with whatever he might need.

"Oh, I know who you mean, so no need to be coy," he hissed.

"What?"

"You know exactly who and what the fuck I'm talking about," he slurred.

"You're drunk," Janus said, "Or high."

"Dammit, maybe I'm both! And so the hell what if I am?" Rayford knew he sounded like a petulant child.

Janus didn't respond.

The jilted lover let his eyes wander to the screen and watched the meandering snowflakes drifting down past the lights on the corners of the house and it dawned on him. "I'll bet you took that glorified bartender bitch with you!" he blurted.

She was probably climbing all over his man at that very

moment.

"I'm getting tired of your antics. You need to chill that shit out," was the answer that came from Detroit, and it was as chilly as the Michigan weather.

The reaction was too calm and Rayford wanted to argue. The combination of the booze and medicine had finally hit like a one-two punch. Floating from above all this, viewing the world through an imaginary fishbowl, he could make Janus verbally knuckle up. Even through the thickening haze, he knew what buttons to push.

"Go on and say it: you're getting tired of me," he'd blurted back in a slurred, accusatory tone.

Only silence ensued.

Desperate for Janus to feel something, Rayford threw a barb, admittedly trying to knock his lover off his game. "Question for you, Superstar—"

"What's that," the DJ growled, obviously annoyed.

"If I could have your baby, would *she* even be in the picture?"

This time, when no response came, the bitter house guest figured his dart had hit the bull's-eye. He heard his lover emit a long sigh. Though muffled from inside Janus's dressing room, Rayford could discern the cheers of the crowd in the background signaling it was time for the musician to do his thing.

"You're a fucking joke," said Janus. "Since the promoter doesn't pay me for domestic drama, I'm gonna let you sulk."

"Yeah, whatever. You're so damn full of yourself, we should be callin' you Narcissus!"

In a flash, the DJ's voice turned into a snarl. "How about this: you need to be gone when I get back home. Soon as you sober up, collect all your crap and get your possessive, bitter black ass out of my house!"

It wasn't the first time Rayford had heard this threat, but it hurt anyway. Throwing the phone onto the bed, he thought about tearing up the mansion—dousing the expensive wallpaper in some garish color of paint, then going from room to room, gathering the masks and framed sketches into a pile and setting them ablaze. He'd even knock the beloved Nefertiti off her pedestal—maybe.

But his vengeance would have to wait until the room stopped spinning.

Collapsing onto the bed, Rayford felt the full effect of the cocktail deliver the knockout blow. When he closed his eyes, his body took him into free fall; when he opened them, the walls and ceiling swam and the huge projector screen blurred.

Purging was inevitable, so he hung his head over the edge of the mattress and emptied the contents of his gut onto the plush green carpet. The sight and smell of his chunky vomit prompted another round of regurgitation. Puke splashed onto the wooden frame of the bed, the wall, and God only knows where else. A couple more times, his body went through the motions, making him wretch so hard his abdominal muscles went into spasm and his heart seemed to beat erratically. Feeling a sense of doom, Rayford thought about calling someone for help. But who? He wondered when the housekeeper was due to come again—tomorrow morning at the earliest.

He needed to get it together. He was a sweaty mess, but the spinning seemed to have subsided a bit. He wiped his mouth on the corner of a pillowcase, and gradually realized that he was no longer alone. A silhouette loomed at the double door of the theater, appearing to watch him there in his chemical purgatory. He accepted without argument that he was hallucinating—until the figure pulled the doors closed, turned, and took a step closer to the bed. Rayford gasped as the shadow leaned in. Through the haze of his altered mind, he could make out white teeth bared in a scowl.

For a moment, the world was silent. The incapacitated performer gazed up at the unexpected guest who stood statue-still next the bed. On the screen, the gently falling flakes had yielded to dancing flurries.

Lacking all mental coordination, his effort to address the uninvited visitor proved fruitless. Perhaps, if he had started screaming at that moment, the neighbors might have heard something, people arriving for a late service at the church across the parking lot maybe, or someone passing by...

The first blow connected with his left eye and caused a constellation of stars before everything went black on that side. Another slam crushed flesh and splintered bone beneath. Blow upon blow followed in rapid succession.

He lost count, eventually feeling the pressure but not the pain of the remaining strikes. He was still trying to beg for mercy through busted lips and broken teeth when he had the sense of an eggshell cracking open.

It was his skull.

Chapter 1

Like it or lump it, the Windy City is my hometown, as it has been for at least three generations of Brandywines before me. By enlisting in the military, I thought I'd made my getaway, falling in love with the stunning blue of the Aegean Sea off the coast of Santorini, and finding that I much preferred Southern Californian sunshine and palm trees to my birth city's frigid winters. But Chicago had tentacles and pulled me back.

An audible gurgle erupted from my stomach and I rolled over in bed, trying to catch the flavor of the dream I'd just left. My mouth watered as I remembered. Today was my day off and a Maxwell Street Polish sausage piled high with grilled onions shimmered in my immediate future. If the city's cuisine could be transported to the shores of Greece or the beaches of LA, I would start packing my stuff right away. I wasn't worried about the heartburn the onions would give me or even the frigid February air I would have to endure while traversing across town on slushy roads lined with dirty snow to go get it. None of that bothered me. Wanting to stay on track with my workouts, I didn't overindulge too often, but this edible delight had been on my mind for the last few busy days at work and today was the day.

Lying still and willing sleep, my eyelids slipped shut and then snapped open! The angry buzz of a disturbed beehive was my phone vibrating across the top of the nightstand.

Seeing Captain Kodjoe's name roll across the digital screen, my heart sank and my stomach growled in protest.

"Detective Brandywine," he stated, shaking me out of a pending identity crisis I may have been about to suffer. Kodjoe was typically stiff and formal but he was a good boss.

"Cap," I said, and tried unsuccessfully to stifle an audible yawn, while he, formal as always, delivered condolences for disturbing my downtime.

"No problem at all, sir. What's up?"

"With Sergeant Perry out of town, I have something for you."

Right now, my grizzled partner was somewhere between a margarita binge and a suntan session with his wife in Cancun. It dawned on me that his absence might have put me in the catbird seat.

"I realize it's your day off," he continued, "so feel free to decline if you have plans."

"No plans," I whimpered, as a thought-bubble image of a loaded Polish sausage went "pop" above my head.

"It's a sensitive matter that requires delicate attention. When, no—if, you take the assignment, you'll understand what I mean."

Assembling the jigsaw pieces of any crime, especially a murder, was always a sensitive matter, but I got the feeling he had something more in mind.

"There's a matter I'd like you to look into."

"That matter happen to involve dead bodies?"

"Yes—well, only one, thus far."

"I'm on it," I assured him, eyes watering as I stifled another yawn.

"How quickly can you get to the 5000 block of South Drexel?"

"Half an hour."

"Make it more like 20 minutes."

"10-4," I said, making sure there was no sign of complaint in my voice.

"Oh," he said, "just so you know, I'm not choosing you as lead on this case just because the Sergeant is away. Him not being around is happenstance yielding an opportunity for you. I'm confident you can get it done."

"Thank you, sir." I was ready to pop a salute. I felt pretty sure he wasn't blowing smoke up my ass.

"Officer Eggleston will be standing by with the patrolman first on scene. They're clearing the house and securing the perimeter now."

"Oh, goody," I croaked, hearing my point of contact's name.

"Yup, and I know how great you two get along. But that's minor compared to the task at hand. Call me if you need anything."

"Aye-aye," I told him and hung up. The digital clock read 7:11.

* * *

I blasted a P-Funk CD to help me wake up and improve my mood. The sun was playing peek-a-boo behind cloud cover while the Hawk swooped down in chilling gusts, disregarding layers of long johns, sweaters, and heavy coats, taking no prisoners. It reminded me that, though I loved the city, I loathed its colder months— which seemed to be everything outside of June through August.

Drexel Avenue skirted the neighborhoods of Kenwood, Hyde Park, and Woodlawn, but was mainly considered an extension—spiritually, if not geographically—of historic Bronzeville. During the Great Migration, upon arrival to the city from the Deep South, many blacks gravitated to this community. As the saying went, if you were fresh off the road from Mississippi, within five minutes of standing on a corner in the so-called "Black Metropolis," you were sure to run into an old friend.

The street was lined with ivy-covered miniature mansions. As a child, I remembered wandering out of nearby Washington Park and across Cottage Grove Avenue to marvel at the stately homes. I was amazed to discover that the fancy houses were occupied by well-to-do people with complexions like mine—attorneys, dentists, and entertainers. This stood in sharp contrast to my run-down neighborhood, infested as it was with hustlers, hoes, hypes, and knuckleheads. I grew up less than a mile to the southwest, but it may as well have been on an entirely different planet. Doe-eyed at the time, I had attributed the difference to education, but these days, I would have to throw equal parts sheer determination and luck into the mix. After all, luck favored the prepared.

I rounded the corner from 51st Street and arrived on scene in 19 minutes flat. The captain would've been proud. "Show time, Brandywine," I told myself, glancing at my reflection in the rear view before popping a stick of gum in my mouth to hide the fact I hadn't had the chance to brush.

I flashed my gold-colored star and creds to the officer posted on the walkway just past the front gate. This was the port of entry into the outer circle of death. He nodded and jotted my arrival time on a pad a paper. He'd done the same with the paramedics, who'd just gotten there a moment before I did. They were standing by, gear in hand, at the ready. Apparently, the scene was not yet secured.

"Forensics arrive yet?"

"On their way, from what I hear," the pimple-faced, uniformed patrolman assured me.

"M.E.?"

"Well, if it ain't my favorite dick," came an older voice in a cynical tone, not giving the gate-keeping youngster a chance to answer my question. But then, Melvin Eggleston was rude and territorial like that. He enjoyed being the pebble in my shoe and reveled in our ongoing pissing contest. "Emphasis on the *dick*," he added with a fake cough.

If Humpty Dumpty had taken up an interest in law enforcement or just wanted the chance to be a prick, the portly, grinning bastard before me would be he. When

I was a kid, I found the neighborhood thugs to be a minor nuisance compared to the Gang in Blue—which represented a real threat to one's life and liberty. Eggleston would have fit right in.

"If the pot ain't calling the kettle black," I volleyed.

"Touché," he said, possibly taking my remark as a compliment or just not giving a damn. Either way, his jowls blushed bright pink.

"Coroner will be a while. Forensics will be here when they get here—they're workin' another scene. I guess all the weekend corpses are surfacing this fine Monday. What else ya need to know?"

"You all still clearing the house?"

"Enough to establish a warm zone on the first floor. Got a couple of guys inside checking closets and cubbies." He turned away from me for a moment and pressed the transmission button on his radio. "I'm sending in the medics."

With that, the EMTs, rushed in with their kits.

Eggleston was trusted enough to where the zone supervisors would take their time, stop for coffee or something to eat, if they knew he was on scene. You could tell he loved being in charge, but he was a senior officer who refused to even put in for a promotion.

Word around the locker room was he pulled so much OT that he raked in more than most watch commanders after taxes. In fact, I was sure Monday was his off day, which meant that the overtime hound was making time-and-a-half as we spoke.

"Who discovered the body?"

"Cleaning lady. She was pretty upset, so I had Smitty take her back to the precinct."

"In cuffs?"

He shot me an incredulous frown and snorted. "Hell no. Itty-bitty thing. Says she arrived at about a quarter to 7, as she always does every Monday and Thursday, using her own key to the back door. Though I'm sure you're gonna check the security system for her entry time and all that jazz, I'd say she's a witness, so no bracelets during transport."

"Beside the maid and the vic, did anybody else have access to the house?"

Here, he hooked his thumbs into his duty belt with a sly grin and a look of mild irritation in his eye. "Now, if I knew all o' that, it would make *me* the detective, wouldn't it?"

He had reached his limit. Good at what he did, Eggleston knew his place in the pecking order. He was a fat frog squatting on the biggest lily pad in a small pond, happily dining on flies.

"Fine. Who was first on scene?"

"Barbosa."

The name was unfamiliar. "Have Officer Barbosa stand by for me."

"Aye-aye, sir" he said, his snarky tone rolling off my back like water off a duck.

I turned my attention to the abode. Felt strange to be walking into a murder investigation without Sarge. I would be lying if I said I wasn't a bit nervous entering the place. Even in muted daylight, the three-story house loomed like a dark and spooky thing, its upper windows glowering down at me like predatory eyes.

Every crime scene was a haunted house waiting to reveal its terrible secrets. I'd seen plenty of corpses—and even made a few of my own during my military career. Each body was as unique as a new lover, though their wide-eyed, open-mouthed looks of surprise issued not of the throes of ecstasy, but of the horror of their demise.

I climbed the ten steps to the wide columned porch and the impressive front door. Disturbing the sanctum of the deceased was to be done with reverence. I paused there and applied booties over my high-top sneakers and donned latex gloves before nudging the heavy door open and stepping over the sill.

Inside, the foyer was dark, and before my eyes had a chance to adjust, I saw something that made me jump out of my skin. Turns out, it was only a mask, a huge and angry-looking African mask.

Opening another door, I found myself in a sunny anteroom of sorts, with a stairway curving up on the right, and a shrine of back-lit framed photographs covering a prominent wall opposite. I could hear the sound of medical hubbub coming from the back of the house, where the medics were doing CPR.

I stepped closer to the photos and noticed that one man—likely the homeowner, and quite possibly the victim—appeared in each picture. Many looked to be promotional shots, with the self-possessed subject wearing various stylish outfits, including distinctive fashion eyeglasses. Several group shots were scattered amongst, one with Mayor Daley, another with Frankie Knuckles and Michael Jackson, as well as a few photos of the man on stage. He looked familiar.

"Who is this dude," I asked over my shoulder, sensing someone else in the room.

"You must not listen to House music, man," replied a feminine voice.

I spun around to face my accuser.

Dressed in CPD uniform, complete with a subdued bun, the officer was short and curvy with bronzed features. She appeared to be Latina; Northeast Illinois boasted large Puerto Rican and Mexican-American populations. But her greenish-hazel eyes were not in common with the descendants of the Tainos or Aztecs. Maybe her folks hailed from Portugal, Brazil, or someplace else—I couldn't assume—and it didn't matter.

"He's a superstar DJ and music producer. Kind of a big deal around these parts."

"Brandywine," I said, by way of introduction while catching sight of her name tag.

She returned the intro, briefly gripping my extended

hand. "Officer Jerilyn Barbosa. Glad to finally meet you, Detective."

"Wait. What does that mean," I blurted out.

"I guess it means that your reputation precedes you," she said, rolling her almond-shaped eyes playfully. Then she straightened a bit and her expression went serious. "His name is Janus. Just the one name."

Of course I knew of the mononymous musician. In fact, I was pretty sure that my House Head captain was a big fan. No wonder he had referred to it as a sensitive matter. Kodjoe, appointing me lead on the investigation into his hero's murder meant I better be at the top of my game.

"Quite the ladies' man—a man's man as well, rumor has it," she said, cutting her eyes and raising her eyebrows. For a moment, I thought she was talking about my boss, which gave me pause. But then she continued. "Janus is rather notorious for that sort of thing."

The voices of the paramedics counting out chest compressions droned on in the background, punctuated by the periodic swoosh of the ambu bag.

"By the way, may I offer my opinion on something, sir?"

"Sure, but you don't have to call me—"

"The person they're pumping on in the theater," she thumbed over her shoulder, "that's not *him*."

"What makes you so certain?"

"Well, Janus is a big guy, around 6 foot 5, or thereabouts, and 38 years old. The victim is nowhere near as tall, and just not as big, or as old. Sure, it's hard to tell, but I think the—should I say *deceased*—is quite a bit younger. I've seen Janus perform more than a few times—even posed for a picture with him once. Hang on..." She was scrolling on her phone, made a click or two, and handed it to me.

It was uncanny. Definitely the same guy as all the framed photos on the wall, right down to the smirk. He towered over Barbosa in the picture—and she was wearing some wicked stilettos. And, I couldn't help but notice, a short turquoise dress with a scoop neck.

I handed the phone back to her without comment and started walking toward the room.

"The EMTs will be giving up soon," she said, following me.

"What makes you say that?"

"He's long gone. Rigor had already begun to set in and he was cold to the touch. And, umm, you know...the gray matter."

I grimaced. So it was one of *those*.

Reaching the doorway, I saw why Barbosa had referred to the room as a theater. The deck was raised. Rather than stepping up and into the room, I leaned my head through the doorway and looked over to where the medics were working on the victim on the floor.

My gaze shifted to the center of the bed where an ugly pool of dark red congelation mixed with pinkish gray tissue, then back to the poor fellow there at the center of activity, enduring this futile attempt at resurrection, with his brain exploded and his limbs gone cold.

We stepped away from the entrance a bit, into the sunny living room, and I asked for a full account of the officer's interaction with the housekeeper. Being first on the scene, Barbosa had met the frightened woman at the curb. Apparently, Mrs. Bilandic had run screaming out of the house without her phone or coat, and rang doorbells until someone called the police. The officer said the housekeeper seemed genuine, and in no way suspicious. I would interview her myself later, so I was non-committal.

Barbosa explained that she'd made entry to the house via the back door—left wide open by the fleeing maid—and had found the victim on the bed amidst a large amount of gore. She hadn't noticed any weapon left behind and, after failing to rouse the man, had backed out of the space and called for backup.

"Wait—the victim was on the bed when you found him?" I interjected.

"Yes, the medics moved him to the floor."

Just then, the trio of medics emerged from their vain lifesaving efforts looking weary. "He's completely unresponsive with absent heart tones, pulse, and respirations," the de facto leader announced somberly. "It appears he was bludgeoned multiple times to the head, but the coroner will have to say for sure."

Barbosa elbowed me gently.

"What do you want us to do with the body?"

"Leave the victim in place for the investigation. I'll intersect with the ME."

"We tried, man," the youngest-looking EMT said. The letdown in his voice told me he was still new at the job—maybe he was in training, which would explain why there were three. They start out all idealistic, wishing that everyone could somehow be salvaged. But people die every day. It was only Monday morning and I was sure that, by week's end, there would be more deaths and births, keeping the wheel turning.

I patted him on the shoulder and marked the time and "failure to resuscitate". The Medical Examiner's investigation, which would include obtaining a core temperature, would decide the time and the official declaration of death. After that, an autopsy would follow to determine the exact cause of demise.

I exhaled and reached into my messenger bag and handed Barbosa gloves and booties. Sarge got me used to carrying extra sets.

"Squeamish?" I asked.

"No sir. Wouldn't have taken this job if I was."

"You got a camera with you, by any chance?"

"Yes—um, yes of course, right here on my phone."

"Oh, right. Well, Forensics is running behind. I want to snoop around and get some pictures of the scene."

I dug out a business card and handed it to her. "That's my email address. As soon as we're done here, forward the pictures to me."

The room was plush, with thick dark green carpet.

A huge screen occupied most of one wall, with several smaller screens and artwork adorning the other walls. A large round bed took center stage, and I mean that literally as well as figuratively. Elevated reclined seating curved around it, like a luxury observation deck. With cameras strategically aimed, it was clear that the space was used for more than just watching after-school cartoons.

The murder victim lay—not prone on that bed as Barbosa had originally found him—but supine on the floor. He was a muscular African American male, naked except for a thong—which looked to be of some kind of shiny cloth in a royal blue—and an elastic wrap on his right ankle. A heavy trail of blood led back to the pool of gore on the bed, marking the spot where the man had died. I activated my portable recorder. "Victim is a bravo mike, mid to late twenties..." I continued to denote physical identifiers, keeping an eye out for tats, scars, and piercings, each of which Barbosa shot as I indicated.

One eye was open, the sclera bloodshot, staring unseeing at the high ceiling. The right eye was swollen shut, that whole side of his head grotesquely misshapen. With his ultra-short haircut, you could make out indentions to his skull. "Subjected to several blows with what appears to be a circular object," I said into the recorder. "What could do that? Too big to be a hammer. A mallet, perhaps?"

"Not a mallet," the young officer opined. "It looks like a smooth crater. Could it have been a bat?"

"Only if the assailant stood over him and rammed the tip of it straight down in a stabbing motion. That might work for one or two hits but it doesn't really make sense. I'm thinking something spherical, like a baseball or softball."

"Yeah, but I'm not sure they would be hard enough. Plus, the stitching might have left marks."

"Possibly. We can figure that out later, though." I paused and pointed, asking her to snap pictures. "How was he positioned when you first encountered him?"

"Face-down on the bed, with his head pointing that

way," she said, gesturing toward the curved bulkhead of the observation deck.

"Um," I hesitated, not wanting to introduce a negative. "You didn't think to take any pictures before they moved him, did you?"

She looked at me aghast, her green eyes bright. "Of course I did, several. I've already emailed them to you. Didn't you get the notification on your phone?"

I subconsciously patted my coat pocket where my trusty old Nokia handset was only available for phone calls or texts. "No, it's fine. I'll look when I get back to my computer." I felt a bit off-kilter for some reason, but I didn't forget my manners. "Thanks."

I crouched near the wall, thinking I would look under the bed but then I got a whiff of something really bad.

Ready for the coppery smell and the splatter, I was caught off guard by a foul odor that triggered my gag reflex. Sure enough, next to the bed reeked a huge, putrid puddle of pink vomit soup studded with multi-colored chunks. I wanted to heave.

I came up for air and stepped away from the area to try to regain control of my olfactory system.

Barbosa snapped a picture of the vomit, sidestepped, and took another.

I squatted by the body and canted my head, checking out the vacant look in the victim's one open eye. "Savage," I mumbled, "the way he was attacked. Dude had to have been pretty threatening to overpower this guy. He is — *was* — in great shape."

"Why are you so quick to assume the perp was male?"

I paused for a moment, rubbing my chin. "Yeah, good point. It's just that . . . well, this guy is chiseled. Looks as if he could have defended himself."

"He does look pretty formidable," she said, snapping another pic. "But what if the killer had an advantage over the victim?"

"Like a gun?"

"Nah. If she'd had a gun, she would have simply shot him or pistol-whipped him to death."

I chuckled. "*She?*"

The officer smiled and shrugged her shoulders. "Hey, why not? Women are capable of some pretty heinous shit."

We were going back and forth, the way Perry and I did when we came to a crime scene. Making suggestions and looking at things from different perspectives is what often led to nabbing the bad guy—or girl, if Barbosa was correct.

"Most women sent to prison felt they were protecting something that was theirs," I posited.

"True. If the most docile mother thinks you are trying to hurt her children, she'll rip your head off."

I nodded, having seen my tiny mother take on my inebriated father as if he didn't outweigh her by almost a hundred pounds. And Thomas Brandywine Senior could be one mean dude when he hit the sauce.

"Likewise," Barbosa said, "it could have been for love."

"It does have the markings of a crime of passion. What do *you* see?"

She lowered the camera, and did a slow pirouette, taking in the screening room, with all its sexually explicit decor. "I see a lot of freaky stuff having gone on here."

"Like?"

She pointed to the prominently displayed paintings of people satisfying their urges. Then she turned to the raised platform behind the headboard. "Look at all the seating."

"What about it?"

"Well, notice all the chairs both recline and are wide enough to support more than one body. The seating at the lower level also faces the bed."

"Think they were into something kinky?"

Barbosa chuckled. "Well, *that's* obvious." She paused, turning her head to consider something. "Being sexually liberated doesn't make someone a killer, though."

"True. But it does look like they perform some sort of weird rituals in here." I looked around, expecting to see a stash of incense, or at least some candles.

"I'll keep my eyes peeled and camera ready for any occult symbols and black robes," she quipped. "My guess is they were just having good clean—or *dirty*—fun."

"Think they were making porn here?" I suggested.

"Probably not for mass distribution, but for private viewing—definitely."

I looked toward the ceiling, where track lighting aimed at the bed. I stepped carefully around until I found two cameras. "Bingo," I said, pointing them out.

"We need to see if anything was recorded," she stated flatly. "Anything having to do with the murder, that is."

I watched as she fished a remote control out of the tangled bedsheets and clicked it on. The large wall screen sprang to life with images of the street and the backyard.

"Looks like we might have some surveillance footage to work with," she suggested.

"You're good at this. Maybe I should just hand my badge over to you," I said, trying to bring the focus back to myself, I suppose.

"Yeah, but in a few years," she said with a grin. And then added, "It's likely that he knew his killer."

"Now, you're just stating the obvious. Most victims know their killers. However we can assume it wasn't a random break-in because there was no sign of forced entry. He—no, *she*," I corrected, playing into Barbosa's hunch, "may have had a key. Or maybe the victim even let the perp into the house."

"I would lean more toward the former than to the latter."

"How come?" I asked.

She squatted to her haunches, taking out her flashlight, and shined it at the puddle of vomit that had so overpowered me. "It's there."

"His last supper?"

"More than that. I'd bet you a cup of your favorite coffee that there's some sort of drug and/or alcohol in it."

"The forensics guys haven't been through here yet," I

intoned, "They'll collect samples. We'll have it examined, plus the autopsy will include a toxicology report."

"You're going to owe me a large hazelnut latte with coconut milk, sir."

"Please, you don't have to call me—*wait*, what does a regurgitated meal have to do with all this?"

"My guess is he was too, um—I'm trying to stop cursing—*jacked up*."

"You were gonna say he was too fucked up. I don't mind the profanity. Just tell me what you think."

"Thanks," she said, taking a deep breath. "The victim was too impaired to open the front door, then stumble back in here to the bed again. Besides whatever he drank, ingested, shot up, or smoked, it was probably in addition to some sort of painkillers or muscle relaxers." She waved her arm at the victim's bandaged ankle, and included the pair of crutches leaning against the wall.

And obviously, we had both noticed the well-stocked liquor cart.

"We'll need to find out who else, besides the housekeeper, has a key to the house." I looked the body over again, picked up and examined his hands, and saw no defensive wounds. The medical examiner would determine what, if anything hid under the victim's nails. When fighting to survive, humans devolved, trading sophistication and high-minded manners in their desperation to live. Even a big guy would resort to scratching his assailant. If he could.

"Am I allowed to touch this?" asked Barbosa. She was pointing at a handbag looped over a seat back.

"Sure, you're wearing gloves, just be careful."

Without disturbing the way the bag hung, she lifted the top and peered inside, snapping a picture before she reached in and pulled out a prescription bottle.

"Just as I thought. Oxycodone, 5mg every 6 hours as needed for severe pain," she read aloud.

"Let me see that," I said, and she handed it over. The

patient was a Rayford Goodbody, the meds came from a nearby urgent care clinic, and 30 of the pills had been dispensed just three days before, on Friday. I popped the top, poured the contents into my gloved hand and did a quick count. All but 6 of the original pills were present.

"Not excessive, but depending on when and how he took them, you could be right about his being incapacitated. Anything else in that bag? Like a wallet?"

"No wallet, just some papers. Discharge instructions from the clinic for Rayford Goodbody, let me see, right ankle sprain, the usual RICE advice, nothing special."

"Rice? What, as in cooking it?" I asked, considering it an odd occasion for a recipe.

"No," she admonished, shaking her head like I was daft. "I guess it's true that men only think about food and sex, huh?"

"That's kinda discriminatory," I said, feigning hurt feelings but finding the humor (and the truth) in it.

"As I meant for it to be," she volleyed with a playful wink. "Anyway, genius, RICE is an acronym for 'Rest, Ice, Compression, and Elevation.'"

"Oh," I replied, acknowledging I learned something new everyday before getting back to the matter at hand. "It's not a straightforward identification but seems pretty likely," I said, unnecessarily.

I walked over to the doorway and surveyed the room to see what else I had missed besides the victim's murse. *Must be the murderer took the weapon with him—or her. Unless...*

I stepped over to the foot of the bed to peak under it and took a knee.

"Dammit!" I exclaimed, realizing I had knelt in another spot of vomit, this one rather petite, and blending into the carpet so perfectly that I hadn't even seen it.

In my periphery, Barbosa was near the head of the bed, peering down between the mattress and the frame. "I think I might have found the murder weapon."

I went to take a look. Rolled up under the head of the bed and wedged so as to be completely hidden from most vantage points was what appeared to be an orb the size of a softball. Barbosa took photos of the thing as it lay from every angle she could reach.

Then, she pulled the pictures up on her screen, one at a time, dismissing some outright, and focusing on others.

Much of the surface was smeared with blood, colored brown at this point. Maybe it was made of metal, or possibly some kind of rock. But it looked perfectly cylindrical. I didn't dare even nudge it to check its heft—Forensics would be livid, since they were on their way, and there was no cause to move it other than my piqued curiosity.

"Try to get some images from the other side, if you could," I suggested to Barbosa, and she went ahead and worked on that, using my flashlight. I felt kind of bad about sending her into that barf-soaked zone, but I got the impression she was plenty tough.

A few of the later pictures showed a bit more. Between the bloody smudges, you could see some contrast in color. I really wanted to get my hands on that object and take a good look.

We moved over to the foul dark green vomit puddle I'd found with my knee and Barbosa snapped a picture of that.

"WHAT ARE YOU ALL DOING IN HERE?"

Even with the room's soundproofing, the volume was loud. Laplaglia and Sorenson had arrived from Forensics. The former was the larger, balder, and slightly more masculine of the two. I speculated that the source of his perpetual crankiness was the stringy comb-over that served as a futile attempt to hide an LZ large enough to set a helicopter down on his oversized head.

I peered up from the patch of emesis and channeled my absent partner: "Well, we couldn't wait all day for you divas to get here."

"Has anything been moved or removed," Sorenson demanded. She was the calmer of the pair, though she kept a steely gaze.

"The body was moved from the bed to the floor by the EMT's," I said right away, provoking angry recriminations from both of the detectives—which I ignored, but I noticed that Barbosa wore a pained expression. I also mentioned the prescription drug bottle.

"Next time, unless something is in jeopardy of being removed or destroyed," said Sorenson, "leave it for us to approach first."

"My bad."

"We'll take it from here, Rook," Sorensen said, running her fingers through her short dark hair and resting her hand on her neck in an irritated gesture.

I didn't like being referred to as a rookie.

"Perry still on leave?" Laplaglia asked.

"Yep. Kodjoe assigned me as lead on the case."

The partners looked at each other, barely stifling chuckles. Laplaglia gave himself a face palm, while Sorenson put her hands on her narrow hips and shook her head.

Assholes.

I gave them a quick rundown of the investigation so far, leaving out the part about finding the murder weapon. I was saving that little morsel. I told them about Barbosa taking pictures of the body before it was moved, which they certainly should have appreciated. They just ordered her to email them the photos. After several more questions about what we'd noticed, they told us to step out, so they could begin processing the scene. Sorensen gave us the green light to look around the house for other clues but warned us about destroying any fingerprint evidence.

As we skirted past his bulk, Laplaglia emitted a guttural noise that reminded me of a mangy stray. "Ya better not have dicked up my scene," he growled through clenched teeth, on the verge of blowing a gasket.

"Oh, by the way," I said, over my shoulder, "you might want to take a look at what's under the right side of the head of the bed."

Once we stepped out, Barbosa asked, "What the f—um, *heck* is that all about? Eggleston is a smart-ass, too."

"Thought you were trying to stop using profanity," I quipped.

"Dammit—*sorry*," she uttered, smacking herself on the forehead. Thumbing toward the duo who was setting up lights and marking evidence, she said, "I know I'm pretty new to this, but is that what I have to look forward to?"

"What, looking as if you could crack a walnut between your butt cheeks like Sorenson or acting as cantankerous as her partner?"

"The one with the bald spot."

"Everybody's different but the toe-taggers tend to be a cranky batch. Ain't natural to keep seeing dead bodies all the time," I ventured.

She nodded.

"Anyway, we can look around and see if we can confirm the victim's identity, among other things."

Back in the sunny living room, I peered at the mural of photos lining the wall with renewed perspective.

Janus was probably the most successful of the crowned "Superstar DJ's," among the chosen few who did collaborations and remixes with household name artists. At least that's what Barbosa told me.

I hadn't really been into House since my days of school dances and basement parties. Since then, my musical standbys had become old school Funk, Soul, Hip Hop and, thanks to Perry, Classic Rock.

But I wasn't clueless. My fair city is notorious for several things. Crime, tourist attractions, and the awesome cuisine aside, we are a musical city, known for innovations in Jazz, our own style of Blues, and the homegrown evolution of dance music. I was still in diapers when fanatics had sounded the death knell at Disco Demolition Night in '79, which prompted the birth of House and its underground nature. What rose from the exploded shards of vinyl at Comiskey Park was a hypnotic, bass-heavy sound that became the worship music in dance clubs from New York to Ibiza to Rome.

Coming to fore around the same time, Hip Hop was more "in your face", and became the more commercially viable of the two. The second coming of Disco remained subversive and its new gaggle of fans, "House Heads", went about their loyalty like members of a secret society or lesser known cult that was not seeking expansion.

Barbosa, gleeful to be standing on what could be considered sacred ground, but more importantly, thrilled that everybody's favorite music producer had not been the subject of our visit, would definitely qualify as a House Head. I had a feeling that Captain Kodjoe also belonged to the club. I hadn't been a detective long, but I could recall him making a big deal last summer about attending both the Urban Music Fest and Battle of the Superstar DJ's in Grant Park.

"So," I thought aloud, "if the vic isn't Janus, then where is he? Maybe he's in danger...And how do we know that he's not the culprit?"

"Could he be on the run, you mean?" Barbosa pulled out her phone and did a few taps and swipes on the screen before handing it to me. "If you scroll down, you'll see his tour schedule. According to this, Janus had a two-day, sold-out engagement in Detroit over the weekend, then he heads to Milwaukee for another show tomorrow evening. The murderer would have known that too—you would think—I mean, if it was someone who meant to murder Janus, but got this guy instead."

Wow. "Good sleuthing," I said, but again I felt that little disconcerting tug. I might really have to take the plunge, upgrade my phone—and my methods.

A public engagement at a city a few hours away did not exactly serve as an airtight alibi. The time of death determination, when compared to the time of the show, would speak volumes. It was still possible for Janus to have been the killer— flying back to Chicago after Sunday night's performance in Detroit, then rejoining the rest of the tour in Wisconsin. Not probable, but far from impossible.

"What time do you get off," I asked Barbosa. "

Why," she inquired coyly, "you asking me out on a date?"

I chuckled. *As cute as she is snarky.* "Yeah, a date with the dead," I said somberly.

"You're a friggin' killjoy. Anyway, my shift ended about," she pressed a button and glanced at the time on her phone, "thirty-seven minutes ago."

"If you don't mind hanging around and helping me out…"

Her eyes brightened. "I would love to! However, OT has to be approved by my watch command—"

I pulled out my own phone and dialed the station.

Captain Kodjoe picked up on the second ring. I informed him that the DJ was definitely not the murder victim, though of course, further verification of the victim's identity was necessary. I heard him sigh in relief.

"Who is it, then," he asked, and I gave him the name from the prescription bottle. In any case, the homeowner had to be notified; I figured that Kodjoe might want to take the lead on letting Janus know what had happened at his house.

He told me he'd put in the call to Captain Malloy, who had the off-going Patrol shift. I informed him about the chest-bumping between me and Laplaglia.

"We got a preliminary statement from Mrs. Mariska Bilandic, the cleaning lady, then released her. She'll come back to interview with you. I'll forward you her number, so you can set that up." He paused, clearing his throat. "As for Detective Laplaglia, he'll be alright, once the swelling goes down."

My boss hung up before he could catch my snicker.

I turned to my temporary partner, who was ogling the curio cabinet. "You're good. Just make sure you log the overtime when we're done here."

Mesmerized, she nodded but didn't look at me. The vintage curio cabinet stood against the wall with its curved glass and dainty little legs. Five glass shelves were filled with all sorts of trinkets, sparkling from the type of lighting used in jewelry stores.

"Any baseballs?" I quipped, directing my attention to the cabinet's handle where I immediately saw that the key had been left in the lock. I wanted so badly to turn that key and that clasp, open that door and examine everything inside. But of course, I didn't.

"Nope. But there are quite a few snow globes."

"Snow globe, huh?..."

Standing next to her, I peered down into the display case, my hands in my pockets. I'd never really given much thought to snow globes before, and I guess I expected to see holiday scenes or maybe a miniature Sears Tower inside them. But these were different. They were artsy and stylized.

"Oh look, there's one with the cover of 'The Black Narcissus'"!

"Eh?" I didn't get the reference, but she indicated a globe sitting on a pedestal on the middle shelf. It was nearly the size of a softball, larger than your run of the mill shake-it-up-and-watch-it-snow plastic toy. Even seen through the glass case, it gave the impression of bulk and heaviness. It looked to be made of solid glass, but I could see a scene etched inside—a silhouette profile of a man holding a flower.

"It's probably his most popular album, and my personal favorite, " supplied Barbosa, and added "it came out 10 years ago when I was a teen."

I looked to the others in the cabinet. "Does each of these commemorate an album? Seems like a lot."

"He has quite a few records under his belt, to include some live performances, remixes, and several compilations. Won a couple of Grammys—oh, there they are on the second shelf," she exclaimed.

"They look smaller in real life than I would have guessed."

"Wait, there's an empty pedestal," I exclaimed. It sat on the top shelf, near the back. "Thief of Hearts, Jack of Spades," I read the metal label affixed to the empty pedestal.

"Oh my god, his new album," she responded, and gave a little hop. "I can't see it—Oh, okay," she said, stepping back so she could get a good look at the top shelf.

"How tall are you, anyway?" I asked, "Or maybe I should say, how short are you?"

Veeeery funny. Tall enough," she laughed, and then looked at me, with all seriousness. "Maybe the thing we found under the bed belongs on this here pedestal."

"You may be right. We need to find out if this key is always left in the door. If not, where was it kept and who the hell knew about it."

Without opening the cabinet, we cataloged the contents, a total of 35 items, (not counting the empty pedestal). I figured that Barbosa's apparent expertise in the area of House Music lore was worthy of the extra effort.

I learned a lot in the process, maybe more than I ever wanted to know about "the great Janus—music impresario and nightclub owner".

We moved down the hall, went past a small bedroom, and into the kitchen. A once-over revealed a dried up partially eaten slice of pepperoni pizza in a splayed-out pizza box balanced on an overrun trashcan. The bin was full of wrappers and containers and was smelling pretty ripe. The spacious refrigerator contained little in addition to the usual condiments in the doors, a nearly-empty juice bottle, some wilted produce, and a couple of Chinese take-out cartons. I thought about the dead man's injured ankle and turned on my recorder. "Garbage hasn't been taken out. Filled with remnants of fast food or delivery."

"He was likely house-sitting," came from the peanut gallery.

"What about all this crap?"

"If you tag it," she said with a sly grin, "Your best buddy with the bald spot will have to take it with him for analysis."

"I like the way your mind works," I told her with a wink. I chuckled at the idea of Laplaglia joylessly carting the bag of stinking trash out to his car.

A peek into the pantry revealed a run-of-the-mill collection of canned vegetables, boxes of pasta and rice. The only thing out of place was a dark skullcap lying in the middle of the floor.

"That's odd," Barbosa commented, snapping a picture.

"What, the image?" I asked, noting that the embroidered emblem facing up on the hat was of a man looking forward and back, resembling a Greco-Roman bas-relief.

"No, of course, I know what that is."

"What do you mean, you know what it is?"

"That's the logo for Janus' club, Duality. Everyone who works there wears one. It's part of the uniform."

"So you've been to this nightspot?"

"A time or two," she said, "or three."

I looked back down at the hat laying there in the middle of the pantry floor. Seemed as out of sorts as it was convenient. I tagged it, made note of it, and we moved on. Forensics would study it for hair and fibers.

"Looking for this?" Barbosa said, pointing at the counter. The leather wallet was parked next to the waffle iron, almost camouflaged against the speckled dark marble.

I nodded and scratched my chin before picking it up.

Rifling through it, I found a gift card, a hundred dollars or so in varying denominations, and, most importantly, the victim's Illinois driver's license. "Rayford Goodbody, 28 years old, Lincoln Park address."

"Hmmnn, that's an hour away by train. What's he doing here?" she asked.

I was looking at the photo on the ID. Then I thought about it further, recognizing the victim's unmistakably athletic physique, as well as his obvious injury. "Maybe he was left behind from the tour," I ventured, and added "Run his info."

"Gotcha."

Done in the kitchen for now, I moved back to the living room. Hands on my hips, I looked up the staircase, which was lined with eclectic paintings. I couldn't really see the victim hobbling up the stairs or down to the basement for anything, but no stone would go unturned.

Though we'd only met that day, I got a good vibe off the young officer. And it had nothing to do with her attractiveness. In fact, I ignored the sway of her hips and rounded butt as she climbed the stairs ahead of me. Most importantly, I noticed that she made sure she didn't smudge the banisters or any other surface that could be brushed for prints. She was good police.

We checked each of the four bedrooms on the second story; all staged and looking un-lived in, as if ready to be photographed for a celebrity homes magazine article.

The master bedroom suite, which took up the entire 3rd floor, was an elegant affair, with a four-poster California king, more artwork, and all the accouterments, including a sumptuous bathroom, a cavernous walk-in closet, as well as a sitting room with a desk. I tried not to think about my unmade queen-size bed waiting for me back at my humble abode.

Back downstairs, Sorenson and Laplaglia looked to be finishing up in the kill room. I saw something I hadn't noticed before—pink residue about the vic's mouth— which probably pertained to the larger puddle of puke off the side of the bed.

"You checked the vomit, right?" I asked.

"Duh," said Sorenson. "We got it, Rook."

"*Both* spots?" I asked, all innocent-like, and I noticed Barbosa's expression change as we watched the pair look back and forth at each other and then around the room.

"Um…"

Now it was their turn to be schooled.

While Laplaglia took a sample of the green stuff, I informed Sorenson about the key we'd found (and left untouched, of course) in the curio cabinet, the wallet, the garbage, and the skullcap in the pantry. Finally, before they moved on, I asked them to show us the murder weapon.

Sorenson sighed, but didn't balk. She went out in the hall for a moment to where they had collected their stuff, and came back in with a cardboard box the size of a basketball. The top was open and I could see loosely packed paper all around the middle object, which now I could definitely see was indeed a bloody snow globe.

My partner grinned in recognition. "That's so *cool!*"

"The murder weapon is cool?"

"Yes. The stuff inside is made of gold—even the snowflakes."

Peering into the box, I couldn't see that at all. Far too much of the surface of the heavy glass orb was obfuscated by dried blood and gore; there was no way of making out that kind of detail.

"Get out of here, Barbosa. You can't see that!"

She laughed. "No, of course not. But that's what it is."

At this point, I noticed Sorenson and Laplaglia taking an interest, and thus encouraged, Barbosa continued.

"It's a stylized playing card, only instead of a mirror image, there's a man on top, portrayed with the suit of clubs, and the woman on the bottom is the Queen of Hearts. The object in the globe replicates the cover of Janus' latest album."

"Ah, so it *does* match the empty pedestal," I exclaimed, and Sorenson's eyes widened as she made the connection.

"I guess we will have to wait until our friends the

forensics experts finish with it, before we can clean it up and see its real beauty," she said, smiling.

"Given this, you should take the empty pedestal into evidence as well. On the top shelf of the curio cabinet in the living room," I said to Laplaglia. "And the key, of course."

"Sure, no problem," he said, like a normal person. Then, in a congenial manner, Sorenson turned to Barbosa, "Give us a chance to analyze this in the lab, and you can come visit it next week for a better look, Officer." Then she and her partner moved on to other parts of the house.

Jerilyn Barbosa's big smile followed them out of the room.

Though I didn't want to, I went back to the vomit. I could clearly see the vast difference between the two upchucks. The small thin dark green one at the foot of the bed was mostly dried, while the large puddle at the bedside was still moist, some of the colorful chunks being readily identifiable as peas and carrots from the Chinese leftovers I saw in the fridge. I made a mental note to check for an empty can of spinach or something else that could have been the dark green. I thought I might toss my own cookies from being so close to it and I stood up, putting a hand over my mouth.

"I should've asked if you had a weak stomach," said Barbosa.

"Blood and gore don't bother me too much, just puke."

"Everybody has that one thing that makes them queasy. For me, it's always been dirty diapers. We can trade war stories on that factoid another time. The struggle is real, son."

All I could do was laugh and shake my head.

"From where I'm standing," she said, not missing a beat, "either the vic blew chunks after two separate meals, or more than one person purged their guts."

"You mean the killer?" I thought about it for a second and then continued, "yeah, I noticed a curdled, pink residue in the corners of the victim's mouth, so it's apparent which puddle belongs to him. I suppose it's possible that the murderer upchucked the green stuff, especially if he wasn't a hardened crim—"

"*She.*"

I shrugged, giving in that it was possible.

"Why not," Barbosa asked. "The female of the species can be a motherf—um, can be worse than the male. Plus, it's not wise to be so chauvinistic—we ladies want equal standing when it comes to that thug life!"

I considered the various domestic disputes I'd attended, automatically assuming that the primary aggressor would be the husband, only to discover, that it was the wife. Despite all the posturing, there were guys twice the size of their women who were softer than hush puppies on the inside.

"Could be," I admitted.

The officer's radio crackled, announcing the coroner was on the way in.

She keyed the mic, "10-4".

"I've got to get down to the station, but if you have a chance before you leave, can you canvas the neighbors for statements?"

"You bet," she said.

"You like this sort of work?" I asked.

"Sure do," she said, all bright eyed. "You're what I wanna be when I grow up."

"What, a tall dude with a big head who spends much of his time alone?"

She laughed and I beamed. She saw that I had a sense of humor, after all.

"No, smarty-pants. I joined the force hoping to one day become a detective. I know I have to put in my time on the street before I'm even eligible to apply."

"That's how it works," I shrugged.

She flashed a professional smile but batted her eyes in a way to suggest her interests may have gone beyond that.

No denying she could turn many heads, but I always keep things above-board at work. I grinned and gave her a small nod.

Then I headed out, only to be met by the Hawk; the frostbitten wind notoriously swoops in from the lake to claim its victims. My breath floated before me in a cloud of condensation and I saw members of the press buzzing about with their cameramen, trying to get the scoop on what'd happened. The Public Information Office could handle that headache.

Off to the side were the common folk, peacefully waving their signs. It took some serious commitment to listen to their police scanners and exercise their right to protest in some of the nastiest weather. They chanted, sometimes sang, but never really got in the way.

Theirs was a world on the other side of Washington Park, where young men who looked a lot like me were arbitrarily taken away in cuffs, only to be returned battered and bruised, if at all. Randomly showing up outside crime scenes, the demonstrators were there to ensure that we, the cops, did our jobs. I owed it to them to not only to do my best at what I did, but also to take care of business professionally and by the numbers. We wanted the same thing—to see justice done. They weren't some renegade gaggle with ill intent; they were just people of the community. And I was one of them: a native son whose position happened to fall on the other side of the crime scene tape.

I'd become accustomed to Sergeant Perry being around to head up the investigations but this time it was me on deck leading the charge, despite the cynicism of LaPlaglia and Sorenson. There would likely be others who thought I was too young in the game to be thrown a bone, but my captain trusted me, and the job felt heavy on my shoulders.

A shiver went through me and I popped the collar of my pea coat, teeth chattering from more than just frigid temps. I imagined strolling over to the folks holding their signs and, like a bleeding-heart TV cop, declaring to them that justice would be done.

But that would've been silly. Deciding to leave the corny lines unspoken, I warmed up my truck and mentally prepped myself to interview the housekeeper. Flag-waving and promises aside, solid investigations hinged on taking statements—not making them.

Chapter 2

Mrs. Mariska Bilandic was a fragile looking woman in her late fifties with sallow skin and graying dark hair put up in a neat bun.

I introduced myself and offered her a seat. "Water?"

"Thank you," she said.

Her arthritic fingers struggled with the cap before she got it off and took a sip.

She affirmed that, though she had only caught a glimpse of the victim before running out of the house, it was not Janus. She was a tiny woman who'd been cleaning houses since before I was born, and had tending to that address for over five years. A quick records check came back negative for petty theft or anything else.

The Drexel house was her first appointment twice a week. Showing up each Monday was a mandate, while she had a choice of either Thursday or Friday for the second. "It's because of the types of parties Mr. Janus has all the time," she said, her voice dropping to just over a whisper.

"What kind are those," I inquired.

"Wild ones."

I could tell she didn't approve but that she also kept hush about the goings-on there. "She explained that she would start in the screening room, since it took the longest to clean" Seeing the dead body on the bed about gave her a heart attack.

"Mr. Janus has many overnight visitors and they are

often still sleeping upstairs when I arrive, especially on Mondays..."

"Who was he," I asked, handing her an enlarged copy of the victim's driver license photo.

Bilandic's hands were shaking and her eyes were tearing up. "I have seen him many times, visiting the house. He is...*was* a nice young man."

She told me he went by Goodbody, though she didn't know if it was his Christian name, last name, or just a handle he used.

I saw no motive she would have to kill. Standing just 4'11" and weighing in at no more than 100 pounds soaking wet, she could not have overpowered and bludgeoned the victim on her best day. But I had to be sure to eliminate her as a suspect or even a person of interest. That meant holding her at the station while calls were made and questions were asked. I shuffled through the shots Barbosa had sent me and found one that showed the less battered side of the victim's face. I wanted to see the older woman's reaction.

Tears streaked her cheeks. "Yes, that's him."

The dam broke and she was inconsolable. Though she didn't know him well, he was the same age as one of her own sons, who had, she said, given his life to drugs and revelry. I held her hand and made sure there was a box of tissues nearby.

Switching tracks, I began a series of questions about the snow globe collection. Mrs. Bilandic attested that once a week she cleaned the locked glass display cabinet but only the outside, never handling the objects inside. She claimed she didn't even know where the key was kept. From memory, she detailed the collection shelf-by-shelf, totaling thirty-six snow globes, awards, and other keepsakes.

"Any empty bases?" I asked, and she made a funny face.

"Empty bases?"

"You know, like just the pedestal, no snow globe or whatever?"

"No, nothing like that. Nothing's changed in that curio for maybe four months. The newest one came around Thanksgiving. It's on the top shelf. It's a big one with an etched gold bar inside—really beautiful."

"Do you remember if there's any writing on the base?"

"Of course, Jack of Clubs, Queen of Hearts."

"So, you don't remember anything else unusual?" I asked Mrs. Bilandic, by way of wrapping up the session.

"I noticed, the basement door was ajar," she said. "That was unusual."

"Is that an exterior door?" I inquired.

"No, it's inside the house. Goes from the hallway near the kitchen down into the cellar. I never clean there, though."

She assured me she'd never noticed that door being open before, and what's more, had never gone down into the basement during the entire time she'd worked at the address. She'd run out of the house as soon as she saw the body, and then found herself outside without her coat or her phone.

"But I wasn't going back in there alone," she said. "I had to ring four doorbells before someone answered and called 911. So glad the police lady came right away…"

Soon, Mrs. Bilandic was free to go. I handed her my card and encouraged her to get a hold of me if she recalled anything else, but I had the feeling I wouldn't see her again until the case went to trial.

* * *

After saying my goodbyes to Mrs. Bilandic, I popped back to talk to Captain Kodjoe, but saw that his door was shut tight. So I decided to return to the crime scene.

I thought about grabbing a bite to eat, but I wasn't in the mood for anything from a drive-thru window. Of course, Maxwell Street was too far away; I shook my head to try to exorcise the glorious image and delightful aroma of that treat from my head. I guessed I would be fasting.

I was familiar with the neighborhoods to the north and the west of the mansion, but thought I could use a better feel for the immediate layout. I drove in a couple of concentric circles then spiraled in to the city block featuring the murder house. I drove slowly around the block, observing everything. A church was located to the north of the residence, with a paved parking lot between.

I was working under the assumption that the murder had occurred on late Sunday evening, or during the night—this had yet to be confirmed but was the most likely interval.

Maybe the church was holding services and its members might have seen or heard something. The latter was doubtful, considering the pains the owner had taken to muffle any sound escaping the orgy chamber.

I parked my SUV and saw that, after the initial discovery, the only police representation left was a single unit parked out front. Even Eggleston had packed it up and headed home. The reporters had gotten what they needed to sensationalize their papers and broadcasts for the next few days. I imagined a TV anchor stating "Murder and mayhem on S. Drexel Avenue. More news at 10."

I tapped on the window of the marked cruiser. The officer was checking text messages but wasn't startled.

"Evening."

"Hey, Detective," he said, sitting up straighter. The tag on his jacket identified him as Pasternak. He was sipping something hot from an insulated mug. With the chill in the air, I couldn't blame him.

"How long you been here?"

"About an hour or so. Everyone else left already."

"Forensics?" I looked around for their truck, which was gone.

"Think they got another call. Maybe they went to get some chow. It's not like they'd tell me anything."

I recalled my days on the street and how there was a distinct separation between cops in uniform and those in plainclothes.

My attention veered to the other side of the street, seeing a single stalwart individual pacing back and forth with a sign. With the sun down, it was hard to read what it said.

"Keep warm," I told Pasternak, and made my way toward the pacer who was stomping his feet to generate warmth. He had to be either determined or demented to be out in the cold.

"Good evening, sir."

He was a bearded, man, about 50 or so, wearing a tattered military jacket. An unkempt Afro peeked out from the places his knit skullcap didn't cover.

"You investigatin' this thing?"

I nodded, taking a closer look at his sign, on which was scrawled, "Just Desserts." Seemed he was advertising for an exclusive bakery or he spelled it wrong.

"Sure am. What happened to the other folks who were here with you earlier?" I asked.

He leaned his sign, which was on a wooden stick, against a nearby light pole. He stomped his feet and rubbed his hands together in the freezing cold. "For starters, only someone as stubborn and crazy as me would be out here in this kinda weather."

Took the words right out of my mouth. "Definitely not the warmest of days," I agreed.

By February, even folks who didn't mind the single digit and negative temperatures so much have grown tired of the constant chill. I hated the cold from the time it began to rear its ugly head in November until, like a rude party guest, it finally left, long after spring had officially set it.

"Them other people was just nosy," he continued. "I know what goes on in there."

"What do you mean?"

"Ahh," he waved his hand, dismissively, "You live in sin, you die in it. I say good riddance to bad rubbish." He paused, digging into his woodland camouflage jacket. "D'ya mind," he asked, producing a dinged and dented up flask.

"No, go right ahead."

He took a swig, wiping a wayward trickle from the side of his mouth before offering me a pull. I shook my head politely, to which he mumbled, "Suit yerself."

I could have told him that liquor would only make him feel warmer while dropping his body temperature, but it would've fallen on deaf ears.

"What's your name," I inquired.

"I got nothin' to hide," he said, puffing up his chest. "Army Specialist Elias Washington, medically retired! I proudly served then, and I serve a higher callin' now."

"And what's that higher calling, Mr. Washington?"

"Tryna alert the city to the nasty shit that goes on in that house over there." He thumbed toward the crime scene with disdain. "Somebody died and everybody is goin' on with their day as if that's normal. I'm telling you, it was some sort of say-tonic ritual!"

"Satanic ritual? What do you know about it?"

"Nothin' at all. Only what I heard on the news: unidentified victim. However, I suspicion y'all found his head turned around, facing backward. If so, that pompous bastard *deserved* it!"

Washington rambled on, imagination fueled by an occasional swig of alcohol, to tell me how Janus and his followers were a cult. He slurred the word "debauchery," pronouncing it "duba-cherry," in his description of what sorts of things he thought went on inside. For a moment, I considered he might be jealous he was never invited to one of the wild parties.

Since he said he lived in the neighborhood, I asked him about the Greater Mount Zion House of Worship, the church that sat across the lot from the den of iniquity in question.

"In cahoots," he exclaimed, vigorously rubbing his hands together before blowing onto them.

"How so?"

"They share that lot with the sinners who cohabitate in that place." He pointed to the paved parking area between the two buildings. "Let them put their bus there all the time to support their devilish shenanigans. The Good Book says to shun the very appearance of evil and it will appear!"

The man was clearly drunk, but instead of having him arrested for public intoxication, I determined he was no more a menace than a slug found under a rock. I let him go back to his vigil, though I encouraged him to go home. I went back toward the house, passing Pasternak who still sat in the car, absorbed in his cell phone. Even so, his presence should discourage the stray fan who might try to gain entrance. I left him to his text messages and took a walk around the property.

The three-story structure, sat with its main entrance to the west. A wrought iron fence with a gate marked the property line. A narrow sidewalk skimmed the side of the house closest to the mansion next door where Dr. Elaine D'Arby, an orthodontist, lived.

When Barbosa had questioned the dentist earlier, she had readily denied seeing or hearing anything out of the ordinary the night before.

I took this path, trying to figure out where the assailant had made entry.

The rear of the property boasted a yard full of snow and a sun room that doubled as the porch. There were no signs of footprints across where the grass would've been; the walk was salted and free of ice.

Above the back door was a camera, angled outward at anyone who would climb the stairs to the door. It was pretty discreet. There were no signs of broken glass or tool marks pointing to a forced entry. Mrs. Bilandic always came in this door, and had, according to her statement, used her key that morning to gain entrance just prior to discovering the remains. I made note that the backyard faced a narrow alley, then the rear of another row of mansions that faced the next street over.

Working my way around to the north side, which nestled up to the parking lot, I observed a gangway path leading from the front to the back of the house. I descended a short, concrete staircase, which took me down just shy of subterranean level. Another flight of steps led to the front yard, with an additional, perpendicular set leading down between the two to a door that led to the basement. I pulled out my portable camera and began taking pictures. If the security cameras in the front and back didn't catch the killer, he or she likely entered here.

The door was painted a faded red. At a glance, nothing about it seemed to be kicked in or tampered with; I looked for the requisite scratches and marks, finding none.

Nobody had dropped a crowbar or lock-pick set, or even a hairpin. Something about the darkened gangway was unsettling, nonetheless. I dismissed part of that feeling as a holdout of a bad childhood memory.

It was dusk, and the lights to the parking lot had come on. There was no light directly over the gangway door, so the only illumination would come from sources in the lot and, to a lesser degree, the street lamps lining the avenue. A short concrete wall, denoting the lower path, rose to about waist level, before giving way to the fence. There was a ledge of about a foot between that fence and where the church property began. The pathway wasn't bricked in, so someone could have scaled the chain link boundary and slipped into the gangway.

Everything seemed dingy, the rafters overhead covered with dust. It didn't appear the entry point got much use. Areas to the right and left of the door were festooned with filthy cobwebs that had been spun before the weather got chilly.

I imagined the color of the door had been a vibrant crimson at one time; now, cracked and faded, the paint had taken on the look and hue of dried blood.

"Excuse me," someone said behind me. I spun in his

direction, startled. Looking up from the lower level, I saw a bear of a man was eclipsing the lights of the parking lot. He was wearing a fur hat and a partially zipped parka.

His face was in shadow, and it took me a moment before I noticed his clerical collar.

"Evening. May I help you?"

"You're a cop, I take it."

"Yes," I admitted, holding up my star for him to clearly see. "And you are?"

"Curtis Nieves, head deacon of Mount Zion." He thumbed over his shoulder toward the house of worship.

"Brandywine, detective, Chicago PD. How can I help you, Deacon Nieves?"

He was a brown-skinned man with a square jaw. Looked like, maybe forty years before, he could have given folks hell on the gridiron.

His voice was matter-of-fact. "I was here Sunday night, cleaning up the sanctuary after service. Was taking out the trash when I saw somebody scale this here fence and disappear into the gangway, where you're standing."

"What time?"

"Oh, about nine."

"Man or woman?"

"Can't be sure. It was from across the lot and the person was wearing dark clothes."

"Short or tall?"

"Well, this fence is a six-footer, like myself."

I nodded for him to go on, and noted that the top of his fur hat peaked an inch or two above the horizontal pipe.

"The person was kinda short, because it took them a couple of tries before they made it over. Come to think of it, she was a woman."

I raised an eyebrow, not expecting that.

"Even though she was wearing a lot of clothing, she was small overall but kinda wide about the hips, if you know what I mean."

"How tall would you say she was?"

"Welp, the parking lot is about four, maybe four-and-a-half feet above where you're standing. I could hardly see her after she got down in the gangway. So, I'd say she may have been about five-foot-three, give or take a couple of inches."

"Did you see her come back out?"

"No, but that's not something you can see from over there."

"What else did you notice?"

"Not much. Like I told you, I was taking out trash. It was cold outside, so I didn't linger."

"Did you call the police?"

"You kidding? Why would I do that? People hop that fence all the time. It's a shortcut to the alley. If I buzzed y'all every time, you'd think *I* was the problem. Calling the cops while black—that's not one of my hobbies."

"But somebody's dead."

"Well, the next time I know somebody is gonna get killed, I'll drop whatever I'm doing and pay closer attention. God's kingdom don't wait, son. Whether it's something as simple as wiping down the pews or as important as delivering a sermon, it trumps much of the stuff going on out here in these streets. Now, is there anything else you need, Detective? We've got a meetin' tonight and I've got stuff to do."

I couldn't make out every detail of his face but sensed his dour expression. He was lit up at the edges of his bulk, with me in his shadow. Not sure if he set that up to be a metaphor of our supposed spiritual differences, but with me in the dark and currently occupying a lower level, it would have been an interesting coincidence otherwise.

I handed him my card, pushing it through the diamond-shaped space formed by the chain link, and asked if I could get an official statement from him for my report at a later time. He nodded and told me I could find him at Mount Zion almost any day of the week. He was turning to go back to whatever chore awaited, when it dawned on me to ask if the sign-wielding, hooch-sipping Mr. Washington was as dedicated to his post as was the deacon.

He came about as slowly as an aircraft carrier, seeming to me not that he couldn't move fast if the situation dictated it, but for *this* he would not. His irritation didn't seem to be toward me, but his frown looked as if I'd asked him to consider cockroaches equal to human beings.

"You mean Ol' Lyin'-Ass Washington over there?" He jutted his chin and tossed his head with disdain.

"The protester across the street, yes."

"That's who I meant. He probably told you some hogwash about the pastor and ministers here being mixed up in some damn cult conspiracy with the souls who partied and orgiated on the other side of this fence."

I didn't realize "orgiated" was a word, but I kept that thought (and the sudden urge to snicker) to myself. I cleared my throat, ignoring his dislike for the Army vet, but realizing that Nieves had some sort of clue as to what went on in the mansion next door to his church.

"We pray for these fools every day, but each man has to make up his own mind to follow the one and only truth. Not all religions support the morals we hold dear."

Religion? Earlier, I'd asked Barbosa whether or not she thought the apparent, um, *orgiating* seemed ceremonial. If that was so, maybe—at least to the deacon—his church represented the positive side of the spiritual scale, while the murder house was the negative. That would make the parking lot something akin to purgatory, though that was a concept generally associated with the Catholics.

I turned my attention back to the gangway, where that red door stuck out like a sore thumb, and fired up my flashlight. I observed the rusted hinges and the dust that seemed to have settled onto the horizontal surfaces. I turned to the parking lot, which appeared to have a rather fresh layer of blacktop.

"When did you all set up this parking area, Deacon?"

He was still standing there, as if he knew I'd have

another question. His demeanor had changed from its previous intensity, dialed back to just mild annoyance.

"The house that stood here was condemned and torn down a couple of years ago. We acquired the empty lot last spring and had it properly paved and marked this past fall. We finished in October, just before the cold began to set in."

"So when did the owner of this house start parking his tour bus on your lot?"

He didn't answer right away, probably digesting the idea that he and his church may have inadvertently gotten wrapped up in a murder investigation.

"Well, that was something already between him and the previous owner, back then it had an extended driveway next to the house. Long before we bought the lot. We're just trying to be good neighbors; we let him use it on days we aren't having service and he donates a few dollars to our coffers. We don't judge the fact that he produces secular music and we've always kept out of whatever goes on in there. They're grown, consenting adults. And, contrary to the beliefs of your dingy-ass friend over there," he pointed to Washington, who was still making his rounds, "we ain't part of some cult or conspiracy."

I thanked him and bade him good evening, making a mental note to check out recent large charitable contributions to Greater Mount Zion.

There was dust all over the gangway, not just from years of neglect, but most likely from all the dirt that was moved on the other side of the fence when they scrapped the condemned house and paved the lot. All those earth-moving machines would send most bugs scattering.

Spiders would seize the opportunity and set up shop in spots that would allow them to capture more prey. The cobwebs were plentiful in a nook to the right of the door. The hinges showed a few tendrils still intact, while traces of broken webbing clung to the side that swings open.

I knelt to observe the doorknob at eye level, using my

flashlight. Aluminum does not rust. The grimy layer covering the metal had taken on a pattern, as if the knob had been recently turned. Laplaglia and Sorenson hadn't submitted information on what they'd collected and I wanted to be on the safe side. I pulled my fingerprint kit from my bag. An application of magic dust would reveal a good thumb print and maybe some partials, if they were there.

They weren't. So, the fence-climber was probably wearing gloves. Given the frigid temperatures, I wasn't surprised.

I stood on my tiptoes, a lot taller than Nieves guessed the suspect to be. I fished blindly between the rafters and above the door, happy that any spiders that might call the place home in the warmer seasons were off hibernating, or doing whatever arachnids did in their downtime. I was looking for a spare key but found nothing.

Walking around to the front, I snapped a picture of the octagon-shaped sign sticking out of the ground near the stairway, noted the hidden camera over the double door, and made myself another mental note—this one, to contact the Gold Coast Security Company.

Inside the domicile, with no one else there, it was spooky as hell. Not so scary that I needed to pull out my weapon and clear each room, mind you. Still, I owed it to the investigation to ensure nothing had been overlooked.

I went to the basement first, so I could see what was on the other side of the gangway door. I had to make my way through a narrow path between stacks of boxed vinyl records, paper files, and lots of old music equipment.

On the floor near the doorway, I found what I was looking for. Lying between a file box and the lintel, the key was most likely dropped by mistake. There was also an open hasp that would have allowed the option of securing the door from the inside. It was odd that there was no padlock.

Pulling the door inward was easy. Typically, with the

cold, the hinges would squeak and there would likely be some sort of resistance from disuse.

Nope.

I didn't have to pay attention to the cobwebs this time around, and the key slid easily into the knob from the outside. I bagged it, and made note of where it had been discovered. I turned the doorknob lock from the inside and climbed the stairs.

I returned to the kill room, from which the body, the linens, the victim's bag, and a few other choice items had been removed. Carpet swatches containing samples of each of the puke puddles, had been neatly cut away and seized by Forensics. The stench of vomit overrode that of the blood; I breathed through my mouth as best I could. Nothing to be gained by staying in there any longer. I stepped out and closed the door.

Standing in front of the curio cabinet, I noticed that the "Queen of Hearts, Jack of Spades" base had been removed, as well as the key from the lock. Knowing they had already dusted the handle for fingerprints, I gave it a little tug.

They'd locked it before taking the key; good on them.

I decided to make a final sweep of the house and call it a day. I had lots to do back at my computer, as I'd been plotting my investigation in my head, like chasing down the info on the front and back cameras, and researching Janus, his friends, employees, and fans. I lingered for a moment in front of the shrine he'd made to himself. What kind of man was this? I figured I would soon find out.

Back on the 3rd floor, standing in the middle of the master bedroom, I took a page from Perry's book and let myself be still for a moment, paid attention to the details, and allowed the room to speak to me. The oversized mirror on the vanity and the gauzy canopy on the king size bed whispered a woman's touch, while the dark color palette and all the wood seemed overtly masculine. One thing for sure, I was picking up the strong sense that the owner loved his image.

The HVAC system did its job to keep the house at an even 70 degrees. When it completed its cycle, the steady hum of air rushing through the vents paused, allowing me to pick up on another, similar sound. It was a soft whirring coming from somewhere nearby. I stepped into the large walk-in closet and continued to listen. My ears directed me towards a bunch of full-length stage outfits stored on hangers. Stacks of shoe boxes further obscured what was hidden behind. Digging through these collections, I tracked the muffled high pitch to something outside the ordinary: a running computer. A CPU tower, actually, without keyboard, mouse, or monitor.

Like finding the skullcap in the pantry, sometimes it's not the item itself that seems strange, but the way it doesn't fit into its surroundings.

Everything at a murder scene is potentially evidence. I could seize anything that might be key to the investigation. Better safe than sorry, so I put the CPU on my evidence list. I snapped pictures of its location and the way it was connected to a cable that ran through the back wall. Later, I would have that line traced.

As I moved the boxes and clothes away, I noticed a portable external hard drive connected to the front USB port. I captured an image of it, along with its make, model, and serial number, before putting it into a sealed plastic bag and dropping it into my shoulder bag along with the other smaller pieces of evidence. Then I carried the heavy computer down the two flights of stairs to the main floor.

I set the tagged computer on the kitchen counter—our agreed upon retrieval location—and dialed Captain Kodjoe, while noting it was already closing in on 9 pm.

I provided him a rundown of my findings, giving ample credit (where due) to Barbosa. "She's sharp and energetic—good police. I could really use her help going forward—well, at least until Perry comes back."

"I'll see what I can do on that," Cap offered, making no promises.

"Thanks, I'll be in at my regular time tomorrow, if that's okay."

"No. We contacted the homeowner; he has a sound check tomorrow afternoon in Milwaukee for his evening show. He agreed to come in for questioning bright and early at eight a.m., so I'll see you at the precinct at seven," he said and hung up, leaving no room for negotiation.

Chapter 3

He arrived at the precinct fifteen minutes early, looking every bit the character from a Blaxploitation-era movie. Whether he was up for the role of the hero or the villain remained to be seen. Draped from head to toe in an off-white ensemble, Janus stood as tall as a professional basketball player. He wore an oversized turtleneck beneath a chinchilla-collared, three-quarter-length cashmere coat. His pristine cream-colored suede loafers must have been specially treated to withstand the city's filthy winter muck. Perhaps to ensure a dramatic entrance, he paused just inside the foyer, doffed his ridiculously cool, old school applejack hat and mink-lined gloves, and asked the desk sergeant for me by name.

Later, the officer would delight in describing the musician's entrance for anyone who was willing to listen. Everyone loves meeting celebrities.

I was up late into the night researching, as well as compiling a list of other possible witnesses. I was on the computer reviewing Sorenson's notes when I got the call from the front desk. "You have a visitor, Detective."

"Thanks."

My supervisor, usually stiff and emotionless, was acting downright giddy. His confident, authoritative posture had been replaced by the wide-eyed awe of a schoolgirl. He beat me to the lobby to pick up our guest.

I didn't have an office of my own. Like all nonsupervisory dicks, I was relegated to a desk in the bullpen and was grateful for that. The captain had ensured the conference room was clean and furnished with comfortable chairs for the interview.

Everything about him, save the fact that he'd arrive alone, *sans* an entourage of fans and attorneys, suggested he was urban royalty. I'd done my homework and realized Janus was a proud man who lived life by his own rules. James Delbert Porter, who'd had his name legally changed to its present mononym, started out in the Wild 100's, the neighborhood where his parents grew up and got married. They had rented an apartment off of 114th & Michigan Avenue and proceeded to build a multi-level marketing empire. That led to the family making an upward move to the residence on Drexel. Able to afford it, Mr. and Mrs. Porter enrolled their only child in private schools, then financed his higher education at a prestigious performing arts college.

His only run-ins with the law were misdemeanors involving possession of marijuana during his college years. It was suspected that he got a cut of recreational drugs moving at his night spot, but that had never been proven.

Janus was a talented and ambitious teenager during House music's infancy, which proved to be perfect timing. As a young DJ, he found success producing underground artists and doing remixes of songs by a handful of well-known acts. The genre never achieved the same commercial viability or widespread appeal of Hip Hop, but it was popular with the club scene, over which he held sway. He was able to grow his net income into the seven-figure range, but his debt-to-income ratio was reportedly high. He liked to make the money, which he spent with extravagance. He maintained a robust touring schedule, occasionally flying overseas for shows all over Europe and in Japan, locales where urban music had found a niche. When not plying his trade on the road, he presided over Duality, the hottest dance club on the South Side.

Janus maintained a bigger fan base than I could rightly imagine, but to me, he was just a man. His chosen handle was that of a Roman deity and he was considered a god of musical production, but that didn't send me into hysterics.

My boss was quite the opposite, though. Captain Kodjoe held the door and made the introduction. I was waiting to see him bounce on his tiptoes and admit to having all the DJ's albums, but he retained some of his usual decorum. The captain did, however, insist on staying for the interview.

Our guest was as lean as a young cat in his twenties, though he would be turning forty in a couple of years. Hair dye ensured that his processed coif was shiny black and void of gray. His handshake was strong, though he didn't grab my hand with the typical grip. Instead, his fingers more or less enveloped mine and squeezed tight. It felt disingenuous, as if he was trying to display his diamond-encrusted pinky ring for me to kiss. Though I'm sure Cap would've happily puckered up, I passed.

"Before we start," Janus said, "I'd like to see the photos."

It was something we typically waited to show—not only to spare the victim's acquaintances the shock, but also to gauge their reaction, as I had done with Mrs. Bilandic the day before. I glanced to my superior and he gave an approving nod.

Based on his statement, Janus was performing at the venerable Fox Theater in downtown Detroit, three hundred miles way, when the murder had occurred. I considered his absence only a partial alibi at best; resourceful criminals, especially those with power and influence, often got others to do their dirty work. I let the thought slide and produced a manila envelope that contained prints of some of the photos Barbosa had taken at the scene. He perused each grisly image, giving no emotional response that I could see. Done, he slid the pictures back across the table.

"Mr. Janus," I began, "Thank you for taking time out of

your schedule to come down today. We'd like to discuss the tragic incident that occurred in your home on or about February 22nd. Any information you provide in that regard will be used to further our investigation. Do you have any objection to this interview being recorded?"

"I make my living being recorded. This is no different," he yawned. "Forgive me. I hit the road early so I could get here on time; I don't like being late. I'm here for whatever you need but would like to wrap this up as quickly as possible." He preened a bit, straightened the lapel of his jacket, and smoothed out his processed hair. "Of course, I'll fully cooperate and hope to see justice done. Now, what do you need to know, officers?"

Kodjoe, who sat next to me, leaned in. "There is no question as to your whereabouts when the crime occurred." That part was true. The ME had put the time of death roughly concurrent with the Sunday night show.

"Listen," said Janus, with a dismissive wave, "you can stop referring to what happened in vague terms. Goodbody was killed, as I'm sure he couldn't have crushed in his own head. No need to beat—no pun intended— around the bush."

"We're sorry for the loss of your friend," I said. Condolences are mainly reserved for family members, but I wanted to see what the pompous superstar had to say when it came to his feelings about the dead man.

Janus exhaled and leaned back, cocking his head. "I wouldn't have necessarily called him a friend."

"Oh, then how would you characterize your relationship with the deceased? With Rayford, I mean."

"He was an associate. Goodbody choreographed and danced in my stage show, since about three years ago," he said. Then added, "sometimes he was my lover."

Kodjoe squirmed almost imperceptibly, and straightened his tie.

"He lived up to his name: Goodbody. The dude was ripped and prided himself on his...*prowess*."

143

"Was there anyone else," I asked, "lovers, I mean."

"Sure, quite a few others—but nobody special. I'm not ashamed to admit I'm both promiscuous and uninhibited."

Janus spoke in matter-of-fact tones, not caring what we thought. From his posturing and eye contact, he seemed sincere, as if he had nothing to hide concerning his sex life. I wondered if it was a distraction. Most people wouldn't be so forthcoming about their proclivities, just as some cops would be thrown off the scent by such an admission. As Perry would say, 'everybody is a suspect until proven otherwise'.

"Will you miss him?" Kodjoe asked.

Janus leveled his eyes in the captain's direction. "I'm going to have to find someone to replace him on the stage," he answered, "and I'm sorry that I'll no longer have him in my bed, if that's what you mean."

Then his gaze returned to me. "I don't lament his death. I hate that he went out the way he did but we're all slated to go at some point."

Dude was coldblooded.

"Any clue of who could have done this?"

"Nope," he said, spreading his legs wide and placing his hands on his knees. It was a body language power move.

It was likely that he was lying through his teeth. My mother used to say that whenever my sister and I used any other version of "*no*" when just that one word would have sufficed, we were being deceitful. Plus, our interviewee had made a casual response to a very serious inquiry. I made a mental note; collusion would need to be ruled out.

"Besides the housekeeper, anyone else have a key to your house?" queried Kodjoe.

"Just Rayford and Nina."

"Nina?"

"Yes, Nneka George. Nina is her nickname."

"What's your association with her?"

"She works at my club—she's the general manager. Sometimes lover, too. She, Rayford, and I would often…

y'know, *party* together."

"Any issues with jealousy between your, um...partners? Is it possible that Ms. George could be responsible for Rayford's death?" I asked, without missing a beat.

"Nah," he said, fanning his hand before placing it back onto his knee. "Nina wouldn't hurt a fly."

He went on to explain that, while Rayford choreographed shows and toured, Nina ran Club Duality. He did much to prop her up: she, like he, had pulled herself up by her bootstraps and made something of herself. He took credit for recognizing her talents and giving her a chance.

"Ever since she's been working for me—five years or so—she's stayed out of trouble," he said, laughing, though I couldn't see what was funny. I thought it sounded rather conceited that the height of her rise was determined by servitude under his umbrella. His words, intentional or not, raised a red flag, citing "trouble" in her past.

"So they were both down with your bedroom activities?"

He smiled like a cat pondering how deep to stick its paw into the fishbowl. No doubt he was replaying their greatest hits in his mind.

The concept of three being a crowd was typical of love relations. From the smug grin on the DJ's face, I could see this was a tumult that he orchestrated and enjoyed. Two people constantly vying for attention would definitely boost an already-inflated ego. I just wondered, with Goodbody out of the way, if he was planning to replace that leg of the love triangle.

"Nawwww," he answered. "Everybody was pleased as punch."

The look on his face definitely revealed his own pleasure, though I wondered if the others felt the same.

I requested Nneka George's contact information. "You don't mind if we speak to her?" I said, knowing I didn't need his seal of approval in the matter. It might give him a false sense of control, which I could use to my advantage.

145

"No problem at all," he responded, magnanimously.

Something occurred to me: a murder had taken place in his house and Janus was completely laid back about it. He hadn't asked when he could go back home or who was going to clean up the crime scene after it was fully processed. Most striking, he expressed no concern for his own wellbeing. What if the perpetrator had killed Rayford as a message to Janus? Or what if Janus had been the intended victim, and the murderer would return to finish the job?

Why wasn't he worried? *Because he'd done it?* Though people react to death in different ways, his response seemed a bit off.

It was unusual to come in contact with a person so apparently lacking in empathy, though someone else did come to mind. Last year, Perry and I had responded to an emergency call at a university: jealous husband and his much younger, cheating wife. The woman was terrified as her husband held a glass tube of acid above her face. When the man chose to kill himself instead, I couldn't help but watch her reaction. Much relieved for her own safety, she displayed no sense of concern or remorse, but watched him wallow in agony until death finally claimed him. Perry had noticed it too. We'd interviewed the new widow for the post-incident follow-up, and her heartless attitude was unsettling, to say the least.

I went through the other standard questions, like when was the last time Janus had seen the victim alive and if there was anyone who wanted to do the dancer harm. Janus never asked how the murderer had gotten into the house. Instead, he was more concerned about the snow globe seized as evidence in the case.

"Was it damaged?" he inquired.

It was a ridiculous question, considering someone had been killed with the thing. But it revealed what he considered important.

"No," I answered, "I don't think so."

He smiled. "Had that globe specially designed to commemorate my most recent record."

"Carjack of Diamonds, Queen of Busters, right?" Of course, I knew the album's proper title; I just wanted to get under his skin.

"It's *Thief of Hearts, Jack of Clubs*," he admonished.

Just as I thought: *some*thing mattered to him, though not the folks in his inner circle.

"And, I must admit," he continued proudly, "it *is* my greatest album to date."

I waited for him to add a shameless plug about his album being available for download—and everywhere records, CD's, and tapes are sold—in a cheesy announcer's voice, of course.

"Is it true what they say?" Kodjoe asked.

Janus relished the spotlight. He turned to my boss as if he was a reporter seeking a sound bite at a red-carpet event. "What's that?"

"The 'snow' in the globe is made of gold shavings."

"That's true," he said, with a big smile. "Had it made in Dubai. Very expensive."

"Who has the other one," I asked.

Suddenly, the spotlight dimmed and his smile faded.

"Because, rumor has it, there are two," I added, drawing from the hours I'd spent researching his fan forums the night before. "One has platinum and the other has gold flakes."

He was silent, as if he was working out an algorithm in his head.

"Janus?" prodded Kodjoe.

With a sigh, he knuckled under. "A private collector whose name I'm not at liberty to divulge. Is that relevant to this investigation?"

"Could be," I said. "Maybe the perpetrator broke in to complete his collection, expecting you to be on tour and no one at home."

"That doesn't make any sense," he exclaimed with

aggravation in his voice. "Why the heck would she …"

"She?" I recalled Barbosa's hunch that the killer was female.

"Or he," Janus corrected, realizing his fumble. He proceeded with trepidation bordering on contrived humility. "I was about to say 'she or he' before you cut me off. That was rude."

"You're right. My bad."

"Women are just as capable of doing dirt as we guys are, right? And how would I know the killer's gender?"

"Indeed," I said. "How would you know?"

Kodjoe leaned in, his stare fixated on the DJ, who was looking more suspicious by the minute. "Detective Brandywine is just curious."

"Yeah, that's me—always curious." I pasted on a shit-eating grin and reclined in my chair, interlacing my fingers behind my head. I could hardly wait to see how he was going to wiggle his way out of this one. Janus took a deep breath and placed his palms on the conference table, fingers splayed. It was a gesture denoting honesty, or at least an attempt to look that way. His nervousness was thinly veiled, and I was willing to wager a dollar's worth of penny candy that sweat would leave ghosts of his hands.

"Listen," he said, in a voice just above a whisper. "I took time out of my touring schedule to fly back here and see how I could help you all catch…whoever did this. I'm tired and have to get to Milwaukee for sound check and tonight's show. If you're going to charge me…"

"Whoa, who said anything about charging you?" Kodjoe blurted. He frowned and waved away the idea of it.

"I have an attorney," the DJ said, his voice drifting. Sure as shit, when he took his hands off the table, I could see the perspiration, which soon began to evaporate.

"No need, unless you have something incriminating to confess. We haven't advised you of your rights and, thus far, I see no reason to suspect your involvement."

I gritted my teeth, wondering where the captain was

going with this. Janus was involved all right, it just wasn't clear to me how. Not yet, anyway.

"Am I free to go, then?" His tone was that of an emotional appeal.

"Cameras," I said suddenly, ignoring his plea to be finished.

"What about them," he asked. He'd already stood, expecting to be let off the hook. Barbosa hadn't been wrong about how tall he was. His height was imposing. But I wanted to cut him down a notch or three.

"We noticed there were a couple of small cameras inside the theater—"

"We only film there on special occasions. And there are only willing participants in those activities," he said, his voice edgy.

"Understood. What about security cameras outside the house? How many and where?"

"It doesn't matter. They're broken," he exclaimed. "Off-line. In fact," he continued, his voice changing to that of someone either absentminded or obviously lying—I figured the latter. "I've been meaning to get those repaired."

"But there are what? Two? Three? More than that?"

"Just the two: one at the front and another at the back door."

"One more question for the road," I said before Janus could skitter out of the room like a human cockroach. His eyes kept darting toward the door, telegraphing his intentions.

"What's that?" His response was terse, as if I was trying his patience. I relished the idea.

"Do you love her?"

"Who?"

"Never mind."

My boss took that moment to rise to his feet with a smile and offer his hand to the interviewee. "We appreciate you coming by," he said.

I followed suit, wanting to pass on the handshake. However, I'm glad I didn't. Initially condescending, his grasp was now flaccid and moist with sweat. This time around, the deflated superstar didn't bother trying to impress me with his oversized mitt in a "mine-is-bigger-than-yours" gesture.

"Will I be able to return to my house?" He almost sounded sheepish.

"Sure," Kodjoe remarked, "as soon as we get the green light from Forensics, we'll let you know. They tend to go over every nook and cranny."

"Sounds like that will take a while. I'll need to get some stuff sooner than that," he said, his tone casual.

"There's still quite a bit of…" I paused, picturing the blood-and-tissue-spattered walls in the screening room, "…work to be done."

"Fine, I just need a few things from my bedroom closet, like shoes and clothing items. It should only take me a few minutes."

"I think we can arrange it," my boss said.

Though I understood, I wished the captain hadn't been quite so accommodating. Something about our visitor raised my hackles. Arrogance aside, it was hard to put my finger on it. But the silver lining to that cloud was that following him back to his domicile would be an opportunity to observe him.

"Give me a couple of minutes," I told Janus, once we were in front of the precinct. "What are you driving?"

He motioned to the large, mother-of-pearl Cadillac SUV which had been warming the entire time he was being interviewed. As soon as his driver saw him, he jumped out and opened the rear passenger's side door. The wheelman was a solid, dark-skinned dude dressed in baggy jeans and a heavy leather coat.

Once I was following the other vehicle, I called my supervisor. "I don't like the idea of going into his house with him, especially with his chauffeur."

"Didn't realize he had a driver with him. There's still a patrolman posted outside the house. You can take the officer inside with you, and I can send backup."

"Not necessary. As long as the second guy stays in the car, I should be good. I just don't want to be outnumbered."

Minutes later, I tapped on the window of the cruiser and told the officer what was up. I informed him to come into the house if anyone else got out of the Caddy. He nodded.

I cut through the police tape, which would be replaced once we were done.

Janus mentioned going upstairs to retrieve items from the master bedroom. "This is only gonna take a few minutes," he assured me as we stepped into the foyer. His smile was a little too friendly for someone who'd already shown conceit. I think he was trying to draw attention away from the anxious look in his eyes. It was that shifty way drug addicts looked when they were either foraging for a hit or afraid you were about to discover their stash. He removed his hat, loosened his scarf, and wiped sweat from his brow.

"Man, is it hot in here or is it just me?"

I unfastened my coat in an empathetic gesture, though I felt absolutely fine. The move would put him at ease while giving me ready access to my firearm, just in case. "It is a bit warm in here."

"Want something to drink? Whiskey maybe…" he asked, making like the host, but fidgety.

"Not while on the job, 'preciate it, though."

Then he tried walking into the theater, there was another line of police tape waiting at the closed door.

I stepped between him and the crime scene. "Sorry."

"I understand. It's just that the bar is in there. Wish I had something to calm me down a bit. Y'know, being back here, where my best friend was killed, it's…surreal."

It wasn't lost on me that, just an hour before, he'd made it plain that Goodbody was not even his friend, now he'd

151

become his best bud. I didn't apologize for blocking his path. "You said there were some items you wanted to retrieve?"

"Yes," he said. "You don't have to follow me upstairs, do you?"

"No, sir. I'll just hang out down here," and I made a show of being intensely interested in the photo shrine on the wall.

He tried to be cool, but he couldn't get up the steps fast enough, taking them two at a time. I saw desperation in his stride.

As soon as he was out of sight, I beat feet to the kitchen and saw immediately that the CPU was gone; someone from Forensics had picked it up. I let out a sigh of relief.

Back to the living room, I kept my eyes on the staircase. Though it wasn't likely he would appear at the second-floor landing holding a semiautomatic shotgun in each hand, I wanted to err on the side of caution. That is to say, I didn't trust his ass.

There was thumping and the muffled sound of objects being moved about. It was a lot of action for someone who just wanting to retrieve clothes.

I crept up the staircase without so much as a creak and tiptoed into the master suite. "Everything okay?" I called out.

Janus was rummaging through the master closet, back in the corner where I had found the CPU the day before. He was sweating profusely, the look in his eyes almost feral. When he saw me, he screamed and nearly jumped out of his skin. "Man, don't be sneakin' up on me like that!"

"Looking for something? Can I help?"

He tucked his bottom lip, gnawing at a sliver of skin with manic energy. He was working hard to stay calm, but his cool was growing frazzled at the edges. Keeping a straight face, I made a mental note to have the techs give the computer special attention.

"I-I can't seem to find something I left in my closet."

Internally, I chuckled. "What was it?"

"Somebody stole my shit!"

"Anything removed is to help solve the murder of your friend. And I *know* you want that."

He'd been squatting when I happened upon him. Now, he stood, appearing even larger than he had at the police station.

"Hell yeah I want that," he exclaimed through gritted teeth. "But what do you need my music for? I store projects and mixes on that machine."

"Anything we took as evidence has been bagged and tagged. We'll give you a receipt which will allow you to get your property back once the investigation is complete."

His height made him formidable. With his jutted chin and clinched teeth, I could have interpreted his demeanor as pre-assaultive. His nostrils flared; he was clearly sizing me up, trying to decide his next move.

"You need to take a seat," I half growled. Most cops would have rested their hand on their holster as a threat. My 1911 could stop a charging rhino but it would take more than a hissy fit and a glare to make me clear leather.

Janus stared at me a long time before he blinked. Maybe that was his realization that I'd already summed up any move he could make and how I would counter it. It could be that he sensed that I'd loaded my right leg and was already prepared to place a quick, yet highly effective kick to the left side of his head. He had the reach on me, and the home court advantage, but I don't scare easily. His hands, which remained at his sides, below his belt line, were free of any weapon I could see.

Eyes measured, but hands killed.

"You're understandably upset," I said with the even tone of a therapist. "Your buddy is dead and your house has been rendered a crime scene. That's got to be tough. However, you gotta realize we're just here to help."

His eyes fluttered and his chin retracted to its normal position. His brow furrowed and he licked his lips.

"S-sorry," he said, his shoulders relaxing. He rubbed his eyes and the bridge of his nose, before taking that hand and sliding it down over the rest of his face. "I'm just tired."

"You need to relax, man."

The DJ plopped down into a desk chair. I quickly identified the pens, a pair of scissors, and a letter opener within his reach.

He leaned forward, cupping his face in his hands, feigning grief. I let him go through his act and push his fake tears. I played along so that he would believe I bought it. I even reached into my pocket and handed him a couple of tissues.

He bemoaned the pressures of touring and made sure he threw in a comment about just seeing Rayford a few days ago. The lowest point of his vapid thespianism came when he shouted out Goodbody's name, as if we were in a movie, and as if I was going to be impressed. He sniveled, blew his nose, wiped his eyes, and let out several quivering exhalations.

The whole performance was an eye roller, but I stayed in character as the sympathetic witness to his counterfeit meltdown, knowing his specialty was music, not drama. With nothing of any substance having been accomplished by his pseudo-tantrum, I simply asked, "Did you get everything you needed?" The question was twofold.

He dried himself and looked up at me with reddened eyes and a sour face. Realizing his mask had slipped, he furrowed his brow and gave his best impersonation of a sad clown. "I-I just need to grab a few things."

He avoided eye contact, knowing I could see the lie in his face. He found a suitcase and began tossing random garments into it, whining on and on about the loss of his friend.

Downstairs, I bid him adieu and watched the DJ pile into the back seat of the Escalade. The beefy driver shut the door and tossed the suitcase into the back. The tires spun defiantly, and they had to slam the brakes once for traffic, before speeding off heading north on South Drexel.

Janus hadn't said it, but he wanted me out of his house—which is why I was determined to find out what that computer had been hooked up to and what information it held.

The department had personnel who specialized in electronics, IT, and all that other stuff to which I had little understanding. However, even with the captain's urging, it would take at least a day or two before the request was fulfilled and somebody came out to check the connection.

I kept a man named Bridgeforth on speed dial, buzzing him whenever I got a new gadget that needed setting up at my place. He plied his trade for the Board of Education, but also used his skills as a side hustle.

He answered after the second ring.

"Sherm," I said.

"Well, if it's not Chicago's Finest! Good morning, Detective."

"Need your help, bro," I said meekly.

"For business or pleasure?"

"The first one. It's a hot button item." I gave a quick explanation.

"You're killing me, sir—*figuratively*," he said, with a nerdy chuckle. "Send me the address and I'll be on my way."

"Wait, aren't you at work?"

He let out a fake cough, which was on par with the paltry melodrama Janus had meted out. "I'm feeling a cold coming on."

"Seems like you only take sick days when I call."

He snorted, stifling a giggle. "Funny how that works, right?"

We both laughed and I texted him my location.

* * *

Forty-five minutes later, my phone rang.

"You need to call off your watchdog," said Sherman Bridgeforth. "Seems Officer Chamberlain has been instructed not to let anyone enter without your express permission."

"Damn straight," I told him. I stepped onto the porch and signaled for the patrolman, who stood outside his cruiser in a field interview stance.

Sherman had the pleasure (or misfortune) of being named after an actor who had portrayed a cranky character from an old TV show his mama used to watch. Oddly enough, he was more like the cartoon character (by the same name) who ran around with a talking dog. It didn't help that, like his animated counterpart, he had an oversized head, wore thick glasses, and was as painfully intelligent as he was socially awkward. He must have seemed like an easy mark, and the young thugs in his neck of the woods harassed his mother about her monthly state check with no worries—before I caught wind of it, that is. It was a few years ago when I was assigned to patrol. When I ran down the perps, I put the word out that Sherman and his mother, Mrs. Shirley Bridgeforth, were off-limits. Since then, I could always call him whenever I was in a pinch and he would come through.

It didn't matter that Afros went out of style some time back; my cohort sported his proudly. He wasn't very tall and his poor posture brought him down at least two more inches. He also didn't bother breathing through his nose, always wheezing through his mouth, instead. An anime addict, he always wore t-shirts featuring his favorite characters; today's tee was of a gigantic kaiju monster going toe-to-toe with a hero in mechanized armor.

Though I would never be able to convince him of the importance of a nice suit and we would never congregate in the same social circles, Sherman was my friend. "Glad you could make it," I told him, outstretching my hand.

Then I remembered that he didn't particularly like being touched, so we ended up greeted each other with a fist bump instead.

"What do you have, sir?" He insisted on calling me that, no matter how much I protested. After a few years, it no longer registered.

"Need you to trace a line for me."

"That's easy. I could've talked you through that one."

I chuckled. Though simple for him, this sort of stuff was far from my specialty. "Hell, I know my limits. Besides, you're the best."

He grinned, repositioning his thick glasses, which had begun to slide down his nose. "Point me in the right direction."

I explained that we had to be mindful of the crime scene. He nodded and followed me up the stairs with his tool bag, a multimeter, and a flashlight. I led him to the area of the closet where I'd found the computer and indicated the cords I'd disconnected.

While my buddy did his thing, I continued to snoop around the house; I felt drawn back to the red basement door. Again, I found myself down in the gangway, reaching into the rafters, searching with a tentative hand. I tapped something hard, but so smooth it couldn't be wood or brick.

Using some impromptu ingenuity, I placed my feet on the ledge opposite the door and angled my body above the lintel, hoping I wouldn't fall. There was a small space up and to the left. I broke out my flashlight to find an electronic eye staring back at me. The camera lay in a shadowy recess, hidden from casual observation. I imagined it could record anyone who wandered through the gangway or decided to jump the fence.

Keeping that device in mind, I added to my sketch diagram of the house's exterior. The camera I'd just discovered gave a completely different vantage point than the others at the front and rear of the house. As those were covered with dark-colored glass domes, this one seemed to be different. It had a hard plastic construction and a rectangular shape. I would've wagered my next paycheck that it wasn't monitored by a security company. Of course, Janus had insisted the monitored cameras were broken, which didn't make sense based on my own observations in the screening room. I would get to the truth.

An hour later, I had confirmation that the connector at the back of Janus's closet led to three cameras: two in the orgy room and one the device I'd located above the gangway side door. Sherman had also found an audio line, which he thought might go to a microphone located somewhere in the house, though he would need more time and tools to locate that one.

* * *

"Hey Cap, remember that CPU we snatched up as evidence?"

"What about it?"

"I think we made the right call."

"Good."

I was about to hang up when Kodjoe told me to hold on. "Forensics seized the victim's cell phone from the scene. It was discovered in the bed linens."

"Okay."

"The vic sent several texts and had a conversation with Janus shortly before his demise. That reinforces the DJ's whereabouts in Detroit. Now, I'm getting curious about who else Janus may have talked to leading up to the murder. Though he didn't pull the trigger, I have a notion he ordered it done. Find me the evidence and we'll be able to charge him with conspiracy to commit."

"I'm on it, boss." I hung up with and looked at Sherman. "So, what do I owe you?"

Using his breath, he fogged one of the lenses of his glasses, then wiped it with the hem of his t-shirt. When he put them back on, they sat a little crooked. "I haven't eaten yet."

I smiled. "Then lunch is on me."

* * *

"Arrogant bastard isn't he?" said Captain Kodjoe later that afternoon when I walked into his office.

I smiled. "I was going to say it if you didn't."

"Enjoy his music but I would pass on being his friend."

"Yeah," I said, "we see what friendship with Janus can get you."

I could hardly wait to tell him about Janus' behavior back at the mansion but curbed my impulse and let my supervisor lead the conversation.

He plopped down into a chair, loosening his tie and top button. "Jealous lover, you think?"

I nodded. "I'd bet my paycheck on it. Not only is Nneka George the manager of his club, but she's also intimately involved with him. I'll see what turns up on her before setting up the interview."

"Good thinking, Detective," he said, and then added, "You're probably wondering why I didn't have you advise our guest today of his rights and begin an interrogation."

"It definitely crossed my mind, sir."

"Well, arrogance doesn't equal stupidity. We don't currently have enough information to label him a suspect. His prints are expected to be all over his own house, naturally. And his alibi is pretty airtight. Being an asshole doesn't necessarily make him a murderer."

"But what if he paid someone to do it?"

"It's possible, even probable," he said, scratching his chin. "We can snoop around public records to see if any large sums of money have moved in the last couple of weeks."

"The problem is, we can't access his bank accounts without a warrant to do so."

"Exactly. And he'd lawyer up in a New York minute. Besides, there are other ways to barter, aside from money."

"Like?"

"Love—or what passes for love," Kodjoe said, leaning

back in the chair, forming his forefingers into a steeple. "Just because he doesn't love Nneka George doesn't mean she isn't over the moon about him. That emotion makes people capable of some pretty crazy things."

An image of Vickie floated through my mind. Then, Maurice and Shauna Bolduc—it got no crazier than that.

"Nice work, coming up with that tidbit about the two globes, Brandywine. Sure caught him off guard."

"Yep, that went better than expected. I wonder who has the other one."

"Me too." He swiveled in the chair. "Let me ask you something."

"Shoot."

"If someone had been beaten to death in your house, would you act that nonchalant?"

"*Hells no!* But I'm also not in the habit of giving my house key out to just anyone, especially folks I wouldn't even call friends. It all sounds fishy to me."

I filled him in on the temper tantrum Janus had thrown when we'd gone back to his house. I showed Kodjoe the diagram I'd drawn of the exterior, which included the projected visual patterns of all three of the known exterior cameras. I also shared Sherman's report, implicating the side camera, which I had visualized, and the as-yet-unconfirmed microphone, in addition to the screening room cameras. This reminded me that I needed to turn the hard drive over. But I hadn't had a chance to look at it all the way though yet.

"So, what's the strategy? What do we do next?" I asked.

"First, check to see if the monitoring company has any footage from those cameras. We'll continue interviewing witnesses. And then we'll wait for him to fuck up."

I was shocked to hear my strait-laced supervisor curse, particularly dropping the f-bomb. He didn't respond to my chuckle, his eyes unblinking.

"Did you see how he went on the run when you began to corner him?"

"Yeah, with his lyin' ass."

"It's only a matter of time before he puts his foot in it and can't wipe the crap off. Proceed with a background check on Nneka George and schedule the interview. I have a feeling Janus is already on the phone, schooling her with what to say and what not to reveal. Look at any other known associates and, when you get a chance, check out his nightclub. Never know what might turn up."

"Shall do."

* * *

Social media is awesome. Nine times out of ten, I can find much of what I need from online profiles. Nneka George was no different—the woman Janus bragged about as a sex trophy, but whose name he couldn't recall when talking about love.

Damn shame, too. The woman's beauty transcended the physical—she was gorgeous. Her skin was brown, her build athletic, and her smile was wide and seemed genuine. She was a short, stylish lady who seemed to enjoy posing for the camera with friends, family, and other revelers. She was conscious of her looks. Her hairstyles—always natural, often locked or plaited—changed like her nails with different outfits. She seemed fun-loving and interesting.

Perusing Nina's public feed, I came upon a photo that spoke volumes. It was captioned "The Three Musketeers." In the center, laughing and playing to the camera, stood Janus with his long arms around each of his lovers. On his right was Nina George, wearing a form-fitting red dress and a forced smile. On the DJ's left, the dead man, caught just as the camera froze him, wore a look of hurt, gazing—not at the lens—but up at Janus.

I looked through her list of friends, but Goodbody's name wasn't listed, though maybe he didn't go in for social media—not everybody did. George had posted several times since the murder: an inspirational quote about love, a selfie with her cat, a picture of a fancy cocktail. No hint about the death of the young man in the picture.

Her relationship status read "It's Complicated" and, though her feed was full of compliments from men who were clearly interested in her, she encouraged no one. No, she only wanted one man, it seems; the question was if she'd been willing to kill to have him for her own.

I hated the fact that I often suspected the worst in people.

"Hey, it's alright to go home," I heard come from over my shoulder.

I turned to see Detective Vargas, who was heading for the door with an attaché in hand. "Don't be like your partner," he said.

"How's that?"

"Perry practically lives here," he said with a chuckle. "Escape while you can. The case will still be here tomorrow, my man."

I sat forward, rubbing my face, stifling a yawn. "Y'know, as much as I hate to admit it, even a broken clock is right twice a day!"

"Yeah, but I'm right more often than that. Take your butt home. Don't you have a girlfriend or something?"

"I do," I said with a smirk, "but your sister wants me to take it to another level and actually marry her ugly ass!"

Vargas paused, giving thought to my joke. Then he shrugged and admitted, "Yeah, she does look like the product of a gorilla mating with a dump truck!"

We both laughed.

He didn't have a sister that I knew of. If he had, his response might not have been so humorous. We ribbed each other like that, meaning nothing by it.

He waved good night and went home to a wife brave enough to be seen in public with him. I smiled and decided to save that remark for next time around.

It was almost nine but I had to prove to Cap that I could lead an investigation. As much as I liked and learned from Perry, I needed to start pulling my weight.

But Vargas was right too—it was time to go home, even if it was to nothing but a television and a bathtub. I sighed and wondered what I would be eating for dinner. This reminded me of hot dogs, for some crazy reason, and I made a mental note to take a daylight gander around Washington Park next chance I got, and see how my as-yet-unnamed friend was faring. Then, glancing at the phone, I figured I should do one last thing before I called it a night.

Ms. George didn't pick up on the first ring, or the second, or the third. When she did, I was greeted by a sultry alto as sweet as her image. "Hello."

"Ma'am, I hope I'm not disturbing you. This is Detective Brandywine from Chicago Police Department."

"I've been expecting your call," she said.

Chapter 4

Social media should get its ass kicked.

Okay, let me clarify that statement: I love using this new method to dig up the goods on people, but it flat-out failed Nneka George. The photos posted online did not do her beauty justice—not by a long shot. Much like Janus the day before, but without the peacock stance, she had paused in the lobby and surveyed the scene. Then, every pair of eyes in the place watched as she removed her outer coat—a long, dark, flannel affair—and folded it over her arm.

"*Clawd hammercy,*" I muttered under my breath, recognizing her immediately. Had to blink to both wet my eyes and break my stalker's gaze. She was dressed in a sharp navy pinstripe skirted business suit, which revealed her shapely legs and did not disguise the fact that she was well endowed on top. Her high heels lent her some significant height and made me wonder how she pulled off the balancing act. Her burnished hair was styled in a plaited crown and framed the loveliest face.

Looking that hot, could she possibly be Rayford Goodbody's killer? I sure as hell hoped not.

She stood for a moment just inside the entrance, perusing the controlled chaos in the vast room. Instead of elephants, clowns, and trapeze acts, these rings featured a desk sergeant fussing into the phone, a baby hollering in its black-eyed mother's arms, and a wannabe pimp in cuffs kicking and screaming as he's dragged to Booking.

Looking past all the ruckus, Nneka's eyes rested on me. Maybe she recognized that I alone seemed unaffected by the circus around me. "Detective Brandywine," I presume.

"Ms. George," I said, shaking her hand. "Thanks for coming. Right this way."

Flipping the tables from the day before, it was my turn to provide the escort and make the introduction. Kodjoe stood when we entered the conference room, extending his hand. He offered her a bottle of water.

"How was your ride over," he inquired, as we took seats at the table, she on one side, the captain and I on the other.

"It was good but kind of slippery," she said, bringing up an issue we were all dealing with. The temperature had dropped, turning the slush into a bumpy sheet of ice. "I'll be happier when spring finally sets in."

"Agreed," I admitted.

"Will I be needing an attorney?"

"No, ma'am," Kodjoe said. "We're just trying to get a feel for what you know about the case. We have no reason to suspect your involvement."

Not yet, anyway, I thought. I knew that, if she slipped on the figurative ice, she would soon be requesting legal representation.

She opened the bottle, took a cautious sip, and squared her shoulders. I knew she was uncomfortable, and I wanted her that way. Though I displayed the facade of amicability, we didn't call her in to be friends.

The small talk came off as robotic. She was not interested in chatter about the weather, but things loosened up a little when I asked about her background.

She was proud of the fact that she'd gone from being a homeless high school dropout with no prospects, to club manager, while earning a business degree from the local college.

"That's quite an accomplishment," I commented.

"I owe it all to Janus," the beautiful woman across the table told me.

"He is a rather remarkable guy," I suggested. "But you probably should take credit where credit is due. It sounds like you worked hard."

"Oh, yes I did. But I have to hand it to him for recognizing my potential. Not only is he a musical genius, but a wonderful humanitarian."

"He does put out some great mixes," my division officer agreed. "I've got each of his albums from as far back as the early '90s. Many of them are collector's items."

"What's your association with him," I asked, leaving no air between the captain's compliment and getting down to business.

"As far as work goes, he's my boss. He initially hired me as a bartender at Duality. Since then, I've made myself indispensable, you might say."

"And personally?"

"We're in love," she said without hesitation, her eyes bright. She crossed her legs, adjusting the skirt so that it approached her knee. "We're getting married next year."

So says you, I thought, considering her boyfriend's lack of enthusiasm for romantic exclusivity.

I nodded, then hung neutral for a while, letting the silence expand into the hollow room.

"I heard about what happened," she finally said.

"What was that?"

"About the…death," she said, shifting in her chair. "Isn't that why you had me come here?" Her tone was annoyed, but what I noticed most, is how she avoided mentioning the victim by name, though they were obviously well acquainted.

I said his name and asked her how well she had known him.

She nodded in a dramatic way, and suddenly remembering the water bottle, reached for it with both hands. She unscrewed the cap and took one sip, and then another. The move seemed practiced, as if part of a rehearsed series of motions.

I leaned forward, coming at her, as she wanted to distance herself. Her features hardened a bit.

"How did it make you feel—to hear of his death?"

"Sad, of course," she quipped. At that point, most friends and acquaintances would become emotional, speaking about the last time they saw or talked to the deceased. Nina knew more than she was letting on, I guessed. She still managed to avoid saying his name. "He was a friend," she said. "I'm devastated, of course."

But he wasn't her friend, was he? Quite the opposite. Rayford may have been the expendable third leg in a love triangle, the person who stood between Nina and her man.

"He is already missed. God rest his soul," she announced.

I imagined her as a ventriloquist's dummy, propped up on the DJ's knee. The words were not her own. Like with the man throwing his voice and pulling her string, there wasn't enough on which to charge or hold Nneka George.

"By the way," I began, "about the snow globe . . ."

Her eyes widened and then cut to the side, full lips pressed into a thin line. "Snow globe," she said, giving nothing away.

"You know, the one with the gold flakes inside . . ."

"Yes, I know. What of it?"

"You've seen it, of course."

"Yes."

"Held it in your hand?"

"Um," her face had gone pale. "I, um, no. I mean, I've seen it for sure, at Janus' house. But no, I've never held it."

"Right... Who has the other one, the one with the platinum flakes?"

She gave a little pained gasp. "I don't know. He didn't give it to me."

"But he gave you a key to his house, didn't he?" I shot back. Kodjoe and I exchanged glances.

"Um, yes, sure. Long time ago."

"And you still have it?" I asked, to which she nodded.

"Did you use it Sunday night?"

"No, no, no, of *course* not," she said, raising her voice.

"Where does your fiancé keep the key to the trophy case?" I came out with next.

"The what? The trophy... I don't know. Wait, you mean the curio? The key is... um..."

I leaned in, and so did the captain.

That's when she laughed. But the sound held no humor. "You all aren't trying to put some circumstantial thing on me, are you? I didn't kill Goodbody and the more time you waste on me, the longer his murderer will be out there."

By the time we concluded the interview, all she had given us was that she'd stayed at the club all of Sunday evening, until closing, which had been one in the morning. I would check that out to be sure.

Nina ignored the hubbub as I escorted her out, her mind apparently occupied with other thoughts. She didn't exactly wriggle like a worm on a hook, but I could sense a strong desire to get away.

"Thanks for coming by."

Her eyes were sad, though I doubted it was for the death of Rayford Goodbody. Like deep down, something inside her wanted to be free. Possibly she was regretting whatever involvement she had with the crime. Or maybe she was beginning to wonder if the "promise" of love dangled before her like a carrot would lead to her happiness or a life of misery.

I had a feeling it was an empty vow and she was just being led to the slaughter. I couldn't warn her, only allow things to play out until either she or the DJ slipped. If and when they did, I'd be waiting with a pair of handcuffs for each.

As I watched her rush toward the parking lot in her high heels, I was glad I didn't offer to walk her to her vehicle. At this point, my gentlemanly actions would have been less than welcome. The headlights came on and, without bothering to warm up her modest sedan, she drove off, ignoring my goodbye wave. Just as well. I was sure we'd be seeing each other again soon.

I stepped back to my desk and analyzed the possibility of Nneka George as the prime suspect. Whereas Janus's alibi placed him five hours away at the time of the murder, hers was shaky at best.

In my mind, charging Nina with the crime depended on proving the triumvirate: intent, opportunity, and capability. I asked myself if she had intention to kill Rayford. That would take further interviewing. However, if I was a betting man, given what Janus himself had said about the threesome's antics, and her contrasting emotional ties, I might go with that. The photo of the three together suggested a smoldering anger that very well might have resulted in the most drastic of measures. After all, as Cap said, people do crazy things for love.

The opportunity to do the deed was definitely there, since she had a house key, and she could have been physically present. Duality did most of its business on Friday and Saturday nights, when the hardcore partygoers came out to dance, drink, and play. Though opened on Sundays, business was quite a bit slower, according to Barbosa. Both the club and the residence were located on the South Side of town, though roughly a half hour apart by car. It was within the realm of possibility for her to slip out of work, go to Drexel Avenue, commit the murder, and be back at Duality within an hour.

Finally, there was capability, which was a bit more nebulous. This element depended on an array of abilities and characteristics, in addition to the driving distance. It involved her knowledge of the house, the choice of that particular weapon, and her physical strength, among others. But as Barbosa had mentioned, the victim's impaired condition would also influence the assailant's capability.

I walked over to the wall and stood staring at the map of the city for quite a while, considering all the angles.

I went back to my desk and drew a hasty picture of the dialed-down area in question — the kill house, the club, the airport, the major roads. I opened my steno pad, read my notes, and sat staring at my diagram of the mansion until my eyes crossed.

I turned a page in my notebook and began to make a list of things I wanted to check on and do. Probably of highest priority, I needed to follow up on finding and notifying the family of Rayford Goodbody of his demise. I would start by going to the address on his ID and see what I could find out. I also planned to talk to the ME about the autopsy. I would visit Club Duality and try to get intel on the victim and who might have wanted him dead. I'd check on Nina George's alibi, gather information on Janus, and consider other suspects.

I needed access to the camera feed at both the club and the house. I still needed to contact the security company about the front and back cameras. I had to follow up with Forensics about multiple items, like the CPU, the skullcap, the trash and vomit, and the murder weapon itself, for starters.

Then there was the home itself, with the audio wire still not found, the feed for the third camera over the side door, statements from all the neighbors, taxi drivers in the area that night, security cameras on neighborhood houses and the church, and background checks on everybody that worked at Duality or with the tour.

I considered the murder weapon. Why did the killer choose that particular item — a limited-edition, custom-made snow globe? Was the object itself symbolic of something more? Did it have something to do with that album? Someone who had worked on it wasn't happy?

This was one of those times I wished my big, mustachioed lug nut of a partner was around to help. But I planned to have this case in the bag before Perry came back with his farmer's tan and tales from the beach. Still, if I planned to be successful — and I did — I would need some help.

I texted Cap and asked for a meeting. He said he'd let me know. My desk terminal was hit-or-miss, at best. So, despite the fact I'd put in a work order to get it fixed, it was no surprise I got a blue screen with an error code when I turned it on. Had Sherman worked for our department, he'd have easily accomplished whatever update or replacement was required but, for the time being, I was ass-out. Fortunately for me, I'd gotten used to the walking relic that was my partner. He didn't believe in relying too much on computers, preferring to go low-tech. Knocking on doors didn't take a password to log in. Rather than letting technology limit me, I grabbed my messenger bag and hit the streets.

I spent the afternoon performing my investigation the old-fashioned way, driving to various locations, looking around, flashing my badge, talking to everyone who would talk to me, making notes, and snapping pictures.

The landlady let me into Goodbody's place, which was compact and neat, and yielded some leads on next of kin.

Duality's parking lot was empty in the early afternoon—both the main area to the side of the building, and the smaller section in the back. Two cameras were mounted on a central light pole to cover most of the side lot. I walked over to the section in the back and didn't see any surveillance cameras there. I circumnavigated the large building on foot, and thought I saw someone through a slit of visibility in a back window, but no one answered the door or the phone.

Flyers advertising a "Memorial Tribute Fundraiser" for Rayford Goodbody were plastered everywhere. The event would be held the next day, on Thursday night. I pulled my portable camera out of my bag and took a picture of the invitation. I would definitely plan to attend.

I drove over to the crime lab, and caught Barbosa just getting into her patrol car. She was wearing a happy face and said that Forensics had decided to cooperate. When I asked her what she meant, she just laughed and waved me off, saying she had to get back to her post, which happened to be at South Drexel Avenue.

She tooted her horn in a friendly gesture as she drove off. I humbled myself and went in and sought out Sorenson and Laplaglia, and ended up learning answers to several of my questions, as well as a lot more about what those guys in Forensics do all day. It wasn't till later in the shift when I finally strolled back into the precinct bullpen.

"Cap wanted you to go to his office when you got in," Vargas announced when he saw me plop down at my desk.

"'Bout what?"

The burly investigator shrugged and returned his attention to the stack of files on his desk. The office was buzzing with the normal amount of business, so the world hadn't ended just yet.

I tapped twice on Kodjoe's door. "You wanted to see me, sir?"

He was a handsome man, built like an Olympic track-and-field star who'd shaved his head and facial hair to cut down on wind resistance. Propped up in his gray herringbone suit pants and pink shirt, he was staring out the window over a dreary cityscape, probably wishing for warmer weather.

By the end of February, most of us were worn out from the relentless advances of Old Man Winter, who, like a boorish guest, couldn't take a hint it was time to leave.

"Detective," my boss said. "Have a seat. Give me an update."

I did as I was told. First, I brought up my intention to talk to Janus and everyone who worked for him. I planned to check out the club before it opened the next day. I also informed him that no footage had been recovered from the fore and aft vantage points of the house. The security company said they had been taken off-line the same day Janus and his crew had hit the road for Detroit. This made the DJ a liar, as he'd told me that the cameras were broken. It could also indicate premeditation.

After I briefed Kodjoe on my visit to the club and the thus-far futile effort to notify Rayford Goodbody's family, he asked, "Are you getting all the assistance you need?"

"Honestly, no. Besides the computer problems, I could use an extra set of eyes and hands. Sergeant Perry picked the perfect time to go on leave."

"Murder never takes a holiday," he said coolly. "Besides, his absence gives you the chance to shine. Officer Barbosa assisted at the house. Was she helpful?"

I nodded. "Very," and I filled him in on Barbosa being a self-proclaimed "House Head," which was an added benefit.

To this he nodded for a few seconds, as if to a beat. "Nothing wrong with that," he said, and continued, "Actually, I've already talked with her watch commander, and he's given me the go ahead. I understand they're short on manning, so I won't be able to pull her away completely. However, I will authorize the overtime if she is willing to put in the work before or after her shifts."

I smiled. "Thank you, sir."

"I'll leave it to you to inform her, Brandywine," he concluded, or so I thought. I started gathering my things together. "By the way, when was the last time you've been out clubbing?"

"Not really my thing," I answered honestly.

"Well, make it your thing. Tomorrow night's event is a pretty big deal."

"Oh, you already knew about it?"

"Yes, I have my own sources. It promises to be sold out, so I went ahead and squared that away," he said, handing me two tickets.

I mumbled as I read the print on the laminated slips of card stock, "Rayford Goodbody Memorial Fundraiser... Join Janus at Duality to help the family of his choreographer, dancer and good friend... February

25, 2010…doors open at 10pm…$75 open seating," I read aloud.

"Sorry, the VIP seating would have broken the budget," he said with a chortle.

"Are you coming with?" I asked.

"Oh, no. But I expect you can get Officer Barbosa to go with you.

"Yeah, unless she's washing her hair tomorrow night."

"She's not my type, but I'm guessing she could pass as someone you'd date?"

"She could."

"Good. I'll authorize $100 to help you two blend in." He reached into his desk and retrieved something. It was a debit card in a sleeve, which he slid across the desk. "Any drinks you order will be non-alcoholic."

My frown was playful.

"You'll carry your weapons. Though I don't think anything will go down, if something does and you two get into some gunplay…"

It was standard practice to take bodily fluids from officers involved in shootings to rule out anything that would have clouded judgment. When casing a joint in undercover status, officers were allowed to consume a couple of drinks. However, Kodjoe was speaking from experience and wanted to avoid the headache in advance. "No funny business, either," he added. His statement held double meaning and he stared at me, ensuring I understood both.

"10-4," I acknowledged, standing and pocketing the tickets and the debit card.

"So do you think that Janus knows how to get in touch with Goodbody's family? If so, he's holding out on us," I suggested.

"Or cashing in on his friend's death…" said Kodjoe, giving voice to my suspicion. "Oh, that's right, they aren't friends. He barely knows the guy."

We both shook our heads.

Chapter 5

Thursday afternoon, I swung by Duality. A liquor truck was parked out back and several employees were moving the inventory inside. With Janus on the road and Nina not yet at work, Head Bartender Julius McGovern was willing to talk, once the delivery was completed and the truck had driven away. Despite the chill in the air, we remained outside to give us a bit of privacy. He asserted that he had seen the general manager there for several hours that fateful night. However, because Nina was his boss, he didn't keep up with her whereabouts every minute. As far as he knew, she had been there from opening to closing.

McGovern shivered, rubbing his arms.

"It is kind of cold out today," I said in agreement. "Not too bad when I'm in motion," he said, referring to the liquor delivery he'd just helped to hump from the loading area into the nightclub. We were standing still and little clouds of steam rose from our mouths as we spoke. "I never got used to it but Nina likes it."

"What do you mean?"

"She'll go for walks in temperatures low enough to make a polar bear think twice."

"What about the night Goodbody died," I asked.

McGovern paused for a moment, dipping his head while raising the glasses from the bridge of his nose. He used a thumb to wipe away the wetness forming at the rim of one eye. When he leaned back onto the brick facade and looked at me, I knew it was more than the negative wind chill affecting his eyes.

He cleared his throat. "Damn shame what happened to that young man," he garbled through an incorrigible patch of mucous. He hacked it up and launched a loogie in the other direction.

"It was," I said. I posted my shoulder up on the same wall in a show of empathy. "You knew him?"

The man nodded slightly, wiping at a tear in his other eye. "Yes."

I fished a tissue from my pocket and handed it over.

"This'll break his mother's heart. And no matter what his daddy may have thought 'bout how his son lived, he's bound to be busted up too. But that's something for the preacher to work out with his god."

I gave the bartender a moment, not hitting him with a barrage of questions. There was a subtle art to setting the stage and just waiting.

And just like that, the story of poor Rayford's life spilled out. The younger man's plight was having parents whose god would not allow them to accept him.

"Not that St. Louis is a small town by any means," said McGovern, "but Rayford figured that, shy of New York or LA, he could hone his craft and ply his trade here in the Big Windy. That's why he chose that college, but then he quit to join Janus' troop, which I can see would be a plum position for any wannabe choreographer. But that little bit of notoriety wound up being his demise, I guess."

I nodded, trying to banish an image of the dancer's corpse from my thoughts.

"Can I confide something in you, Detective?"

I stood up from the wall and agreed without the standard caveat that my discretion didn't absolve any wrongdoing on his part. He could read it in my eyes, though.

"No, I didn't have anything to do with the murder," he said.

"Got it."

"You ever work for a boss you didn't care for?"

I feigned a cough into my gloved hands, so he wouldn't see the sarcastic grin. Working for Kodjoe got no complaints from me but I'd had several asshole supervisors in my military career.

"Yeah," Julius acknowledged with a sly smile of his own. He'd read me. "You know what I mean."

"Problems with Ms. George?"

"No, not at all. She and Rayford didn't necessarily get along, but I'm already sure you're aware of that tilted love triangle."

"Then who do you mean," I questioned, already knowing the answer. With Nina being his immediate supervisor, there was only one other person who sat at the top of the chain of command.

"I'm talking about the apex of that little fucked up pyramid."

"Janus."

"Mmm hmm. Nothing outright, though. Between his focus on the studio and touring, my dealings with him are minimal. But then, he also knows who he can test."

McGovern took a deep breath, puffed out his chest, and squared his shoulders. Not many people were anywhere near as tall as the club owner, but to be sure, Janus kept his bullshit and intimidation tactics to a minimum with Julius. Hell, I thought, giving the older, barrel-chested bartender another glance, I was taller, and probably quicker, but I wouldn't run up on Julius, either. Nothing in his demeanor said he had time to play games.

"Are you saying the DJ did it?"

"Not directly. I'm saying that, seeing how he would pit Nina and Rayford against each other, I wouldn't put anything past his ass." He spat again.

"Are you telling me you suspect he had something to do with the killing?"

He exhaled an exasperated cloud, pained that he had

to say the words but happy to get his theory off his broad chest. "The man orchestrates records, careers, and keeps the drama on full tilt."

"Doesn't make him a murderer, though," I proffered.

"Naw, it don't. But then, the man ain't the type to get his hands dirty when he can have somebody else do the work."

"Nina?"

He shook his head. "That's not what I'm saying, either. Like Rayford, that young lady dragged herself up from the dirt and accomplished a whole lot. She may not have liked the constant competition with Goodbody, but that don't make her no killer."

I was also hoping she hadn't caused the death.

"Listen, don't get any of this twisted, Mr. Brandywine. I don't have no proof of who did that boy in and I don't want you putting in some report that I do."

"No suppositions without proof," I said, lifting two fingers. "Scout's honor."

"Thanks. Whoever did it, I wanna see their asses fry. Whether he liked other boys or not didn't give anybody cause to take him out."

"Do you know anyone to whom Rayford owed money?"

"I didn't get into the man's business like that."

"Any enemies?"

"Not that I know of. But I do know Janus was tryna put some distance between himself and Ray. Again, I cain't prove it but I also wouldn't rule out that MF pullin' the puppet strings."

His words lent weight to one of my theories. Though I didn't want to, I had to consider Nina as Suspect #1 until I had more to go on.

"Listen Detective, as much as I'd love to stand around out here and shoot the shit with you, I got work to do and it's cold as a witch's tit out here."

"Gotcha," I said, thanked him for the information, and was about to leave. As he placed his hand on the door pull to go back into the club, I turned back as if something had just crossed my mind. "Just one more question, Mr. McGovern: Any of your security guys here?"

That's how I met twins Horus and Anubis Jenkins. One of them had been Janus's driver the day before, though I couldn't tell which. They were identical with the exception of their hairstyles: that is to say, one of them had a headful of dreadlocks and the other was completely bald.

Having gotten their names from McGovern a few minutes before stepping out of the alley and into the building, I feigned having to make a phone call. Well, I did buzz the dispatcher and had a wants-and-warrants check done on the twins, along with McGovern. The bartender came back clean. However, of the brothers, Anubis had a warrant for overdue child support that I could've run him in on. And neither of them appeared to have an Illinois driver's license. With that, it wasn't hard to convince them to play ball, though they did so begrudgingly.

They led me to a small room behind the stage, where several monitors displayed camera feeds from inside and outside the club.

Bingo.

It didn't take me long to find the black-and-white parking-lot footage of Nina walking out the side door of Duality at 8:32 Sunday night, and heading toward the back parking lot before she walked out of the frame. She returned the same way at 9:47, over an hour later, appearing in the frame from the back of the building. I reviewed the interval carefully, to be sure I didn't miss anything. It sure busted her alibi.

Switching to the inside feeds—I watched her go into her office at 8:30 and emerge moments later in a long-haired light-colored coat and carrying a large purse. A pair of jaunty white earmuffs contrasted dramatically with her flowing locks, while a scarf wound around her neck. *Where was she going?*

"Which one of you drives the boss around," I asked.

"We take turns," the one with the dreads said. "It was me, yesterday."

"Well, keep this under wraps."

The clean-shaven one, Horus, grimaced. "Why should we cooperate with you?"

"Because neither of you holds a valid driver's license."

He was silent, while Anubis sucked his teeth. As wide as linebackers, neither had a neck.

I expected that, between the bartender, the twins, and the handful of other employees, word would get out that a cop was sniffing around the club. When the manager and her pompous boyfriend heard, they might get sloppy. And that's exactly what I wanted.

I didn't have a warrant for the footage, but I wouldn't need it if they gave me a copy of it willingly.

"Do these feeds go into a computer?"

"Yeah," one of the despondent brothers admitted.

"How could I get copies of the internal and external feeds?"

"We can burn it to DVD," the other suggested.

"You all mind?" I said, real nice.

They did, from their childish pouts, but they nodded in unison.

"Do it, then," I demanded. "Give me everything from 5 o'clock until closing that night."

One grunted while the other exhaled. But they complied and, a half hour later, I had two discs I could review back at the precinct.

"I'll be seeing you again soon," I said with a tip of my newsboy hat. Then I was gone.

* * *

"Been waiting to hear from you," Jeri Barbosa said after the first ring.

"Good afternoon to you, too."

"Thanks," she said, voice full of excitement. I know that feeling of enthusiasm for being chosen and given a role, so

I get it...

"It was my captain's decision to—"

"Doesn't matter," she purred. "I'm happy to help if I can be of use with your case."

"Well, now that you're going to be officially involved, that would make it *our* case," I corrected.

She pulled the phone away but I could clearly hear the girlish squeal. I imagined her jumping up and down with delight. "Do you think they might consider me for a permanent position when it comes available?"

"Slow your roll. Let's see how well you do on this one before you start rockin' the Sherlock Holmes getup!"

"Okay, okay," she said, "Where do we start?"

Her eagerness was a breath of fresh air, and I told her about the problem notifying the murder victim's family, and the information I'd gained from Julius McGovern. "I'd especially like your help with that," I said, "for starters."

She answered with some good comments, and I was sure that she was the right person for the job. Some officers loved the streets and relished the constant interaction with the common folks, even if it meant the occasional foot chase. Though my thirtieth birthday had come and gone, I could catch anyone in a foot chase, but I didn't want to spend the rest of my career in pursuits, responding to alarm activations, and directing traffic. It wasn't beneath me but I liked the idea of wearing a suit, certain things being flexible—like hours— and the opportunity to take my time solving larger cases. I could picture Barbosa doing the same in a couple of years.

"So, they're having some kind of memorial event for Rayford Goodbody at Club Duality tonight..." I began.

"Yes. You should go. *We* should go," she interrupted. "I wish I'd thought about it, I would've gotten tickets. Now it would mean standing in line..." she continued.

"I'm a step ahead of you," I cut in. I half-expected her to squeal again, but she was quiet, waiting.

How about this," I said, "Let's get a bite to eat on our

way there. We need to discuss what's what before barging into our assignment."

"Alright."

"Do you have the appropriate attire?"

The diabolical chuckle worked its way up from deep in her throat. *"Do I,"* she remarked huskily.

"Well, I'll pick you up at around nine, then."

"I'll text you my address."

"Works for me. See you then," I said, about to hang up.

"One thing before you go, Detective."

"What's that?"

"This is a work assignment, not a date."

"Hell yeah," I said, trying to make it sound as if I wasn't a bit disappointed. "Strictly business."

"Mmmn, better make it nine-thirty," she giggled. "You know how us ladies fuss over our hair and makeup."

"Twenty-one-thirty, it is then."

* * *

I had enough sense to stop by my place, shower, and put some different clothes on. I didn't want to admit it but I cringed at the idea of Jeri Barbosa poking fun at my fashion sense. I decided against another suit and went with a cable-knit sweater in a merlot shade and dark khakis. I chose a pair of charcoal leather high-top sneakers made by Conglomerates, a brand that was lately replacing my Chucks. At a glance, they could pass for "smart casual" instead of sportswear. I topped off my ensemble with a felt porkpie in the same tone as the shoes, wearing it slightly tilted, which I thought made me look like a jazz saxophonist "hep cat." For the weather, I went with my light gray pea coat and a gray plaid cashmere scarf with a merlot stitch running through it.

* * *

She didn't emerge from her apartment until 9:45 but boy, was off-duty Barbosa worth the wait! I clenched my teeth so as not to allow my mouth to fall open. She had slinked into a form-fitting little black dress with stilettos and had layered on a silver metallic cape. She was brilliant.

No funny business, I heard echo in my mind.

I began to get the sneaking suspicion that I was being tested to see if I would fail. Kodjoe claimed he wanted to give me some shine by letting me lead this investigation, then he sent me a female officer who made me want to act like an animated Tex Avery character.

"Sorry I'm late," she said, climbing into the passenger's seat of my SUV, while I tried not to ogle her gams. She'd just tiptoed through the slushy half-frozen ruts in those bejeweled heels with her clutch placed strategically over her head to protect a little from the sleet. I suppose if it was a real date, I would have been out there with an umbrella.

"No problem at all," I remarked from the driver's seat, keeping it together, albeit barely. I was almost mesmerized by her flowery perfume—had to concentrate on my driving. I put on my blinker, studying her from the corner of my eye while waiting for the traffic to clear. Her plum lipstick accentuated her wide smile and a touch of eyeliner made her hazel-green peepers pop. But it was her hair that really got my attention. I hadn't really noticed it before, I would have said it was brown and she wore it in a bun under her police hat. Now it was loose and wavy, and hung to the middle of her back, while on the top and front, she sported a solid faux hawk.

I wanted to pay her a compliment without embarrassing myself. "You look nice. Definitely different from the job," was what I came up with. It sounded about as awkward as it was corny.

"That's funny, because you look about the same," she laughed. I wanted to let her know that I chose my outfit with her in mind and even dabbed on some cologne to impress her, but I kept my mouth shut.

"The hat is a nice touch, though," she said.

"*Gracias,*" I replied.

"*De nada.*"

As I pulled onto the street. I needed something to take my mind off her stunning physical beauty. "Fluent in Spanish?"

She laughed. "Not really. I do know some Portuguese though."

"Oh." I had no more, knowing little about the language that sounded to me like a mishmash of Spanish, German, and French.

"You're curious about where my people are from."

"It has crossed my mind."

"Most folks assume I'm part of the Mexican population of the city, though my skin is dark enough to appear to be Puerto Rican, maybe even Dominican."

"True," I half-sang.

"I could be of El Salvador," she teased, batting those eyes in slow-motion.

"Maybe even from Panama. Lots of beautiful sisters down that way," I offered.

"Ever been?"

"Yep. Drug Ops with the Navy. But they don't speak Portuguese in Panama, Salvador, or the islands."

"Sure don't, though they do speak it in Brazil," she said, winking. She knew she had my interest.

"Well," I asked impatiently.

"Well..." She was smiling from the attention. "How about we discuss it more over dinner. After all the nonsense at the job today and not getting any lunch, a sister is hungry!"

Try as I might, I couldn't hide my smile.

* * *

One deep-dish pizza later, we were rubbing our bellies as we lumbered back to my Chevy. Though we both insisted it wasn't a date, I had come out of pocket anyway, assuring her she could get the check next time.

She left the tip but told me that, no matter how great the

meal was, she could give the chef a run for his money.

"You can make deep dish?"

"I can make *any*thing you want," she said.

"What's your specialty?"

She laughed, as if I didn't believe her, repeating, "I can make anything you want, man!"

"I'll have to take you up on that one day," I insisted.

"Good. I look forward to it!"

I let the truck heat up for a couple of minutes, then pulled into the street, heading toward Club Duality. Jeri Barbosa was checking her phone.

At the pizza place, I'd gotten a better look at her deep chestnut hair and had noticed a smattering of henna highlights. Put me in mind of an old shipmate of mine who hailed from Boston. We were fresh out of boot camp and he was always singing the praises of Cape Verdean women. I'd found out at dinner that Jeri descended from the inhabitants of that island chain that sat to the left of the Dark Continent. Her genetic mix of West African and Portuguese genes yielded breathtaking features as a result. But, with ice pellets sprinkling my windshield, I had to keep my eyes glued to the road.

"So, we're just looking around," she said, as we came within a few blocks of the spot.

"That and showing presence."

"Sounds good. Not one of my frequent haunts but I admit I have shaken my booty there a few times."

I tried not to recall the roundness of her butt nor the supple curve of her hips. "I was there earlier today, so I have a basic idea of the layout."

"You haven't seen it at full tilt then."

"Full tilt?"

"You'll see."

We drove past the venue on the way to the parking lot. Neon lights lent a soft glow to the freezing rain in the night air. A line of dedicated partygoers spilled out the door and wrapped around the block. I was beginning to get the notion it was more of a church than a mere hangout. With the building filled wall-to-wall with congregants, many of the faithful were willing to stand outside in an ice storm for a chance to—*what?* Well, I would soon see.

"You've got the tickets, right?" she asked as we climbed out of the car.

I tapped my chest to indicate they were in my coat pocket and patted my gun at my waist for good measure. We parked and walked around the rear of the building to approach the front door opposite the queue. Arriving with tickets in hand, we were admitted into the inner sanctum without having to wait in line. I felt a mild sympathy for the patrons shivering in their paltry outfits, waiting to get in.

We dropped a layer at the coat check—I declined to give them my hat and kept it on my head. And, as I'd arranged during my earlier visit, one of the twins slipped me a radio and a fresh wireless ear piece. I put it on mute so I could listen in on their internal communications without transmitting.

Folks were grinding it up, with the earnest movement extending beyond the borders of the dance floor, into the aisles and between chairs and tables. A DJ occupied the booth, spinning records and working the boards, while the crowd anticipated the arrival of Janus.

Of course, the excuse was the commemoration for Rayford Goodbody, but I suspected the real draw was Janus's short return before resuming his Midwestern tour. With Milwaukee and Detroit down, he still had Indianapolis, Toledo, and Dayton over the next few days, with Cleveland and Pittsburgh following a bit further down the line.

The place was abuzz and after several fruitless efforts, I gave up on getting us drinks. At her insistence, I handed off the card to Barbosa and posted up at our private booth. Without a trace of arrogance, she claimed that, as a good-looking woman, she would fare better at gaining the bartender's attention.

Had we been on a date, I might not have given in so easy. But we weren't. She'd made herself clear and I respected that. Besides, Captain's orders.

Duality thrived in a transformed theater from a time when the neighborhood was known for more than rampant gang activity and random shootings. According to public records, Janus had bought the burned-out shell for next to nothing, just before the neighborhood started its upturn. He'd financed the overhaul and renovations with record sales and money made from touring.

The club had once been a popular movie house. Abandoned and damn near forgotten, it became a drug den for some time. The DJ had it cleaned up and transformed it into a reputable venue and community pillar again. Nearby businesses could thrive because of the club's revenue stream. From what I could tell, business was good.

The interior architecture included ornate caryatids appearing to support the high ceiling. The row of feminine figures, which lined the wall opposite the stage, effectively separating the expansive lobby and the even larger audience area, had been restored and stylized. The columns were inspired by the city's Museum of Science and Industry, which had, in turn, copied its pillars from the Athenian acropolis. But instead of flowing robes, the gigantic figures were scantily clad in sexy lingerie.

From above the stage, with faces turned to the left and right, was a bas-relief pseudo-stone carving of Janus's Roman namesake. It dropped down from the ceiling in dramatic fashion, seeming to levitate above the crowd. It was the same image I'd seen embroidered in gold on the black beanie we'd found at the crime scene, and on every club employee I'd met since.

I vaguely remembered the icon from my Mythologies and Religious Studies class. The god denoted transition. Maybe that was the superstar DJ's reason for having

Goodbody murdered: it was time for a change. Could it be that the proof of his bisexual hijinks cut into his professional reputation?

I pondered this while my partner fought through a throng of scantily clad ladies vying for beverages. When she finally made it back to our spot with the libations, the only evidence of her struggle was a single strand of hair gone rogue.

"Y'know, maybe I should have gone back and just waited in line for drinks," I yelled over the music.

She placed my glass down in front of me and leaned toward my ear. "Then, instead of it taking 20 minutes like it did for me, you wouldn't have come back for an hour."

"Point taken."

Earlier, I had shared my theory with her that Janus had put someone up to the killing. Though he could have hired a hit man to get the job done, my best guess was that he liked to keep things in-house, either paying his girlfriend outright or promising her something more than money. I had also filled Barbosa in on Nina's claim to innocence and the gaping hole I'd discovered in her alibi.

The bass was bumping, and the club was teeming with activity. Folks were grinding it out on the dance floor and, since that was packed, revelers found anywhere they could to move their bodies.

At dinner, she insisted we use first names while at the club. "Sounds suspicious to be referring to each other by our surnames in a casual environment," she'd said between bites. "So, you can call me Jeri."

"Okay."

"And, unless you want me constantly calling you 'detective' or 'sir,' you'd better give me something else."

"Brandy."

"But that's not your first n—"

I looked at her sternly. "Just Brandy will do."

We were huddled in our booth, leaning in to hear each other, trying to ignore a couple writhing just a few feet away. I was looking for something to distract me from my partner's formfitting attire.

"So," I halfway yelled over the throbbing beat, "I heard back from the victim's family."

She took a sip of her drink, frowned, and cupped her hand to my ear. "What did they say?"

"They're down in East St. Louis. Said it's going to take a couple days before they can come up to identify and claim their son."

She looked puzzled. "I would hope my family would be a bit more eager to get that sort of closure if it was me on the slab."

"I think there are some things going on behind the scenes that point to disapproval of Rayford's lifestyle."

Jeri shook her head, turning down the corners of her mouth. "Damn shame. You'd think they would push their feelings aside—especially under these circumstances. I mean, the dude is *dead*."

"Staunch church folks. The father is a pastor, in fact. Mentioned something about a revival, which is probably why it was so hard to get in touch with them. Said they would drive up on Saturday and meet me at the morgue in the afternoon. I almost thought he was going to hit me with a sermon before we hung up."

"Did they at least seem sad?"

"I heard Mrs. Goodbody wailing in the background but Pops kept his composure. He quoted some scripture about the Lord giving and taking away."

"Book of Job. Some real somber stuff that probably justifies piety in the midst of his suffering." She paused, then chuckled. "Don't be surprised if they show up in sackcloth and ashes."

I shook my head with a smirk and changed the subject. "It's a good thing there is no alcohol in that drink." Jeri winked and gave me a coquettish smile.

* * *

My companion moved to my side of the booth. Her excuse was so we wouldn't have to holler above the music as much. Whatever the reason, it felt good to be that close to her.

"I considered your idea and it makes sense," she said.

"How so?"

"A woman just might do the dastardly deed for love. She had the motivation, if it meant being with the man she cherished."

I took a sip of the concoction, which was ginger ale with a splash of grenadine for color. "But why would he risk all this," I asked, indicating the nightclub, his albums, tours, and production deals.

Jeri smiled and I found myself turning away after staring too long into her eyes.

"It feels good to be admired," she said, nuzzling up to me a bit. This was a surprise.

"Wait, I thought this wasn't a date."

"It's not. I'm making a point."

"Which is?"

"Brandywine, there's a definite attraction between us."

I nodded.

"It's intensified by the fact that, according to departmental guidelines, we shouldn't be involved with each other. It's taboo."

"Okay, so…what're you getting at?"

"What if Janus set up the sense of competition between Goodbody and George on purpose? Keep in mind, he is a bisexual man in a world not quite ready to accept such things."

"Yeah, but people don't make the same fuss they used to about that, anymore. It's 2010, not the '70s."

"Um, you're not right about that. My older brother's not the flamboyant stereotype of what some folks consider gay, but he definitely plays for the other team. He's a professional and keeps his lifestyle under wraps for the sake of his privacy—and he's nobody famous like Janus."

"I'm following you but wondering what that has to do with you getting all close to me."

"I keep my ears open for rumors and the latest news. Well, you've met Janus already and can agree that his personality and fashion sense are over-the-top. He craves attention and probably loves his own reflection. I imagine it would be hard for him to get married and settle down."

I nodded, trying, and failing, to imagine the man I'd met with a young family.

"Doesn't really fit with the Black Narcissus image," I mused.

"Yah, anyway, his parents were successful entrepreneurs; they were also big philanthropists. Their estate contributes to several educational and artistic Chicago area endeavors."

"Keep going," I urged.

"When Mommy and Daddy died in an accident, Janus was shocked to discover a catch to the windfall he expected to inherit. The will stated that he'd get the Drexel house, of course, and would continue to receive a generous monthly stipend, but in order to inherit the bulk of the family fortune, he would have to produce an heir by his 40th birthday."

I whistled. I hadn't picked up any of this from reading the fan forums. "You sure about this?"

She just gave me a withering look and continued. "No offspring and most of the fortune goes to charity. Janus loves the spotlight and all the sex, but his window is quickly narrowing. He's 38 now, and he has to ensure he gets the right woman, someone who won't hit him with the baby-mama drama. As fond as he was of Rayford, there was no way that union could produce an heir."

"So, why have him killed?" I wondered.

"You just mentioned the name of the record that put him back on the map," she said with a sarcastic grin. "Just wait until you see him take the stage at midnight. The other part is that Goodbody could ruin his reputation. Word on the streets is Janus has been tapped to run his own record label, which could yield him all kinds of money, or…."

"*Or?*" I looked at her as if she had all the answers. She gazed back, her plum lips pouty. Maybe she did.

"Or, he was just bored, and he's lost touch with the rules for everyday life. I don't know, there's so many possibilities…"

"Where does Nina fall into all this?"

"She's probably willing to do just about anything. My guess is that she wants to bear his child but I don't think that will be good enough. Men like him are never satisfied, always trying to upgrade to something better." She paused and looked me dead in the eye. "How about *you?*"

I was caught off guard and felt my face flush. "What do you mean," I asked with a suspicious grin.

Jeri didn't blink. "Are you looking to upgrade or trying to experiment?"

Gazing at her, why did I suddenly think of my mother, the human lie detector? She would sense if I wasn't being honest.

"Neither. Look, Bar—um, Jeri, you already know I like you. But I'm a lot more focused on catching a killer than trying to ease my way into your panties."

She blinked slowly and it was impossible to read what was going on behind those eyes. Her voice was low, but it was close to my ear and I could hear her just fine.

"Don't get it twisted; a little role play helps us blend in with the crowd. I take my job seriously, though. I'm not hanging around hoping to be somebody's jump-off or get a locker room rep. Got it, man?"

I sat up. "You're serious."

"Like they say in New York, *dead ass.*"

"Got it." I rubbed my goatee and resumed our conversation on the previous subject. "Well, I hope you're right about our suspect. If Janus did something to break her heart, she might be willing to spill the beans."

"Maybe. Hell hath no fury, which could work in our

favor."

She settled her head into my neck for a while and it felt good. It was so that we could hear each other over the hubbub, but it didn't negate how great her hair smelled.

"So, what's the other reason?"

"Hmm?"

"Oh, nothing. Just thinking out loud."

She lifted her head and studied my face. Hers was a mask that meandered between passion and concern. "Please share."

"Just wondering what all that had to do with you laying your head on my shoulder."

She sat up straight. "Keeping up appearances. People might notice if we don't come off like a couple." Barbosa smiled widely and gave a quick, playful wink. "Besides, I was really getting into your scent. Just try not to read too much into it."

I was about to explore that topic further, when an animated brick wall approached our booth. He was an inch or two shorter than me but twice as thick. It wasn't that his dreadlocks hid his neck—he just didn't have one. Looking past Jeri, who was sitting toward the aisle, his tight eyes settled on me. "Evenin' Detective," the bouncer grumbled.

"What's up?" I asked Horus. Or was he Anubis?

"Mr. Janus and Ms. George request your presence." He said it with the grimace of a representative of the Lollipop Guild, but he was a lot more intimidating than a munchkin.

We'd flashed our badges upon entry, so the security folks never patted us down for weapons. I'd clipped the radio to my belt, the wireless bud in my ear. My 1911 resided in its pancake rig, tucked neatly under my top. I could only assume Barbosa's was in her clutch. "This is my partner," I told our beefy escort. "She's coming too."

The big man paused and whispered into his ear piece. He listened for the response, then gruffly said, "A'ight, follow me."

Standing guard at stage left, his bald headed doppelganger punched in a code then let us go ahead, his muscular arm holding the door and pointing the way. They were quite the intimidating pair.

Backstage, the cacophony of thumping bass grooves from the club proper was muffled. A non-slip rubber pathway led to the recesses and a narrow stairway slipped down into the depths. Descending the steps, I was greeted by softer lighting and heard another type of music playing; something smoother and more melodic. It was an old school slow jam, better known as baby-making music. Judging from the look of post-coital satisfaction on Nina's face, something of the sort had been going on. She grinned and walked past us, into one of the sound booths located behind a panoramic window.

"Good evening, good people," Janus said, wrapped up in a smoking jacket and reclining on a sofa at the rear of his subterranean studio. A smell of sex intermingled with incense, barely masking the stink of marijuana smoke.

I acknowledged his greeting with a reversed nod, wondering what to expect. Barbosa stood just behind my right shoulder, her thumb casually resting on the snap of her clutch.

"I heard you'd come out to see the show tonight," he said smugly. "Heard you were sniffing around here earlier today, too."

"Verifying a few facts," I said coolly.

The scant leftovers of two joints in the ashtray suggested to me that neither the DJ nor his lover would make any sudden moves. I relaxed a bit but maintained situational awareness. After all, straight indica cannabis could mellow the user out, but if the spliffs had been dipped in embalming fluid or laced with coke, you could get the opposite effect.

"That's good, good," he slurred, obviously high as hell. "I would offer y'all some of this herb, but something tells me you don't partake."

"We could drag you in," Barbosa said, like a feisty Chihuahua.

"Over this little bit?" he asked her with a grin, holding up what was left of a dub sack. He looked at me, eyes bloodshot. "Shit, I was trying to be polite. Just wanted to officially welcome you to Duality and hope you enjoy the show. I go on in a little bit."

Nina made herself busy. She was wearing a long t-shirt and not much else, arranging some of the instruments in the larger of three padded booths. When she bent over and messed around with a bass, and some brass and woodwinds, I noticed she wasn't wearing any panties. I tried not to stare but it was a losing battle.

"I'm working on some new, *profound* shit," the producer bragged, making me grateful for the distraction. "Getting bored with traditional House, so it's time to push the envelope. We're adding actual instrumentation, not relying strictly on keyboards and samples."

"We won't worry about the weed," I said, ignoring his soliloquy about musical innovation. Frankly, I didn't care. Though I did note that when talking about himself and his work, he really got animated. He probably whacked off at the sight of his reflection, too.

"So, why the fuck are you here, then," he hissed. "Trying to bring another brother down? Jealous of my success?"

"Man, ain't nobody jealous of your success ," Jeri said with a dismissive wave, as if speaking to a petulant child. "Your friend just got his head bashed in the other day. We're here to make sure the killer isn't after you, too!"

"He wasn't my friend!" He shouted the statement angrily, like he thought his booming volume would convince everyone. But he was trying harder to convince himself. His attention turned to the woman beside me.

"And who the hell are *you*, anyway?"

"Officer Barbosa. I'm Detective Brandywine's partner."

"Partner as in..." he insinuated. Humming lasciviously, he leaned forward, glassy red eyes unblinking. "Does that partnership extend beyond normal working hours?"

Her thumb popped the snap to her purse before she replied. I placed my hand over hers to keep her cool. Even an un-flushable turd like Janus didn't warrant such an easy way out.

"That's none of your business," she said, relaxing her thumb.

"I mean, if not, maybe you can come back and see me after the club closes tonight."

"How about you watch your damn mouth before you lose some teeth?" I blurted before thinking. I hate misogynists. And, though it went against policy for me to smack him in the face with my .45 for his lewd comment, I was giving it some serious consideration.

Janus knew I wasn't playing, so he locked his lip, probably trying to think of a good comeback. I was surprised he didn't threaten to sic his team of attorneys on me for hurting his feelings, but then, maybe he was too high to notice.

The DJ's phone buzzed and issued a brief, feminine-sounding melody. His eyes darted nervously to Nina before picking up the device to read the text and type a response. Whatever the message was, it had brought a wicked smile to his face.

I looked beyond the panoramic window and mixing board to see Nina dusting horns and drums, oblivious to what her boyfriend was saying and doing behind her back. I wondered what kind of hold he had on her and why she stuck around to take his shit.

My father had my mother under his spell for years. It finally took a night where he'd beaten her and threatened to do the same to my sister before I put my hands on the gun he kept in his shoe box. He didn't realize I knew where it was, let alone how to use it. But I was 15 and close enough to manhood to try to stop the abuse. I was as tall as my dad, though not as strong and nowhere near as mean. As bad as he was, he knew he couldn't contend with hot lead. It made my mom, bloodied and bruised, finally admit that we'd all had enough, and she put him out for good.

"When will *she* have enough," I asked, coming back to the present reality. I watched his woman, cleaning like a maid, but with her private parts readily on display.

"Who, her?" he asked with a dry chuckle, not bothering to look in that direction or even say his lover's name.

Reducing Nina to an objective pronoun told me everything I needed to know.

"She'll *never* get enough. None of these bitches can!"

With that, he allowed his robe to fall open, revealing the erection underneath.

"Back out," I told Jeri.

"He doesn't scare me," she said defiantly.

"Let's *go*," I demanded with a bit more emphasis.

I didn't take my eye off him, wondering if his excitement was because of me, my partner, or just the idea of confronting the law. I almost wished he would've made a wrong move. Being a deadeye shot, I knew I could blow his nuts off and leave him a bitter, impotent shadow of a man. Hell, I might've received an award for performing a public service.

"Enjoy the show," he called out as we made our way up the staircase.

Barbosa frowned, holding up her forefinger and thumb to where they were an inch apart to let him know she wasn't impressed.

I half-expected the twins to be waiting on top of the stairs but, according to radio chatter, they were on the club side, dealing with a couple of wily customers. Lucky us.

"You know," she said, "we should've gone on and run his ass in for possession and indecent exposure. Bet he wouldn't be giggling then."

"That would've been a waste of time, jeopardizing the big fish for a shrimp cocktail." It was something Perry would've said.

"Speaking of Mr. Cocktail Weenie," she rifled off. She

closed her eyes for a moment and shook her head angrily. *"Never-fucking-mind.* Anyway, arrogant as Janus may be, do you actually think he's fool enough to slip up?"

"Let him be. He'll do something that may bring about a turn in the case. He's too intelligent to get caught committing an outright felony. He likes the idea of being defiant—hence the cannabis and his little 'wardrobe malfunction', but he's riding the edge so he doesn't get into any major trouble." I rubbed my beard. "However, everything about how he was acting says cocaine..."

"We could get a search warrant," she suggested.

"Yeah, we could, but we won't. We can let a few pawns go for a bigger piece."

"I don't play chess. What's our next move?"

"Let's enjoy the show, like he said, though it would be better if we could find a seat," I said, as we had lost our booth when we went backstage.

"No problem," said Jeri, settling into the wall near some filled tables.

"Question."

"What's that?"

"Were you actually going to draw your gun back there?"

Barbosa grinned and delayed her answer. "As much as I could have let one off an inch from his balls, no. For your information, like every other woman in Chicago, I carry pepper spray in my purse, whether or not I'm packing my firearm. And I'm not afraid to use it!"

I had to laugh. As it played hell on the eyes and the other facial orifices, I imagined that a good dose of oleoresin capsicum to the nuts could send a dude off howling. I chuckled at the thought of him cutting backflips like a cartoon character, smoke trailing behind as he sought a bucket of ice to cool the burn.

Barbosa's frustration had nearly shut her down. She was understandably pissed and was ready to call it a night. Part of me wanted to roll out too, but I felt I needed to watch the guy in action, to see what all the hype was about.

"Wait, let's see if we can salvage this," I said, knowing the main event was about to begin.

The MC made an announcement that the superstar was soon to take the stage, causing folks to abandon their seats and rush to the fringes of the already-packed dance floor. In that mass exodus, we asserted ourselves and nabbed a booth.

Leaving my faux date to hold our seats, I worked my way to the bar, which was fairly empty, and ordered us a round of drinks. Though Julius McGovern seemed to be pretty cool when I'd met him earlier in the day, I still watched closely to ensure the bartender didn't spit or put anything extra into our glasses. Against the captain's order, I'd gotten a cognac for me, and sangria for my partner. We could both use a little something to dull the edge.

The attendance level was likely pressing the upper limit of the fire code. A glance at the door showed patrons still jockeying for a way into the club. It was an indicator of how Janus' mind worked: he created a demand that only he could supply. It fueled his ego and fed his god complex. I had a feeling his stage show was going to be more of the same.

As I made my way back to our booth, something caught my eye: an oddly familiar young lady heading toward the bar. Against an animated canvas comprised primarily of darker tones, the woman's pale complexion and light-colored hair stood out like a beacon. Eschewing men's advances, she passed within an arm's reach but took no notice of me whatsoever, as I stood there transfixed, trying to place where I'd seen her face before. Then it dawned on me. *The hell is she doing here?*

"That was quick," Jeri said upon my return.

I handed her the sweetened, blood-red concoction but didn't take my eye off the white girl. "We should've stuck to something non-alcoholic."

"Why is that?"

"I got a hunch that the show is going to feature fireworks."

She had no clue what I was talking about. "That's ridiculous. They don't have a permit for —"

"I just ran into somebody who can*not* be here by coincidence."

"A suspect?"

"Not exactly. More like a twisted muse, maybe another queen bee. And you can't have two in the same hive."

Barbosa shrugged her supple shoulders. To her, I was babbling nonsense.

"Remember how you said men like Janus can't be satisfied?"

"Uh huh. And?"

My gaze shifted to the crowd and sought out my quarry in a sea of brown faces. I thumbed in her direction, knowing the attractive blonde woman would stand out to Jeri as well. "Got a feeling that she's the upgrade."

"That text he got…"

"More than that. You hear about the professor who killed himself in the chemistry lab a few months back?"

"Just scuttlebutt. Doused himself with gasoline or something like that, right?"

"It was sulfuric acid."

"Do you know that for sure?"

"My other partner and I responded to a mutual aid call from the university campus. It was some nasty business over the professor's young wife cheating with several dudes, including someone he referred to as her 'busker boyfriend.'"

Jeri snorted. "And you think the boyfriend is this butt hole we just left in the studio with a dick harder than Chinese arithmetic? Ol' reefer-smoking DJ Deez Nuts?"

I stifled a laugh but paused in homage to her awesome metaphor topped off like a cherry with a Dr. Dre allusion.

"Could just be mere happenstance, but I doubt it. After all, what's the probability of her dead husband's suspicions being true? Why else would a lone, trailer-park princess like Shauna Bolduc come down to the hood to shake her augmented ass?"

Barbosa rose to her feet, pulling the hem of her dress down toward her knee. "Pass me the company card. I'm going to get us a couple of colas and then you are going to tell me this story. We need to be as clear-headed as possible, and I have to understand what the hell is going on between this doe-eyed chick and Mr. Superstar."

"Exactly," I said, handing her the plastic. As I watched the sway of my partner's hips in her wonderful, formfitting outfit, I considered how much easier on the eyes she was than Perry. Then I laughed and pushed my cognac snifter aside.

From my seat in the shadows, I could see Shauna across the way, cavorting with a bouncer the size of Deputy Muscle Head, who was trying to mean-mug in front of a heavy velvet curtain leading backstage. I say *trying* because being the object of her attention would have the average guy giggling like a schoolgirl. Not me, though. I'd be cool, like I was last year when I'd interviewed the new widow following her husband's demise. Of course, even I couldn't deny what a knockout she was in her red swing-jive halter dress—so very Marilyn Monroe.

"So, Detective Brandywine . . . enjoying yourself?"

I turned to see what kitten was purring in my ear, but I already knew. Nneka George had apparently forgotten that, not even an hour before, I'd gotten a gander of her heart-shaped patch of pubic hair—or maybe her not giving a damn was the entire point. She wore the club staff's requisite emblemed black beanie, jeans, and t-shirt combo, but with her double D's and narrow waist, she rocked it a lot sexier than the beefed-up security dudes. I tried not to let her looks distract me, or the recent memory of watching her do her housekeeping duties *sans* thong.

Glancing back at the velvet curtain, I saw the bouncer standing there alone, pushing a button on his ear piece and talking into his mic.

"Sure, I dig House music," I told Nina, giving her my full attention with a smile.

"Is that what brings you out on this chilly night—your love of the beat? Name your favorite artist or song," she challenged.

I was caught red-handed but kept my poker face in place. Hell, though I didn't mind the genre, I could never say I was a true fan. I was a *funkateer*, with my tastes being more akin to George Clinton's sonic experiments. However, I knew something about classic House from what many considered the golden age. Just as James Brown was the Godfather of Soul, the bass-heavy, illegitimate child of Disco had its own.

"Frankie Knuckles," I told her with a sly grin.

Her smile was wider and just as mischievous as the Cheshire Cat's, minus the playfulness. Her expression was fixed and disingenuous, with a bit of disappointment bordering on disdain showing in her smoky eyes. I hadn't given the right answer. It would be a few more years before Knuckles' death and the renaming of a city street after him but, in Nina's eyes, even that legendary DJ couldn't hold a candle to Janus.

She sauntered off, her braided, auburn ponytail swinging as she cackled sarcastically over her shoulder. I found myself pondering the reality of jiggle physics and trying not to pay too much attention to her glorious backside. It had already mesmerized me before. Combined with that forced grin of hers, it brought to mind a rather comical lyric from Bell Biv Devoe . . .

If my hunch was correct, I'd soon be slapping cuffs on her dainty wrists for either murder or conspiracy to commit. *Maybe she should laugh while she still can.*

Jeri set two Shirley Temples on the table and fell into her seat. "Now talk."

I filled her in on the Bolduc incident, from the hostage call at the university lab and Maurice's suicide, to the follow-up interview with Shauna the next day.

"The way she talked about him was so cold. I don't think she actually said 'good riddance' in so many words, but the message was clear."

"So, that poor bastard killed himself for a chick who could care less?"

"*Couldn't* care less," I corrected. "Love, jealousy, shame—strong emotions."

"I didn't put it together until tonight, but now I understand what Bolduc meant by 'ersatz musician.' It was his wife's affair with Janus that pushed him over the edge."

"Too many people getting jacked up over that repugnant motherfucker," said my partner.

"I thought you were trying to stop cussing."

She took a deep, frustrated breath. "Yeah, about that…"

Chapter 6

Cinderella's magic spell wears off when the clock strikes 12, but at the Temple of Janus, midnight marked just the beginning of the magic. The music stopped and an announcer took to the stage, hyping the congregation from excitement to frenzy. There were calls and responses, chanting, and people leaping as if they were possessed.

With all the hand waving and shouting, I thought I was in church until the special effects began. A thick fog rolled in, accompanied by flashes of lightning and a peal of thunder. Like green fingers, laser beams cut through the mist. A huge monitor descended slowly from the ceiling; an enlarged image was projected at a movie screen behind the DJ's station.

To the sides of the stage, blown-up versions of the latest album cover materialized: the stylized Jack of Clubs in the upper half, with the Queen of Broken Hearts beneath. I considered Janus's ugly disregard for women or anyone else fool enough to fall for him, counterbalanced with his love of self, above all. How appropriate.

Two dancers, a man and a woman, stepped from the back of the stage and took stations on either side of the booth. The sound effect of thunder was almost deafening, the MC's voice nearly lost in all that noise, as he enthusiastically pointed toward the overhead.

In unison, all eyes followed. Floating to earth on an almost-invisible set of wires was the man of the hour, the self-proclaimed High Priest of House. Janus hung suspended above the crowd, a theatrical cape billowing behind, a spotlight illuminating his form. The wires brought him down, pausing for a moment above the stage, giving him the appearance of levitation. He crossed his arms like a pharaoh, minus the crook and flail. At the moment his feet touched down, a simultaneous explosion made the revelers cringe.

The lights went out for a moment, then came back on in a flickering, epileptic nightmare. Janus outstretched his hands and the surreal looking dancers doffed his cape. The superstar stepped into the booth where his image was magnified and broadcast on the screen behind him and on the overhead monitors. Folks went absolutely nuts when the music started. His voice echoed into unintelligible demands that they toss their bodies about in sacrifice to him. They did as they were told—hopping, leaping, and contorting to the thumping bass and hypnotic beat.

Jeri, who claimed to have seen him in action on several occasions, was obviously still in awe. She got up as if in a trance, jacking and grooving with the rest of the crowd.

The music was good, but I didn't get what they all saw in the arrogant DJ. His stage presence was all about getting attention. Though the advertisement said the party was in Rayford's honor, it was just an excuse for the cult to gather and pay homage to their false god.

As patrons forgot themselves in the sweat-drenched ecstasy of the dance, my head was in another space. I could easily understand why someone would have wanted to knock off Janus. Maybe they even mistook Rayford Goodbody for the DJ and bashed in the wrong man's head. Given a snow globe and a bit of impunity, I might find myself tempted…

Nah. I was just talking shit to myself. Even a haughty slug like him didn't deserve to go out like that. After a while, I noticed that the swindling preacher was no longer in his pulpit, but his congregation kept right on with their writhing, dipping, and swaying to a pre-recorded mix.

At that moment, the security radio chirped to life with a distress call. It was just the break I'd been hoping for—at least, that's what I thought.

"Let's go," I told Barbosa, tipping over my glass as we sprang into action. She was ready to roll, pocketbook in hand. I was amazed at how well she could move in those heels.

Several muscle-bound roughnecks had rushed through the backstage door and stood frozen at the top of the staircase leading to the studio. All they were allowed to carry was pepper spray.

"She's got a gun," Horus yelled.

"Who," I asked, drawing mine.

"Nina!"

Barbosa had already unsnapped her clutch, revealing the secret blue steel inside.

I heard shrill screaming and another voice whimpering.

At first, I thought the high pitch was from another lady, but it was Janus sniveling and begging for his life, like the punk he was. After he'd concluded his first set, he decided to hole up in the studio with his upgrade: Shauna Bolduc.

"*Please*, baby," he cried. "It ain't what it looks like!"

I was wondering if Janus had moved from playing House to singing the Blues.

"Don't give me that 'please, baby' shit, negro! After all I've done for you—for us—*this* is how you repay me?!"

"I hate stairs," my partner grumbled. She had a point: stairs, windows, and doorways were fatal funnels of fire. "I've got the watch commander on speed dial! He can have SWAT on their way—"

"No," I said. "It'll take too long and this thing will probably be done before they get here. We've got this." I turned my attention to the basement. "Nneka," I said in a calm, authoritative voice.

"Don't come down here! This ungrateful, cheating-ass black bastard and his cave bitch belong to me! I caught their asses dead to rights!"

Whispering to my partner: "On second thought, if I give you a nod or things suddenly go south, call for the cavalry."

One hand on her weapon, Jeri hit speed dial with the other. It was a preemptive move and she was right to do so, but I still frowned.

My attention focused back to the unfolding soap opera. "Can we just talk?"

I was trying to keep the jilted woman speaking while getting a bead on where everyone was located. I couldn't see the trysting couple, but Nina's voice had come from near the soundboard, where the engineer and producer would have sat. It was to the left of the staircase. That meant that Janus and Shauna were on the sofa at the rear-right side of the space.

"Talk, yes, but don't you bring your butt down those stairs, Detective. I'll see you before you see me and I don't wanna to have to hurt you!"

I cursed under my breath, realizing my vest was in my bug-out bag in the back of my truck. A lot of good it was doing me there.

"Speaking of which, are you injured?" There was no sound of a gunshot and, hearing Janus and his mistress both whining meant they were alive. They weren't my immediate concern. I had to control the hostage taker and worry about the hostages after.

"Only a broken heart," she lamented, her voice quavering. I heard her sniffle but imagined her bracing herself to stay strong.

I was grateful that the staircase didn't have a turn or a landing, but it was so steep, it didn't give me a good vantage point. Nina was correct when she said she'd see me first. My legs and lower torso could very well get shot to shit before I could even make it into the basement.

"What about the other two?" Though I truly didn't care, I had to ask as part of the job, and successfully negotiating meant gaining trust and information.

Her voice dropped an octave, taking on a steely tone. "I smacked Miss Thang in her pretty little, dick-sucking mouth. Gave her a deeper shade of lipstick but she'll live."

Nina's aggravation grew and for a moment, she forgot about me, yelling at Shauna, "How do I taste, heifer?! I was just with him two hours ago!"

Janus's outburst followed, hollering to me: "You gonna keep chattin' it up or you gonna save us from this crazy-ass b—".

He must of thought better of his last word and censored himself.

"Say it," Nneka yelled, no doubt pointing the gun at him.

Then, in a tone that would make Samuel L. Jackson proud, she hollered, "I double-dare you, motherfucker!"

I ignored his plea, addressing the woman with the weapon, so I could bring her focus back onto me. "Now, Nina, I'm going to need you to keep cool. Don't listen to anything he has to say."

There was a cracking sound, followed by Janus crying out in pain.

I wanted to laugh. Though my partner was ready to storm the room, I put up my clenched fist to let her know we were holding still. If the DJ was yelling, he was still alive.

"What the hell happened," Barbosa whispered loudly.

"She just pistol-whipped him upside the head, I think."

My partner was wide-eyed. "We need to get down in there and stop it!"

"Nah, there were no gunshots and he'll survive with a knot on his oversized head."

According to standard operating procedure, we could go down with guns blazing to stop loss of life. For the moment, the self-proclaimed deity had been reminded of his mortality. It wasn't a life-threatening reminder, from what I could gather. Still, to be sure, I asked, "You alright, Janus?"

"She *hit* me, man!"

"Miss Bolduc, what about you?"

"My mouth is bleeding," she mumbled through wet, swollen lips. "I just want to go home."

"My goal is to get us all home in one piece. Nina, why don't we do it that way?" I had to be specific with my task directions. If I'd told her to place the pistol on the console, either Janus or Shauna could grab it. However, I didn't want her approaching the steps with the weapon in hand, either. "Place the gun on the bottom step and face the sound booths."

"He *hurt* me," she exclaimed, her voice softening to a sob when she repeated her statement. "After everything I've done to...*appeal* to him, he goes off and betrays me with this trailer park trick!"

As the two captives blubbered, I thought about Shauna and how her selfishness had led to Maurice's jealousy, shame, and ultimately, his suicide. The chick was about as caustic as the acid that sealed her husband's fate. Janus was poisonous to anyone who got close to him. The two cheaters deserved each other, though I would have had a hard time convincing Nneka George of that fact. And *she* was the one with the gun.

Maybe I should've allowed Nina to enact her vengeance and put everyone out of their misery. However, her life would unnecessarily be turned to shit if she didn't decide to go out like the old professor, turning her weapon on herself. Just as important as saving the lives of the two reprehensible hostages was to save the life of the jilted lover. Beneath all the pain and confusion was a beautiful person who might find love further down the line. I didn't want Janus's emotional disregard to bring about her final act. Nneka didn't have to die.

I gave my partner the nod. "I'm coming down, Nina."

"Don't," she said tearfully.

I placed my foot on the first step. "I have no choice."

"*Please don't*, Detective!"

My tones were measured, my voice loud, but not threatening. "You still have a choice."

I was on the third step, wishing I had my vest. "Put down your weapon, then," she said. "

Can't do that."

Her shoulder was visible, then the back of her head.

She was looking in the direction of her hostages, her right hand pointing with the gun. Shauna and Janus's pleas had become a series of squeals, the high pitch of each sounding indistinguishable from the other.

"Then, I guess somebody is gonna get shot," she said, turning suddenly toward me.

The revolver had a brushed-chrome finish and the mouth of it looked as cavernous and soulless as her eyes did in that moment. She dropped to a knee and the weapon barked.

I flattened myself back on the stairs, the dovetail groove of my 1911 lining up with the blade of the front sight. Her .32 popped as my .45 exploded. But it was nothing compared to the unexpected flash and bang of a third weapon going off behind my left ear.

I watched in slow-mo as my partner's faster .40 caliber-round outpaced my slug to catch Nneka George in her right shoulder. Like the thunderous right from a one-two punch combination, my bullet slammed into the woman's chest, propelling her backward.

I was one-third of the way through what I was trained to do before I realized I couldn't feel the weight of my pistol nor my right hand. I wasn't able to complete the sequence of a double-tap delivered center of mass, followed by a single shot to the head. It was just as well. Prior to that day, I'd never hit a woman, and even as I was going into shock from getting shot myself, I was glad I hadn't splattered Nina's brains all over the wall.

Being that I'd laid back on the stairs to get off my only round, my 195 pounds had nowhere to fall. With the ringing in my ears, everything was muffled.

I remember seeing my partner, my fantastic, beautiful partner, as she knelt over me, mouthing the words that I was going to be all right.

Bullshit, I thought. *That was something we were trained to say.*

I smiled at her, wanting to tell her how pretty she looked, all dolled up in her sexy black dress. I watched her try to stop the red liquid gushing from my arm. I didn't feel any pain and, in a daze, wondered what all the fuss was about. She covered the wound with a napkin but the blood kept coming, so, grabbing the tie-back from the velvet drapes, she applied a tourniquet above the gunshot wound, then administered direct pressure to the artery and held up my arm. I rested my head in her lap and looked over at her painted fingernails pressing into my skin and then back at her frantic expression. Don't worry, I wanted to tell her, but my mouth was so dry.

The backstage door burst open and a heavily armed stampede of officers in dark BDU's stormed past us to secure the injured shooter, who lay writhing on the floor.

Janus and Shauna cowered on the sofa and got cuffs just in case.

With the overhead lighting shining behind her like a halo, Jeri appeared to be an angel. She was my angel. I'd begun to drift. Before I lost consciousness, I wanted to tell my partner how I wished we'd met outside of work, so I could take her out on a proper date. Wanted to tell her she'd make one helluva detective one day. I just hoped I'd be around to pin her gold star.

A man and woman hovered over me, making a fuss. Though they wore uniforms, they weren't SWAT officers. Wanted to tell them it wasn't so bad, except for the fact that I was completely numb.

And cold.

I looked to the pretty girl, who was smeared with my blood, yelling at the paramedics, "Be careful, goddammit!"

What's her name again, anyway? Wanted to ask her to hold

me—she was so warm and I was a block of ice.

There was a blinding light and I was on a gurney, levitating into a tighter space that smelled of antiseptic. The pretty girl kept her fingers pressed to the bandage the medics had put on my arm. She was right there and whispered into my ear that she wouldn't leave my side.

The wail of the sirens was muffled as we sped off together into the night.

Studio.

Janus.

Thief of hearts, wrecker of lives.

All your fault, asshole, I yelled to the sneering, sarcastic face, though no words escaped my lips. Gonna kick your ass!

His huge, translucent head floated above me like the false wizard, smiling. That was the last thing that registered before my raft drifted over an imaginary waterfall. I plunged below, silently screaming, enveloped in the frigid rush, yet never hitting bottom.

Chapter 7

Instead of rising slowly back to consciousness, I was thrust forth, coming to with a gasp.

"Go get the doc," someone ordered in an unmistakable growl. It was Perry.

Barbosa bolted out the door, running toward what I could only assume to be the nurse's station, as it appeared I was in a hospital room. She came back with reinforcements, her face a mask of relief.

"Don't move, partner," Sarge said, hovering. Though his face lay in shadow, I could make out that ridiculous mustache.

My tongue was a fat, dehydrated slug. I wanted to make a quip about him restyling his facial hair like Salvador Dali's, but the lug nut probably wouldn't get the joke.

Two ladies in blue scrubs turned on the light and buzzed about the room, one of them checking the numbers on a monitor, the other fussing with the IV in my good arm.

"How do you feel?" the blond nurse inquired.

I tried to speak but only a slurred jumble of nonsense came through.

Jeri, who was inches away, used a tissue to wipe the froth from my parched lips. She angled a straw so I could take a sip of water.

"Tank oo," I gurgled, prompting her to address the river running from my mouth. "What happened?" I asked.

"You took one in the arm. Nicked the artery, but you'll

live. Shit, I've had a lot worse," said Perry.

My chuckle turned into a groan. "Hurts like hell."

The blond injected something into my IV that made my head take flight. "Alright, folks," she said, "let's allow Mr. Brandywine some time to rest. He's got some healing to do."

With that, a warm sensation overtook me and everything faded to black.

* * *

"Gotta pee," I said, coming awake hyper-groggy in the dim room. I sat up and moved to swing my leg over the side rail so I could get to the bathroom.

A small brunette nurse at my bedside put her hand on my chest, pushing me back down. "You're on strict bed-rest at the moment, sir. Go ahead and relieve yourself.

You're already hooked up."

Peeking under the covers, I saw the catheter jammed into my wingding. "*Aw, naw,*" I protested.

"What's the matter? Twig and berries still there, aren't they?" came Perry's gruff chuckle from off to the side.

I turned my head to see he'd taken up residence in the corner. "As long as those didn't get blown off, you're good."

"When'd you get back?" I articulated with much effort.

The nurse handed me a cup of water with a straw. The more I had to drink, the better I could speak, but I had to be careful not to bite my tongue, which was taking up too much space in my mouth.

"I must actually like you, squid. Ended my vacation early when I heard you ran off and got your ass shot up." His leathery skin had been tanned to a golden brown and I could see salt-and-pepper stubble on his chin and either side of his face. In a few more days, he'd have himself a nice ZZ Top starter kit.

"Friggin' jarhead," I said, tears prickling the corner of one eye.

There was a silence. Then, just as I was dropping off, I heard him say "Damn bubblehead." I didn't have the mental dexterity to tell him that was a term of endearment to describe a submariner and not a member of the surface fleet.

Maybe I was dreaming, but I wanted to tease Perry about him being caught in the Tet Offensive, though obviously he'd been just a boy during Vietnam. I started to giggle, imagining Sarge as a scrawny kid, rocking the same furry caterpillar over his top lip.

And so, I drifted…

* * *

Morning light filtered in through partially open blinds.

I gradually became aware of the sound of an infusion pump near the head of the bed, and a dull throbbing in my right arm. Looking down, there was nothing to see, just a mass of bandages elevated on a pillow with only my puffy hand sticking out the end. I made an effort to wiggle my fingers but didn't see anything move. I couldn't tell if it was primarily pain or numbness that I was feeling in my hand—it just felt wrong. For an instant, I started to worry about getting my full function back, but then I pushed down that concern—one thing at a time.

The squeak of footsteps announced a presence in the room, and I recognized the straw-haired nurse from an earlier shift. She carried a clipboard and smiled when she saw me awake.

"Just making my final rounds before my shift ends, Mr. Brandywine. How are you doing this morning? Any pain?"

Nurse Beth then taught me how to use the pain scale to give my pain a number. I had to settle on a "5" because I couldn't account for the loss of feeling. She didn't really want to say, but I got her to speculate on what was going on with my hand. "Let's just hope the numbness is a temporary effect of edema," she said.

"Hey, how's it going?" A smiling face with portly jowls popped in the doorway.

"Eggleston?! What's up, man? I know you didn't come all the way out here to see me."

He laughed. "You got that right, hoss! Just ended my shift down the hall. Picked up a little premium OT guarding your shooter."

"Wait, what—Nneka George is *here?*" I realized that I hadn't given her a thought since the wee hours of Friday morning when she'd put a bullet in me. She could have been dead for all I knew. I briefly considered if it was wrong for me to wish her gone but shook it off.

The officer walked to the window and stood staring out at the view till the nurse left the room.

"So, spill it," I said, knowing that Eggleston wouldn't worry too much about patient confidentiality.

"She's as lucky as she is a looker. Both of you caught rounds. She got a two-piece, but the bullets missed the vitals. Word is she'll be dismissed in a day or two—straight to the lockup on 26th and California."

I let that sink in and then thought of something else I wanted to know. "Hey, do you know if Goodbody's family came up?"

"You mean the corpse from Drexel?"

"Yeah."

"What do I look like, Central Dispatch?" he scoffed, ever the smart-ass.

I looked at him and wondered, *Does he?* I pondered that so long, I fell asleep.

* * *

I was standing over Rayford's body, his face a crimson mess, but he wasn't dead. He sat up on the bed where he'd been murdered, glaring at me through bloodshot eyes. The side that'd received the hardest blows was so dark, I couldn't make out a difference between the reddened white of his eye and the brown of his iris.

He pointed to a large window that was not there in real life. His hand trembled but whatever power he possessed parted the drapes like a magic trick. Behind the glass was a silhouetted couple. Goodbody continued to point and the people were illuminated, resembling a brown-complexioned version of the American Gothic painting.

His father was stern, holding his pitchfork with a scowl, ashamed of a son who should have followed him into a life of religious servitude. For all his devoutness, Pastor Goodbody looked angry at his own chosen path. His wife was more forlorn, her face soggy with tears.

The window darkened and, in its place stood a shadowy figure. Rayford's pointing became accusatory and he fell forward onto the bed, his head baptizing the sheets in a sanguine splat.

I cried out, waking myself up in the sterile reality of my hospital room.

"It's okay, it's okay," a feminine voice reassured. It was dim and I didn't readily see whose hand was caressing my forehead.

"Jeri?" I croaked.

"Yes, Brandy, it's me."

"Thank God," I said, trying to sit up.

She shushed me, and kept me down, continuing to run her hand over my forehead in a calming, maternal gesture. "You're safe."

I told her about the nightmare. The painkillers were causing a weird side effect, adding case details into my dreams and hallucinations.

"Wait! I have an appointment with Rayford's parents," I said with desperation, trying again to get out of my bed.

"It's Sunday, sweetie," she cooed, her hand gently pushing me back into the mattress. I was too weak to put up a fight.

"They came yesterday. Captain Kodjoe had me meet with them."

"What happened?"

"They identified their son's remains. It was so sad. Mrs. Goodbody cried uncontrollably. Her husband will probably do his breaking down in private. I could tell that seeing his boy laid out on that cold slab messed him up something terrible."

"Yeah. Parents burying their children falls out of the natural order of things."

With her assistance, I drank some water. I thought of the dark figure in my dream, at which Goodbody was pointing. I vocalized what he was trying to tell me: "We've got to nab the killer."

Barbosa nodded, and pushed the straw back into my face.

* * *

Much later, I came to again. "Well, hello stranger." Jeri said as I surfaced. The room was dark and quiet. "Need anything?"

"Water, please," I said, more bullfrog than Barry White.

She bent and placed the straw to my lips. I took a few sips and thanked her.

"No problem. Nurse says you need to be constantly hydrating."

"Not just for the water but for everything. I appreciate you, Jeri."

"You're welcome," she replied, leaning against the wall with an unblinking stare.

I considered that she was the one who'd taken care of me when I was shot. I still remembered lying in her lap, getting my blood all over her. Though we'd only known each other a short time, it seemed a lot longer—not long enough to start picking out engagement rings or anything of the sort, but enough to forge a bond.

"How long I been in here?"

She held up three fingers, indicating the number of days. "It's Sunday evening. Sergeant Perry and Captain Kodjoe came through earlier. Also, your sister stopped by. Said she'll come back another time."

"Tammy was here?" My face must've showed my surprise.

"The feminine version of you is pretty darn cute," Barbosa said with a chuckle.

What's that supposed to mean? I wondered.

Jeri brought a balloon arrangement up close so I could see it and showed me a get-well card with my sister's signature and phone number.

We had some bridges that needed rebuilding, me and Tammy. Damn shame it took a shooting for the first plank to be laid, but good on her for reaching out. The next move was mine to make. I felt grateful for getting the chance.

Rayford Goodbody wouldn't have a chance to rebuild any bridges.

"Jeri?"

"Hmm?"

"Did his family come? Rayford Goodbody, I mean." I vaguely remembered they were planning to come up from St. Louis to claim the body.

"Yeah, I told you that already," she said, sounding a little suspicious.

Man, they're going to think I'm out of it, or brain damaged.

"Oh, yeah. I thought I'd dreamed that," I said, recalling the nightmare I'd endured with a black gothic couple and their bludgeoned son sitting up in the bed. I tried to force that image out of my head.

The weekend had come and gone with me having little sense of the passage of time.

Sitting up with some effort, I took another pull from the straw. I felt a bit discombobulated. Maybe *too much* sleep. I needed to get control of myself, change the subject.

"How come you're not at home with your man? Pretty lady like you shouldn't be hanging around here with the likes of me." I put my palm a couple inches from my face, exhaled, and cringed. "*Whew!* My breath *stinks!*"

"Bad enough to put you back under," she cackled,

handing me the water. The pitcher was rose-colored plastic and beaded with droplets of condensation. "Can you hold this on your own? I need to straighten my back."

"You gonna answer my question?" In my goofy state, I just wanted to know.

"Well, Mr. Nosy, I don't have a boyfriend, and I don't really want one at the moment. Got some things I need to work on before putting my issues on someone else. Besides, between working my shift and doing overtime to assist on this case, my schedule is *crazy!*"

I laughed out loud. "You're preaching to the choir!"

But she continued in earnest. "Besides, most dudes are petrified at the thought of commitment, cop or not."

"Nah, those are just the knuckleheads you're used to dealing with. I can definitely understand where you're coming from. Don't mean to be getting all into your personal business and stuff, though."

She rubbed my head and winked playfully. "Yeah, you do!"

Jeri sauntered to the other side of the room and began organizing pillows and folding a blanket. She was wearing a thick turtleneck sweater that fell past her hips and sat atop her healthy backside. Though turned away, her words were for me to hear: "I may not date men I work with but, for the record, I can stand the foul stench of your rancid-ass mouth."

I smiled in embarrassment when I caught her comment.

Having not been acquainted with a toothbrush for a few days, my breath was bad enough to make an onion cry.

I could only come back with, "Thought you were trying to stop cursing." "Man, *hush!*"

* * *

My mouth was dry when I awoke. I turned my head slightly to see my favorite troglodyte engrossed in a crossword puzzle, while the prettier of the two tapped at her phone.

"Hey," I croaked. "What time is it?"

My partners sprung to life, Perry dropping his book and Barbosa putting her phone aside. "Good morning, handsome," she said.

"Dunno 'bout all *that*," the caveman grunted.

I chuckled at his feigned jealousy and my lips were so dry, they cracked. When my laughter subsided, I asked for something to drink. Jeri refilled and brought me the pitcher. The cold water felt good, though it stung where my lip had split. "Thanks."

She wrinkled her nose, fanning her hand. She handed me a piece of gum.

"What's that," I asked, a bit groggy.

"She's saying it smells as if you've been snacking on road kill taint!"

They playfully elbowed each other, exchanging snickers at my expense.

"My bad," I said, taking another pull. "Sorry I couldn't have gotten shot with a sprig of peppermint under my tongue."

"Ah, we're just effin' with ya, kid," Sarge said. "Happy to see you up."

"Thanks for hanging around. Seriously."

"No biggie," Jeri said. "Let me go get the nurse."

When she exited the room, I looked at Perry with a bit of desperation. "I need to take a piss, brother!"

"Sorry, dude," he said, pointing at my crotch.

I peeked beneath the sheet and saw the tube still jammed into my Johnson. The cheerful nurse entered and quickly realized the source of my lament. "Morning, Detective. We can remove your catheter soon. But first I need to get a urine sample and send it to the lab."

Jeri smiled and put her hand on my shoulder. I was humiliated to have this conversation in front of her. Without a word, her touch let me know I didn't need to feel so bad about it.

"Thanks," I whispered.

A different nurse came in, this one carrying the clipboard. "How's that arm feeling?"

"Stiff. Sore. Like the rest of me, I guess."

"We'll get you up and moving in a little bit," she said. "How about your hand?"

"Numb. Swollen. Feels like I'm being stuck with a bunch of pinpricks when I flex my fingers," and added, because I knew she'd ask, "The pain level's a 6."

She made a note.

"That's his shooting hand," Perry said, sounding more than a bit concerned. "Will he regain the use of it?"

"Dr. Singh will come by today when she makes her rounds," said the RN. "Do you want something for pain before we get you up for the first time?"

"Heck no! I need to get my head cleared up so I can get back to work," I said, sounding like a boy scout, and sending Perry into a giggling fit. He stuck out his chest and gave me a mock salute, which I didn't find particularly amusing.

"Well, it's up to you. Let us know," the nurse said, making another note on the clipboard.

Though Perry offered to stay and hold my hand, my nurse had everybody step out while she removed the catheter as promised. Fluffing my pillows with a smile, she made sure I had my call light before returning to her rounds. She seemed to love what she did for a living—just like I loved nabbing criminals.

* * *

I wanted to know more about Nina's injuries. I found out that Jeri's bullet had hit her in front of the right shoulder, dropping her lung, and exited under the arm. She'd been lucky; Barbosa swore she'd been aiming for the woman's head.

Bilateral chest tubes inserted at the scene were followed by surgery to remove the foreign body—my bullet—which had lodged in Nina's left breast. She was lucky all right.

I'd been targeting central mass, but laying on my back, my aim was off. As a consequence, she had become one of a handful of gunshot wound survivors who can rightfully say they owe their life to a boob job.

Soon, she'd be transferred from the hospital to the county lockup.

It was the first time Jeri had ever fired her weapon on the job, and, besides saving my life, the action had earned her a few days as a house mouse till they could sort it all out.

"What about Janus?"

"The drama worked to his benefit, giving him some welcome attention in the news outlets," Barbosa said. She wore her uniform; she had been staffing the intake desk at the precinct. "In fact, the incident has fans bum-rushing Duality in droves."

"So, that fool gets to walk around breathing fresh air while I'm left to rehabilitate?"

"Relax, partner," Perry interjected. "He ain't the one who pulled the trigger on you. *She's* laid up in a room down the hall."

I gave the sergeant a frown. He'd only read the file and obviously didn't realize my theory of the DJ's influence in the whole mess. I'd seen Perry go back and forth with the captain over the difference between what was in the police report and what couldn't be conveyed on paper. "I'm gonna *kill* his ass," I growled.

"Whoa, champ! Slow your roll. You've got to recuperate before you start yoking folks."

"*But...*"

"But my ass," Perry snarled. "Get that arm up to snuff, get cleared for full duty, and we'll take him down together. If what I'm hearing is correct, whenever the dude hits the road, he always returns to Chicago for the adulation of his primary fan base. He ain't goin' nowhere."

"Yeah," Barbosa added. "He's so in love with the spotlight, he'll always be easy to find. Like Sarge says, his take-down can be a concerted effort. No rush."

I was pissed. I was itching to get back into it, but how much good would I be with a useless arm? It was going to be a minute before I could put Janus into my cross hairs, both figuratively and literally.

"Well," Perry said, taking a look at his wristwatch, "I've got to hit the precinct. Vacation's over and we obviously have some work to do."

"I've got some things I have to do, too," Jeri added. "You gonna be okay?"

"I'll be fine," I said flatly.

"How about I leave my puzzle book behind for you?"

My gaze was humorless, and the irritation was evident in my voice. "I'm not ambidextrous, Sarge. Can't write with my left."

He harrumphed and tossed the book onto my lap, anyway. "The word 'can't' never got anything done. Work on it with your other hand and stop feeling sorry for yourself. Be happy your ass is still alive!"

Barbosa nodded in agreement and a minute later, they were both gone.

Chapter 8

Tuesday morning brought visits from all my doctors, and conflicting emotions. A dye test was scheduled to check the plumbing in the arm and an electrical test of some sort would check the nerves. Sure, I was lucky to be alive. Lucky I wasn't hit in the head or the chest. The bullet had missed all my bones and major vessels, but it had nicked a branch of the brachial artery close to a major nerve. I'd lost a lot of blood and went into shock. I would have bled out if it hadn't been for Barbosa.

My main emotion should have been relief, but I couldn't stop feeling sorry for myself. I worried that I would need further reconstructive surgeries down the road and certainly weeks, if not months, of rehab. All that and there was no guarantee that I would ever regain full use of my hand.

The injured arm was wrapped up and elevated on pillows across my lap. The nurses frequently came and checked it. Squeezing the thumb and fingers, poking with the head and tip of a safety pin. "Sharp or dull? Sharp or dull?" they would ask.

I could feel the pinky and I could move it—the other fingers, not so much.

* * *

Nobody visited for a day or two. I was left alone with my anger and self pity. Between multiple trips to the restroom—which I was doing on my own now, thank you very much—and watching hours of TV, I had nothing but time to think. And to heal.

Though it wouldn't take the place of a face-to-face apology, I used my left hand to text my partners and admitted I'd acted an ass. Barbosa responded. Perry didn't.

The next day, Dr. Singh came by to check on me. "So, you finally had some decent diuresis," she said, perusing the chart that hung at the foot of the bed.

I laughed nervously. "Dye-your-*what*?"

She smiled, not as stiff and stodgy as I had thought. "Diuresis is when the body gets rid of a lot of fluid through the kidneys. Your I & O tells the story. I've been expecting this."

"My I & O? Wait, let me guess: in-and-out?" Now it made sense why the nurses made such a big deal about measuring everything.

"Bingo," said the doc. "When the edema in your tissues clears, it should take the pressure off the nerves and improve your symptoms. I've gotten preliminary results from yesterday's vascular and neurological testing, and I think we may be seeing some positive signs here soon. Let's give it another day."

My arm was held in a sling to minimize the chance of re-injury. Each time I thought of Janus—not Nina—I tried balling up my fist. My pinky obeyed outright, while my thumb showed a bit of progress, wiggling; still only twitching from the other three fingers.

When I did think of Nneka, I saw her as a pawn doing the bidding of her lover. It was hard to prove but I knew it to be true.

I wiggled my fingers with a bit of effort.

The gelatin dessert I hadn't finished at dinner wasn't so bad at room temperature, though I wasn't a fan of the artificial orange taste.

Fans.

Janus.

More wiggling.

There was a time when television actually went off at night. Obviously an antiquated notion, with reruns, reality shows, and infomercials left to fill the void. The concept of a talking horse was mildly amusing, though watching has-been stars peddling reformatted music collections made me grit my teeth.

Music.

Janus.

Slight movement.

I needed a girlfriend. Barbosa was definitely pretty and interesting enough, though us working together made it a bad idea. I wasn't her supervisor but the department would still frown on a relationship between us. Besides, she said she wanted to focus on her career.

Men and women in relationships.

Janus, Nina, and the bloody corpse between them.

My fingers jerked with a flash of anger. I clenched with all my might, forming a very weak fist. Definitely not ready to contend for the heavyweight championship but it was enough to show me that the wiring between my brain and my hand was sending signals with more clarity.

I continued, carefully flexing and attempting to extend my digits. The more my fingers tingled, the more my mood rose.

Then I got a text from Barbosa that really lifted my spirits. Seems she forgave me for my grumpiness and would come to the hospital that evening—and did I need anything?

I was really glad to get her offer. I was bored to the point of tears. I'd watched almost every commercial and stupid show on the idiot box before I considered strangling myself with my tubing. I'd gotten so desperate, I'd even picked up Perry's puzzle book and attempted a few of the crosswords and word searches; already, working the pencil with my left hand had improved from nearly impossible to just very hard.

"Please try to get me a laptop from the precinct," I texted.

"No," she replied, to which I responded that I was going stir crazy, and "pretty please".

Her response was simple. "Love it when you beg," to which she added a winking emoji.

* * *

When she arrived, she gave me a peck on the forehead and set a greasy bag from a mom-and-pop place on my over-bed table.

"Nurse Beth told me you'll be freed tomorrow."

"Really? Man, it's amazing how they'll tell you stuff and I'm the last to find out."

"Quit yer bellyachin' and dig in."

"First, let me show you. Watch my hand…" I extended my full hand, all my fingers straight, then flexed them into a loose fist. "Huh, look at that," I said happily.

"Wow, that's great. How's the feeling? Is the numbness gone too?"

"Not quite, but it's heading in the right direction."

With some difficulty, I managed to open the bag with my left hand and I was rewarded with a delightful aroma. "How much do I owe you?"

She waved her hand. "Forget about it."

The taco salad was an awesome departure from the bland hospital cuisine. I thanked her and chomped away greedily. "Want some?"

"You're welcome and I'm good."

"I'm still disappointed that you couldn't arrange a laptop for me to use. Could be getting some work done."

She sucked her teeth and rolled her eyes. "You wouldn't know how to use it. I'd have to spend a week just teaching you the basics. Make you a deal: you stop talking about anything having to do with the job for a while and I'll hook you up."

I paused with a queso-covered tortilla halfway to my

lips. "Hook me up how?"

"After I pick you up tomorrow, I'll make you dinner at your place."

"You trying to finish the job Nina started," I asked cynically.

Jeri's smile was both wide and wicked. "Maybe."

"Can you even cook?"

"Already told you before, I can *burn* man."

"Yeah," I said, shoveling more food into my pie hole. "Burn up a bowl of corn flakes!"

"You'll find out tomorrow night. We'll break out your home desktop and get some work done then."

"What's on the menu?"

She shushed me and said with a wink, "Quiet. Enjoy your meal. It might be your last, you know."

* * *

I think "Oh Happy Day" was playing while the attendant rolled me out the front doors of the hospital. Evicted via wheelchair, I was all smiles. Still felt like crap with my arm in a sling and my hand barely working, but I was alive and free.

The doc had given me my walking papers with several prescription medications and a set of rules mostly about what not to do, like not to get the bandages wet, and not to drive or drink or do anything fun. Appointments for physical therapy, dressing changes, and doctor visits stretched into the next month.

Tammy never made it back before I was discharged, but we did have a short phone conversation. That was more than my sister and I had shared for a long time. She promised to stop by my place during my convalescence. Baby steps.

It was early afternoon and Jeri had rushed over following shift change, still in uniform.

"Getting the police escort, I see," the attendant joked.

"Yeah, she's going to keep me in line."

Barbosa grinned. "One can always hope."

It took some maneuvering, but I squeezed into her Toyota. It was a tighter fit than my truck and I leaned toward the middle, so as not to bump my arm.

"Don't get any smart ideas," my driver told me. Her backseat was filled with all the get-well-soon balloons and flower arrangements. She fussed with me about not letting my seat back too much, so as not to crush one of the bouquets.

Once I was settled, Jeri pecked numbers into her phone and passed it to me.

"Hello," I said.

"Detective Brandywine," Kodjoe boomed, asked how I was doing, and proceeded to inform me that Nneka George had been transferred to Cook County Jail.

"That's good news, sir."

"It is. But she's refusing to talk to Sergeant Perry outright."

"He probably scares her."

He chuckled. "I seriously doubt that. Anyway, my guess is she might be willing to talk to someone with whom she's already built a rapport."

Nina and I had a unique relationship, that's for sure, having shot each other. I felt a bit sick to my stomach. Nah, I don't want to see my shooter, I thought.

"Officer Barbosa also tells me you're eager to get back to work," continued Kodjoe.

"I am. But I won't be fit for full duty for some time," I lamented.

"You don't need to be medically cleared just to ask questions. I could set it up."

"Need to rest, Cap. Doctor's orders."

"After you're feeling up to it, then. She's not going anywhere anytime soon."

"That works, sir. I'll be in touch."

The call disconnected as Jeri slid her car behind my SUV, which was parked in front of my 3rd floor walk-up.

I looked over to her and wanted to thank her for getting my car moved.

She looked up at me and said, "I'm going to get you upstairs and head out to pick up some stuff for dinner."

"I'm gonna die," I said with a playful, choking sound.

"Well, I guarantee you'll die happy, then."

She got me positioned on my couch and whipped up a simple lunch of tomato soup—with a dollop of sour cream and a sprig of basil—and a grilled cheese sandwich with slices of bacon. It was a lot fancier than what I would've thrown together, left to my own devices. The thought of a handful of dry breakfast cereal with an unheated hot dog chaser came to mind.

Jeri pecked me on the cheek—an affectionate act—though I wish she had aimed a couple of inches to the left where my lips waited in vain. With a wave, she rushed out the door to pick up groceries.

Though I hadn't known her long, and she'd never come by before, my house suddenly felt empty without Jeri Barbosa's presence. I was quietly grateful not only for her kindness but also for the fact that I'd straightened up the place before going to the club that night.

She was back an hour later. I'd dozed off right where she'd left me, an empty bowl and a bit of sandwich crust remaining on the tray table in front of me. I awoke groggy, and somewhat disconcerted about the fact that someone was walking around in my house. I wasn't used to having company.

"Hey, sleepyhead."

I yawned, stretched and made sure there was no drool in the corners of my mouth. "Hey, Jeri. Need help?"

She'd returned with several grocery bags and something she'd retrieved from my truck. "I picked up stuff for dinner, a few items to restock your fridge, and I grabbed your murse."

"It's a messenger bag."

"Yeah," she replied with a snarky tone. "Anyway, here ya

go."

After setting down the groceries in the kitchen, she swapped out my lunch dishes and flatware for the oversized leather pouch. I was glad to be reunited with my stuff, such as it was. Once I was able to gather my wits about me, I would get some work done. "Thanks," I said, rubbing my forehead, while she reached down and turned my personal desktop computer on so it could boot.

"Those pain meds and muscle relaxers are good stuff," she said, placing several containers on the counter. "You needed that nap, I'm sure."

"I think you're right."

She brought a glass of water over to the coffee table. "Hydration is your friend, and it's probably time to take more medicine. Which shall I open for you?"

Dang, she was right. I couldn't even open a pill bottle by myself. I read the labels and told her I needed a pain pill and the antibiotic. My mind was emerging from its fog and, like my computer, I was coming back on line. "Dammit," I said, looking at the monitor screen.

She stopped with what she was doing, a look of concern on her face. "What's wrong?"

"No biggie, first time it's been turned on for awhile," I said, pointing at the screen. "Updates."

"Gotcha. Well, I'm going to make something you can eat for the next few days."

"And what's that?"

"My deep-dish lasagna."

The spirit of Pavlov's dog suddenly possessed me and I made a disgusting slurping sound to try to stifle the drivel.

She looked at me and nodded as if I'd just given her a huge compliment. "If the idea of it has you drooling, just wait until you actually smell and taste it."

"I'm gonna hold you to that."

Jeri gave me a wink and concentrated on arranging her ingredients. She fished under the cabinet until she found my biggest pot, filled it with water, and put it on to boil.

She added a lot of salt to the water, which was something I didn't know to do.

"Makes the water boil sooner, and makes the noodles tasty," she said.

By the time she was dropping the pasta into the boiling water, my mind had begun to wander to the targets of our investigation. The ex-girlfriend, who was likely the killer, was locked up, while her boyfriend, whom I was sure was a conspirator, was back on tour. I fished in my bag, in search of a pad of paper to jot down notes on Nneka and Janus, as well as to ponder the coincidence of his new lover, Shauna.

My hand encountered something hard and unfamiliar, which had nestled itself into a corner of the bag. "*Oh no*," I moaned with a sinking feeling.

Over the clang of cooking and her humming a tune, Jeri looked up from what she was doing. How she heard me mumble above all that noise was beyond me. "What happened?"

I held up the hard drive, which was still in a sealed bag with evidence tape. "I grabbed this from the scene but forgot to turn it in."

"Is that a bad thing?"

"It's not the worst thing that could happen."

"Has the chain of custody been interrupted," she asked, already thinking like an investigator, which I liked.

"No. It's been in my bag in my truck since I took it from the scene. It's just that the IT guys could've been making progress with it."

"Yeah, that's if there's progress to be made. I wouldn't beat myself up too much about it. I mean, you got shot and were laid up in the hospital for the past few days."

She had a valid point.

"Heck," she said, stirring the sauce in one pot while making sure the pasta didn't stick in the other, "it gives you the chance to take a look at it today."

I nodded in agreement, though she couldn't see me with

her back turned.

"*Us*," I corrected. I'd said it softly yet meant it wholeheartedly.

She'd begun slicing mushrooms and was no doubt eyeballing the onions when she paused, and glanced over her shoulder. From that angle, it was hard to make out, but I was sure I saw the corner of her mouth turn up. She said nothing, gave a quick nod, and went back to work on the vegetables.

Chapter 9

She did not lie. The lasagna was so good, I requested seconds and had to be told to eat my salad. It was a good salad too, but damn it—*that lasagna!*

I was posted up on the sofa, swollen as a tick, both relishing and regretting that I'd engorged myself. Had she wanted a good laugh, she could've easily pushed me over with her pinky, then guffaw as I lay on the floor like a tortoise on its back.

"Oh. My. Goodness," I said, trying to hold back a belch.

Barbosa just smiled. "You know, in some countries, the biggest compliment to the chef is—"

She hadn't even finished her sentence before I croaked like a toad. I laughed it off, embarrassed. "Is it a compliment in Cape Verde?"

She hunched her shoulders. "I don't know. Never been. But I'll take it as a sign of respect for my culinary skills in the Windy City. Now, I made dessert, if…"

I waved my hand, shaking my head vehemently. "No, no—NO! Where the hell am I gonna *put* it?!" I asked, looking at my distended belly.

We both laughed.

"Well, why don't I put the dishes in the sink and we take a look at what's on that hard drive?"

"Yes, let's."

More than recognizing her as a superb cook, I respected Barbosa as an equal. Janus didn't respect anyone as his equal, from what I could tell.

My computer had long before finished its reboot. Initially irritated, I was now glad that my desktop had thoroughly done its thing. One of the updates was for the anti-virus software and I wanted to scan the portable drive to ensure I wasn't introducing anything harmful into my system. It beeped and whirred when I plugged it in, reminding me of an old school song my dad used to play. Without conscious thought, I began to whistle the melody.

Jeri gave a sneaky laugh, rocking her head to the imagined beat. She popped her fingers and moved her shoulders. "I know this song! Just can't put my finger on the name of it... Aw, man, this was my *jam*, too!"

I emulated the synthesized effects and shuffling sound leading up to the first verse. She grabbed the sides of her head, the name of the once popular song on the tip of her tongue, driving her crazy.

The whirring stopped and so did my partial rendition of the song. "Here we go."

The hard drive contained three folders: Echo, Eros, and Tyche. "Sounds Greek," Barbosa thought aloud, matching what was going through my mind. "Of course, Eros I know, and Echo is obvious...but what the heck does Tyche mean?"

"Well, since Janus is into mythological figures, my guess would be..."

"Got it," she announced, having looked it up on her phone. "Tyche is the goddess of luck and fortune."

"Well, I hope Lady Luck is on our side this evening."

Barbosa began to hum the Sinatra classic that served as the gambler's anthem.

I rolled my cursor, deciding to access the folders in alphabetical order. However, luck wasn't a lady that night when I double-clicked Echo. "Shit," I exclaimed.

"Password protected," she said, stating the obvious.

"Ya think?"

"I was hoping you'd start with the middle one, anyway."

"Eros?"

She grinned, running the tip of her tongue over her top lip. "My favorite."

"We need to talk," I said, shaking my head.

"Not if we're going to remain coworkers," she replied, giving a playful roll of her hips.

Flirting was fun, but I let it go, wanting to keep things above board between us.

Dozens of dated video files popped up, all easily accessible. At first, I perused the dates to find that there were no feeds since early February. They were full of videos of the wild parties thrown in the room where Goodbody was killed on the 21st. I randomly selected the feeds, just in case any of the dates had been changed. I played them at 64 times the regular rate, looking on as people copulated like jackrabbits wound up on crack. Little seemed off limits but they were apparently all consensual adults.

Barbosa held her peace, though her unblinking stare and smirk was rather telling. However, she didn't ask me to forward any of the files for her viewing pleasure. Maybe it was seeing Rayford Goodbody alive and participating in some of the orgies that jacked her up. I didn't necessarily enjoy those parts, myself.

"Don't forget," she said, "there could be some hidden files."

"You're right." I considered having Sherman give the hard drive a look but decided against it. It was one thing to have him trace a line; it was another thing altogether to cut out the IT folks and disregard the privacy of the party participants. "For now, let's move on to what we can see."

Tyche opened without issue. This folder also contained videos, most of which were quite short. I watched the first few. The camera feed was motion-activated, with there being files that showed leaves blowing through a fence and across a paved area. "That's the church parking lot," I said, pointing at the screen. "This is from above the gangway door."

Most recordings were snippets of an alley cat or some sort of rodent running within range of the motion sensor, causing it to activate. Unlike with the Eros files, this camera was still operational on February 21st.

"Bingo."

When the silhouette fell into frame, I recalled what the deacon had told me about seeing someone jump the fence on the night of the murder. With the time stamp, this was likely who he saw. The dark clothing and large coat were not enough to hide the suspect's petite feminine form.

Her coat was cinched at the waist, giving the figure an hourglass shape. I would be really surprised if this turned out to be a man.

"Looks like you were right," I admitted.

"Told you," she replied proudly.

After a couple of attempts, the unsub's gloved hands grasped the top of the fence, and twisting her body, she slid down into the gangway.

The intruder disappeared from the camera view for a moment, and then reappeared up close to the red door.

"Is that Nneka?" my partner growled, voice buzzing like a bothered beehive.

"Not sure. With everything so fuzzy and dark, I can't pick up on any distinctive facial features. It's hard to get an idea of her skin tone and hair." In the moment before she used the nearby ledge to boost herself in search of something in the rafters, I could clearly make out the two-faced emblem on her hat, but her face was still cloaked in shadow.

"Look, it's the hat we found in the pantry."

"Hmmn, Forensics recovered a lot of hair from inside that hat, and gave me a preliminary report that matches your shooter, but they cautioned me that it's not a final result," advised Jeri.

It didn't look good for Nina being innocent.

"The hell is she doing?" my partner asked, as the perp

felt around near the camera with gloved hands.

I recalled the abandoned house that sat near the alley in my childhood neighborhood. Much like the place in the video, there was a gangway with a door that sat halfway between the front and back yard areas of the structure. My mother warned Tammy and me not to venture through gangways as, at the least, they contained standing water and, at the most, things little boys and girls would not want to find.

Being a hardheaded child, I was innately curious. From the time Mama put them off limits, I became fascinated with what I would discover in those dimly lit thoroughfares.

Condemned houses on our block could stand for years before the city's wrecking ball got around to reducing them to vacant lots. The city's attentions were on its more affluent residents and their neighborhoods, leaving impoverished communities like Washington Park and Englewood as untended as ghost towns. Gangway doors led to basements and utility rooms, making them the preferred hangouts for the homeless to seek shelter and engage in whatever proclivities they saw fit.

Though it had loomed there with the ringing of Mama's warning in my ears, my curiosity got the better of me one sticky summer afternoon. School was out and with my sister and I being old enough, our mother had to trust we wouldn't get into anything while she was at work all day.

After engaging in a rather sweaty game of freeze tag that lasted all morning, Buck and Terrell, who were brothers, were called into their house for lunch. That left me alone long enough to explore the recesses of a musty old gangway. I'd climbed up on a small, cobwebbed ledge, and ran my fingers along the rafters above the doorway. I remember finding what I was looking for.

"She's fishing for a key," I said flatly, resurfacing into a present in which my partner and I were trying to get a bead on the killer. I didn't bother telling Jeri about the nasty magazines with their pages stuck together nor the hypodermic needles I'd found that day so long ago.

However, before the memory released me, I recalled a stirring at the shadowy rear of the space. The basement windows were so caked with mud and dust, only muted rays of sunlight filtered through the murk. There was the soft splash of footsteps circumventing shallow water.

"Who dat," a hoarse voice whispered, the speaker lumbering slowly toward me. I could barely make out the form, only seeing the vague shape of his head and broad shoulders as he peered at me. I was frozen in place, unable to see into the darkness. But with the alley brightly bathed in August sunlight, he was able to see me just fine. His gait was menacing and, having fantasized the touch of flesh through a heroin-induced haze, the 11-year-old child before him would probably do…

Besides the shabby silhouette, I could only see the illumination from behind me glint off his teeth. His smile was not friendly, half-twisted in a predatory snarl. The stranger reached out a leprous hand from the inky black depths and, in a sand-papery croak, said, "C'mere, boy!"

"She obviously doesn't know the camera is there," Jeri said to no one in particular.

I snapped briefly out of my reverie, having been a scrawny, frightened kid who suddenly realized the time to play freeze tag had ended and this was no game. I would never tell Barbosa of my experience or how I had bounded out of there like a gazelle, scared out of my wits. His filthy fingers snatched at my shirt, ripping the fabric as I ran as fast as my skinny legs could take me…

"Too bad it doesn't show her face," she added.

"We'll have to review the earlier footage at high magnification. Maybe we'll find a better view when she's further away," I said.

We watched it again. The image was herky-jerky, as the security camera captured every few seconds in order to save space on the drive.

Then onto the next feed, we saw, apparently the same person going back out the door, climbing back over the fence, her long dark coat hiking up on her back briefly as she went over. We'd have a study of that scene in zoom when we had a chance. My computer might not be able to do it, but the techs would have a good chance of getting something if it was there.

Even with the poor quality, I noticed her running away from the house with her head still covered. "See that?"

"What?"

I backed up the footage and replayed it in slow-mo.

I pointed at the skullcap, which was pulled down tight.

How is it that she still has the hat on when she leaves?" wondered Jeri. "Maybe the one we found isn't related to the murder, it's a..."

"Red herring?" I suggested, "Or what if it's a plant..." I hypothesized, rubbing my chin with my only good hand, "to implicate someone..."

I tried the folder labeled "Echo" again, tried a few universal passwords I know, like "password", "123start", and "OpenSesame". None of them worked, of course.

After saving the relevant files to my computer, I disconnected the drive and put it into a fresh plastic bag, taping it closed. I dug through the paperwork in my bag before finding an evidence custody document and began filling it out all goofy with my left hand. "I want you to take this to headquarters and hand it off to the IT folks."

Jeri paused before signing. "Since we're talking about things we want, how about you forward some of that video footage to my personal email?"

I shot her a cynical glance.

"Hey, the only stupid question is the one left unasked," she commented before taking the object and shrugging. "Can't blame me for trying."

"You need counseling," I muttered.

Her eyes lingered on me for a moment. "Brother, you don't know the half." She got up to leave and shrugged on her parka. "Early day tomorrow."

"Thanks again for everything." I followed her to the door.

"I'll be around to check on you tomorrow but call me if there's anything you need."

I bowed gratefully and watched her descend the staircase. She stopped on the first landing to wave.

"So, the song you were whistling earlier..." I called out to her. "It was 'Computer Love' by Zapp."

She smiled and snapped her fingers in recognition. "Yep, that was it!" And she was gone.

* * *

Sitting around watching TV that night, I saw a piece on the 10 o'clock local news about Janus. The announcer said that the scandal of a murder, a shootout, and a jailed club manager had propelled his latest project up the dance charts like a skyrocket. Radio deejays kept an up-tempo track entitled "Gone" in constant rotation. They played the "song", which sounded like the producer firing off the title in a meaningless staccato over a catchy, bass-laden, triple-time beat. He'd apparently slapped the single together in supposed memory of Goodbody and it was becoming a sleeper hit. The piece ended with local fans all aflutter that he was setting up another huge bash at Duality for when he returned from shows in Pittsburgh, Philly, and New York.

Ever the fucking showman.

Having to shoot Nina did not make me feel good at all. It went against my personal code to hit a woman, let alone discharge a weapon at one. The fact that she'd rightfully earned the bullets that collapsed her lung and knocked her flat meant little. I didn't have all the details about the breast damage but she owned that, no mistake.

One time, when we'd first partnered up, Perry hit me with a barrage of questions to see what kind of cop I was. He'd asked if I'd ever shot anyone before, to which I was honest. "Did he die?"

"Yeah," I said without pride. I'd put down several folks while on military missions.

"That's a good thing," he said grimly.

I frowned. "Why the hell do you say that?"

"Because you don't shoot a person when a simple hello would suffice. If you find you need to fire your piece, you do it to knock the life out of 'em. If they don't die, you end up tied to them until one of you gets bold enough to take the next, inevitable step. It's better if you don't have that type of bond. Makes for weird bedfellows."

I replayed what Kodjoe had said about Nina refusing to talk to Perry or anyone else. Maybe she was just waiting for the right person.

The captain picked up on the third ring. "Detective Brandywine. Everything alright?"

"Yes, sir." I informed him about the video footage and the hard drive. "Barbosa is bringing it in tomorrow."

"Good stuff. Techs may be able to enhance it and get us an ID. I've got a new preliminary report here from Forensics, that you might not have seen yet. They've verified that the largest pile of vomit was from the murder victim—they're still analyzing the contents, and cross referencing with the food you recovered from the trash, but get this—"

I waited, trying not to think of all that vomit.

"They've ruled out Goodbody as source for the second puddle. Could be the murderer regurgitated," suggested Kodjoe.

"Yes, quite possible. It was a small spot, but it wasn't all the way dried, so it's unlikely from someone days before. I guess I have to be sure it wasn't anyone who came after the murder—the housekeeper or any of the first responders..."

"They haven't ruled out Miss George, either way," he added.

"Great. Hey Captain, is it too late for you to set things up for me to interrogate her?"

"Figured you'd ask. I'll send a car for you first thing in the morning, if that's alright. Will you be ready?"

I quoted a line I was taught to recite as a young Navy Master-at-Arms: "Always ready."

Chapter 10

Gone was the sophisticated lady who had come down to the precinct the week before. There was no bling, no accentuated lashes, and instead of the stylish outfit, her sole fashion statement was a plain orange jumpsuit.

Though even with the light drained from her face, beauty remained. A white band wrapped around the prisoner's small waist and held her left arm across her body to keep the shoulder immobilized while her wounds healed. She'd have plenty of time to recover behind bars.

In keeping with standard procedure, the inmate was secured to the table. Though, even with my own reduced physical capacity, I seriously doubted—in the shape she was in—that she'd be able to finish the job she'd started at Club Duality. With a nod, the deputy shut the door, and posted up outside.

I contemplated the woman, who looked as if she'd been bum-rushed by a rabid gang of alley cats. Though her movements were stiff and limited at best, something seethed from behind her squint.

"I'd like for us to discuss some things. But first, I need to Mirandize you."

"You can read me my rights all day long. I don't need my lawyer here because I don't have anything to tell you.

I just hope you didn't come all the way down here for an apology," she said through clenched teeth, her voice full of venom.

"Not here for that," I replied, shifting in the hardback chair, attempting to find comfort around my own injury.

Using my left hand—the one she hadn't shot—I nudged a sheet of paper toward her, while I recited her rights. "Put your initials there and there, and sign at the bottom."

"So, you came to gloat, then," she said, working the pen. "I admit I shot you, facts don't lie. But you distracted me— next time, mind your own damn business."

I shook my head. She was still pretty without the glamor and glitz, but there was something crooked in her soul.

"No," I said before I could stop myself. "You're the one who might want to take pride in your handiwork. Landed me in the hospital for a stint..." I could have gone on, but doubted it would garner her sympathy.

Her eyes were cold and unblinking. "Then you're here to compare injuries and trade war stories?"

I was glad I'd shot her, which was an uneasy feeling for me to admit to myself, but she would have killed me.

According to departmental guidelines, Barbosa and I were in the clear for our actions. Stripped down with her weave removed and one breast deflated, the perp didn't look too dangerous, but she could very well be a cold-hearted killer. I just needed to get her to admit it and implicate her boyfriend. If the hatred causing the frost in her irises was real, she'd want to serve Janus up on a platter. I pictured the DJ hogtied with an apple in his smug mouth and I chuckled.

"Something funny?" she asked.

I nodded and stifled my smirk. "I'd be lying if I told you there wasn't anything amusing about this moment, though you might not see the humor in it."

"And what's so damn hilarious?"

I leveled my eyes at hers. She'd had her shot and, even with that Medusa's stare, she wasn't going to be the end of me. "I'm trying to figure out why you're in here and he's still out there."

"He who? Be more specific."

"Don't screw around with me, Miss George, because I've got better things to do. You know damn well who I'm talking about—your cheating boyfriend."

That gave her pause, causing her to blink and lower her head. When she raised it again, her lips were balled up tight.

"I mean, you're in jail subsisting on the infamous Cook County cuisine while Janus is out there dining on steak... and lord knows what else..."

She exhaled, the corners of her mouth taking a downturn.

"Has he been by to apologize?"

She shifted in her chair but said nothing.

"At least put anything toward your commissary?" The whites of her eyes reddened and became glassy, though she wouldn't let me break her. But I knew something that would get her talking.

I stood up, turning my back to her as I walked to the window overlooking a courtyard and other parts of the facility. From my vantage point, I perused inmates huddled in small groups, trying to ward off the chill while enjoying the limited freedom and the fresh air. Many of them would be shipped off to serve out their sentences elsewhere. No doubt Nina would follow behind.

"Damn shame," I mumbled, as if distracted.

"What's that?" she asked, clearing her throat.

I paused for dramatic effect before turning my attention to her. "The crime is that a beautiful sister on the up-and-up should land in here with a bunch of lowlife knuckleheads. I mean, most of these folks haven't even finished high school." I looked down at my feet for a second, feigning embarrassment. "Hell, I barely made it out, myself. Geometry had me posted up in summer school before I could get my diploma."

I was lying but she didn't need to know that. I'd graduated with honors, a habit I continued while working on my first degree. I wanted to pay Nneka a compliment that went beyond her physical beauty—I also wanted her to assume she was smarter than me. "I'll bet school was a breeze for you, though."

"No, not exactly," she whispered.

"I don't know about *tha-at*," I half-sang, dragging out the last word so that it had an additional syllable. "Anybody who can plow through an MBA—especially since it involves a lot of math—is a superstar in my book."

When I looked directly at her, Nina's features had warmed a bit. "I had my own set of challenges," she informed me in what could become a soliloquy, if coached.

"We all do," I chimed. "For me, it was anything to do with numbers."

"And that was where I excelled," she stated with pride. "Long before my career afforded me a better quality of life, I found I had a talent for complex mathematics."

I cupped my hand to my face, rubbing downward to my chin. "And there I was, struggling over long division, while you were probably putting a new spin on the likes of Pythagoras, Brahmagupta, and all those other deep cats."

Her reverie faded for a moment and she slanted her eyes, perhaps suspecting I might be playing "country dumb" to gain her confidence. She would have been right.

"History was my strong suit," I said, making an effortless save. "I liked studying the great minds, the wars, and all that stuff. But it's hard to make a living observing the past."

"And yet, you do."

I leaned in, canting my head. "How so?"

"As an investigator, your job is to observe past actions and make sense of them."

I considered her point. "I guess you're right. So, the notes I took in Mr. Teller's class paid off, then."

"We shall soon see," she said, her eyes growing guarded again.

"Indeed. In keeping with that concept, I'm here to try my best to assemble this puzzle. I need your help to do it."

"There's no mystery here: I shot a cop."

"Yeah, I might be a bit daft, but that's pretty obvious. What I'm trying to figure out is why would someone so intelligent and on her grind—not to mention fine as hell—go from having no police record to...*this*?"

"Complex math," she said flatly, as if it was something over my head.

"Touché," I said with a slight bow of the head. "Not my strong suit. Break it down for me in terms I can understand."

"You know, I didn't intend to shoot you, Detective." It wasn't an apology, so much as a statement of fact. "You were standing between me and what I felt I had to do."

"And what was that?"

"I needed to show that arrogant bastard..." Her voice quavered with mucous and she cleared it away. "...needed to show him that he couldn't walk all over me again."

"And who's that?"

"Janus," she admitted with a cough, "The Superstar DJ and the thief of my heart."

The tears were welling up. I slid a hand into my pocket and produced a small package of facial tissues. I opened it and placed it on the table. Even with the restraints, she would be able to dab away the wetness and snot.

"We'd just made love before he was set to take the stage."

I nodded, and she continued, her voice sounding stronger.

"It was, well, it was very special. We were trying to make a baby," she said, raising her face and meeting my gaze. "It was special for me, I mean..." Her voice trailed off for a moment before she told me without a hint of weakness, "Well, it was. I was making love to him, and thinking about our future together, sending positive vibes for the union of our love, for a successful conception, our child." Then her voice changed, going low. "He was obviously just fucking me, like at the wild temple parties."

I tried to hide my surprise, not expecting her to be so

candid. I wasn't going to tell her that I'd already seen her on the video feed. "Temple parties?"

"Yes. The theater room was also known as the Temple of Ecstasy."

"What went on in there—besides what happened to Rayford, I mean."

"Well, you saw the setup with the bed as the central focus."

"Uh huh," I nodded. I didn't really need details on their freaky gatherings—I'd seen enough. "I know it's going to sound like an odd question but, was there anything ritualistic about those gatherings?"

"Let's just say there was pseudo-ritualistic sex magic being practiced. However, the only entity Janus worships is himself."

"What about the cameras?"

"Inside or outside?" "Both."

"Well, the ones in the temple were only turned on so he could watch the activities later."

"Did you watch with him?"

"Not my thing. But he would insist, especially on the rare occasion we were alone. The thrill of seeing other people getting it on got him excited."

"Were the cameras rolling when Rayford was killed?"

"How would I know that?"

"I mean, you already said he likes for you to watch with him. Maybe you two reviewed your handiwork."

She frowned and shook her head angrily. "I didn't like Rayford in the middle of my relationship, but that doesn't mean I would ever kill him!"

"Didn't stop you from shooting me," I yelled. I'd purposefully raised my voice, part was for dramatic effect, but part was fueled by the pain and trouble her bullet had caused. The door cracked open and the deputy peeked in. I waved him off.

"That wasn't my intention," she said. "How frank do you want me to be?"

I crossed my arms. "Let's just say your time for being cute is long gone. Give me one good reason why I shouldn't charge you with murder and let you rot your pretty ass off right in here?"

"Because I didn't do it."

I chuckled, shaking my head. "You'd better come harder than that, lady! Your freedom, and maybe your life is on the line. Janus told us you have a key to his house. Now, where were you on Sunday evening, February 21st?"

She frowned. "I already told you, I was at the club."

"Yeah, but you disappeared for a while, I hear," I said, keeping it purposefully vague, not disclosing that the camera feed from the club had pinpointed the exact 75 minutes she'd been gone. I was setting her up to catch her in a lie. An hour-and-fifteen minutes was more than enough time for her to make it to the house, commit the murder, and return to her job as if nothing had happened.

"I did step out for a little bit," she said. "But I never went toward Drexel."

"So says you. We're retrieving footage from the exterior cameras. Let me find out you went to your boss's house and crushed that dude's skull and I'll make it my mission to ensure you spend the rest of your life behind bars!"

"I DIDN'T KILL HIM!"

"Happy to hear it," I said without emotion. "However, I have a body in the morgue proving that *some*body did. Why *not* you? You have a key to the house and it's not like you and Rayford were friends or anything."

The fact that tears were trickling down her cheeks meant little to me. I'd seen suspects caught dead to rights, eyes leaking, swearing on the souls of their children that they didn't do the deed. They should've been happy the devil himself didn't show up to claim their kids behind those lies.

"I didn't appreciate the fact that I couldn't have Janus all to myself, but I wouldn't do anything to hurt Rayford."

I pulled up a chair and sat across from her, pressing my

lips against my fist, staring at her. I willed her to be honest with me.

"On Sunday evening, when things slowed down at the club, I left for a little while. I needed to make a run."

"Where'd you go?"

"To the drug store a few blocks over."

"The one on Damen?" I asked, to which she nodded. "That's like 8 blocks from Duality, so I assume you drove."

"No, I walked. I needed to get out for a while and think."

"But it was like minus 10 wind chill that night." "Don't mind the cold, as long as I'm bundled up." "I see. What did you need from the drugstore?" "Thermometer."

"Somebody sick?" I asked.

"No, but...is this really necessary?"

"There's over an hour of lost time—conveniently around the same time that the murder occurred." I put up my forefinger for emphasis. "You need to account for it or you're going to grow old behind bars. Imagine getting out fifty years from now, you'd be what? Over 80..."

"It was my break. I walked slowly. I've had a lot on my mind lately."

I left her hanging there with the silence.

"I just needed to take a little puff. Medicinal. For stress, Detective. Besides, I would've had to have been moving my ass off to get all the way across town if I'd..." She shook the idea out of her head. "But I didn't."

"Stranger things have happened," I acknowledged. She brought up a valid point, one I'd already addressed. The drive from Duality to the murder house was a good half hour by street without traffic. Still, there was time for it to have been done, had she hit the I-94 to get from 87th down to the 55th Street exit.

"Which store again?"

"White's Drugstore on the corner of 88th & Damen."

"Cash or charge?"

"Cash," she said.

"Where's the receipt?" I was rapid-firing questions,

wanting to see if she slipped or hesitated.

She didn't miss a beat. "In the purse I had with me that night—a brown Louis Vuitton knock-off. It's at my house."

"We'll check that out."

"I also bought a tin of mints," she added.

"Okay. What were you wearing that night, on your walk to the drugstore and back?" I asked.

"That's what people always want to know—'what were you wearing?'" she snapped.

I was confused. We weren't talking about assault here.

But maybe she was triggered.

"Okay, we'll come back to that. You were going to tell me about the thermometer..."

"It was in my locker on Friday when I took my temperature. Then when I went to use it on Saturday, it was missing. I thought I might have accidentally taken it home, but I only still had the one at home when I checked that night, so on Sunday when I had the chance, I went to White's to buy a new one. I figured I'd just misplaced it," she said, in a complicated explanation that left me confused.

"You take your temperature every day? Are you prone to infection or something?" I had to ask; maybe it was private information, but it could be relevant.

"Yeah, I take it twice a day and mark it on a graph. So when I couldn't find it in my locker, I needed to get a new one right away."

"You don't secure your locker?"

"Never needed to before," she said. "Thought I could trust the people I work with. But now that I think of it, the thermometer wasn't the only thing that went missing last weekend. I also lost a hat."

"Oh, really..." I prodded her to go on.

"We all wear black skullcaps, you know—knit beanies— with the Duality logo on the forehead. It's part of the uniform, actually. Mine wasn't in my locker at some point. I didn't pay it any attention at the time but now it's coming back to me."

I didn't tell her what I had found at the scene, dropped or discarded in the kitchen pantry, or that the crime lab was checking the hair inside for a DNA match. It could indicate her guilt, or not. Working in my favor, and maybe hers, was that a blood sample is taken as standard practice whenever an inmate is processed.

"So, when you walked to the drugstore..." I encouraged. "This again?" she sighed. "I was wearing my uniform from work, obviously: black pants and a black polo. I had on a sweatshirt, too. When I left for White's, I changed out of my shoes and put on my snow boots and of course I wore my coat, which is a beige faux fur, matching the boots. I also wore my red wool scarf and my red gloves. And earmuffs—which are white rabbit fur."

"No hat?" I asked flippantly and saw a funny look flicker across her face.

"No, but I would have worn it if I could have found it. That's why I had to wear the earmuffs."

"I'm sorry," I said, not following.

"Who wears real fur anything these days?" she said, rolling her eyes.

"Ever find your cap?"

"No. But they are all over the place. I just chalked it up to me misplacing it somewhere. I tossed on the hood from my coat and kept it moving."

"What about the thermometer?"

"This is really personal," she said.

"Yes, I know. I respect your privacy, but we need to get to the bottom of this."

She looked irritated. "Detective, this is really none of your b—"

"Like hell it ain't," I blurted, sliding my chair back and standing up. I pointed at her with a grimace. "You're going to tell me everything I need to know to either charge you or absolve you!"

"I didn't want to go into all this," she said with a sigh.

"I'm taking Clomid for… infertility, and you have to take your temperature. In fact, there's this whole complicated program you have to follow. When to take the pills, when to have the blood test, the ultrasound, when to have sex—especially when to have sex."

I paused, taken aback. This was uncharted territory for me. I filed the information she had just divulged into a compartment in my mind to be considered later at length and took a different tract. "Does anyone else have a reason to go into your locker?"

"No," she said quietly.

"Are there any cameras in the, no—*leading up to* the women's locker room?"

She shook her head. "The hallway behind the stage, which is where the locker rooms are located, is a blind zone. No cameras."

I stared at the table for a minute, then decided to tell her. "We found your beanie, Nina."

"Oh?" she was leery.

"Yes. It was at the scene. The scene of the murder…"

"Well, then it isn't my hat," she said, defiantly.

"Um, it appears that it is. It's got strands of your hair in it—preliminary results, but pretty damning."

"Circumstantial. My hat is not *me*."

"But can you explain how it got there?"

"How would I know? You're the detective!" she cried.

I threw up my hands, exasperated. "You might well be screwed, Nina!"

"No, I'm not," she said, defiantly. "I'll take responsibility for the bullet I put in your arm but I'll be damned if I'll go down for Rayford's murder!"

"We will check your alibi. Even if you can't find the receipt, the store should have a record, and probably camera footage, if true. Is there any other way to substantiate your claim that you stayed near the club during that time, and didn't go near the mansion? Did you grab something to eat, did you talk to anyone, did you run another errand that will put you anywhere but on Drexel on the night of Goodbody's demise?!" My voice was booming with anger, to which she became quiet and lowered her head.

"I wanted his baby. What's more, despite his cheating, I still do," she said after an extended silence. Her voice was somehow defeated, but not from my interrogation, I suspected. It was from heartbreak.

During the trial for the Tate-LaBianca murders, ladies from Manson's so-called "Family" were loyal to the point of shaving themselves bald and carving matching symbols into their foreheads to mimic their leader. They had already killed for Charlie and, even as their lives lay in the balance, they could think of nothing more than being with him.

I returned to my seat.

"Poor Rayford. If he could've had Janus's child, he would have. But, more than that, he just wanted to be acknowledged as more than a glorified valet." Nina's voice was monotone, as she recited her view of the love triangle, which had morphed into a trapezoid. "And he definitely didn't deserve to be killed off like he was nothing."

I would analyze the camera footage for the club parking lot. Even if it didn't cover the part of the lot where her car was parked, headlights leaving and coming back might be indicated. I would also pay a visit to White's Drugstore and have a talk with the clerk. Everything in Nina's demeanor told me she wasn't lying. If she never went further than eight blocks away from Duality that night, she couldn't have been the killer.

Then who was?

"I never knew about the white girl until the other night when…when…" She pointed at my arm, dropping her head in shame. "You see, I was happy that Janus was back in town to participate in my 'family-making' plan. I was excited that he would be here in Chicago on our most auspicious day to create a baby. He was excited too! Do you know what it feels like to be desired, Detective?"

It had been a long time since I'd been on anyone's romantic radar, but I knew the feeling of which she spoke. "Yes," I admitted with a nod.

"I was sad that Rayford was dead but I'm not going to lie: I was happy that he was no longer in the running."

"Until what?"

"Her."

"Shauna Bolduc?"

"Yes. *That* her."

She hissed, calling the other woman out by her name. She couldn't quite grasp that the real problem was not her boyfriend's latest plaything, but the man himself. Damn shame, too. Couldn't see the forest for the trees, nor the man for the son of a bitch he was. She could have done a lot better than that cockroach.

Though I had no doubt that Nneka George would have done just about anything to please Janus, I believed she had limits. I focused my mind's eye on the members of the trapezoid.

Rayford Goodbody, who was disowned for his sexual identity, even while being taken advantage of, was willing to accept halfhearted attention from a man who was proving he loved nobody but himself.

Nneka George had been the DJ's loyal booster for years but couldn't prove herself good enough. Though she possessed the physical part that Goodbody only wished he had, her willingness and efforts to carry Janus's heir didn't stop him from hedging his bets with Shauna Bolduc. I replayed how confident and carefree Nina had been, immediately post-coitus, before her new nemesis had strolled into the club.

I recollected the first time I'd seen Shauna. That chick was either a walking curse or a catalyst for bad shit to happen. Probably both.

The more I considered the Superstar DJ, the more I saw how everyone close to him fell like dominoes. Bandaged and deflated, the woman who sat across the table from me at the jail, seeming about as brainwashed as one of Manson's girls, still prayed to carry the producer's seed.

Her tile had already begun its descent, which would be complete if the murder rap fell on her.

I wondered if Janus had set her up. He was smart enough to be conveniently out of town when the crime was actually committed and therefore had not pulled the figurative trigger himself. I sure hoped the tech team could figure out how to break into that hard drive. I kept thinking that it had something to do with all this.

I asked again if the cameras in the Temple had been running. She shook her head. "No. He wanted to ensure there was no evidence of what happened there that night."

I seized upon this. "So, he knew. And so did *you*." I narrowed my eyes and stared at her. Just what was she trying to pull?

Nina's eyes betrayed her stone face. A trickle fell from her left eye. "Yes. He asked me to do it."

Though I knew what she was talking about—or thought I did—I needed her to be specific for the confession. "Do *what?*"

Her face softened and she gave me a twisted smile. "It's not going to be that easy for you, Detective."

I considered my next move. I could switch to "bad cop," and start shouting threats but it would undermine the rapport we'd built. I wondered if she wanted to tell me, but needed to be sure to entangle her ex.

"Do you know how long it's been," she asked, "since a man just sat and talked with me, valued my opinion?"

I relaxed, though I didn't know what she was getting at. "How long?"

She shook her head, furrowing her brow. "Longer than I care to remember. Definitely not in the time I was with Janus and his crazy circus."

"Damn shame."

"So, I wonder if you would do me a favor, Mr.

258

Brandywine."

"What's that, Miss George?"

"I'd like to pretend for a little while. I have nowhere to be and, from what it looks like, I won't be getting out of here for a long, long time. We could act like we're just two people, having a conversation. You're not a cop and I'm not an inmate."

"But you know…"

"I know full well what the reality is," she said, rattling the chain on her restraints for emphasis. "I also know that every incriminating thing I say may be used against me. I just want you to humor me for a while. Make me feel like you're just talking to me because you like Nneka George for the woman she could have been, had we met under different circumstances."

So, we talked. And I listened, really paying attention.

She told about a sexual assault she'd endured while in high school, and how it had affected her, in fact had totally derailed her for a while. She told about taking a bartending course while homeless, and a series of low-paying jobs until eventually getting hired on at Duality, and how that had made it possible for her to finally go to college. She told about dating Janus and about a miscarriage she'd had four years ago, how bad she'd felt, how hard it had been.

Then later, the trouble with conceiving again.

I know I showed genuine concern as I listened to her story, because I felt it. But more than that, I believed her—everything she said.

"Did he ever know?" I asked.

"Oh, he knew I'd had the miscarriage, sure; I think he was relieved—he wasn't ready to be a parent then. But I was. I doubt he noticed how much it affected me. Now he's getting older and he's ready. So when I realized I wasn't getting pregnant easily, I started seeing the fertility specialist right away—Dr. Bono. Though, I guess Janus took a different path towards ensuring ultimate success. Figuring I wouldn't be able to carry an heir to full term, he decided to diversify."

"That's where Shauna came into the picture, I take it?"

"Seems she's been there a lot longer, though for me, this was new information," she said, and then added, "New, and extremely unwelcome information. I've invested a lot into this relationship." She shrugged, as if to negate her feelings.

"Though he never invited her into bed with me, I'm starting to learn that she's been a factor for at least the past year—hanging around even more after her husband died some months back. Imagine this," she continued angrily, "after the constant competition with Rayford, after all the sexual theatrics in that orgy chamber…after helping him build and maintain his business empire, he betrays me with that fucking skank!"

"That's jacked up," I told her. Then, I reminisced the loss of a child I'd fathered with a woman—strategically left unnamed—that I'd loved very much at one time. I changed some of the details but ran down a sanitized version of my own experience, giving Nina a reason to trust me. I admitted that I knew about betrayal and that my heart had been left in pieces outside an all-night diner, when the woman I loved chose a drug addict who didn't care about her, instead of me.

"You have a sense of empathy and discretion I can appreciate. I just wanted to be treated like something other than a prisoner for a little while and you obliged me. Thank you, Detective. The amazing thing is how, even behind these bars and in these chains, I feel freer than I have in years."

"You've been through a lot, Nina. I think I understand where you're coming from."

She smiled. Tears ran down the beautiful brown of her cheeks and she nodded with gratitude. "Oh, how I wish I could have met someone like you years ago! You're a good man, Brandywine and I don't want to keep you waiting any longer. That's why I'm ready to give you my statement. I owe you that at least."

Her account of the details began with a phone call from Janus on the morning of Friday the 19th.

"I was still asleep; I almost always stay at the club till closing, so I was dog-tired. He insisted that I come out to the house. Said he wanted to talk to me about something in person and not over the phone."

"What did he tell you?"

"It's not just *what* he told me but *where*. I'll explain that in a minute, though. His eyes were red when I got there and I realized he was high as hell. He met me in the foyer and started telling me about how this was our chance to get rid of Goodbody. He was trying to shake the recent rumors about his wild parties and Rayford was being quite vocal about a supposed destination wedding being planned."

"Was that true?"

She exhaled and shook her head. "I'm understanding Janus says whatever sounds good at the time. Hell, he claimed that he was going to marry me, and I totally believed him!"

"Go on."

His scheme was half-baked, at best. According to her, the DJ told her about Rayford's injury and how he would be left behind at the Drexel house, creating the perfect opportunity for her to take care of the "problem". He ran all this down in the foyer, before any of his entourage had arrived to prepare the tour bus for departure. He'd spelled out a few details, instructions, which Nina related haphazardly. "The specifics don't matter, because I didn't do it," she assured me.

Even so, just the fact of this conversation, if true, meant we could get him for conspiracy to commit. That was almost as damnable as carrying out the murder himself.

"And he gave me a gun," she added.

I gasped, in spite of myself. "Not the revolver?" I managed.

"Yes, the same one I shot you with," she said, her voice

deadpan.

I let that dwell in silence for a minute, my arm suddenly aching worse than usual.

"He just handed you a piece. A firearm with the serial number scratched off, and you took it?" I shook my head, almost not knowing what to say. "Didn't you know that just having such a thing in your possession is illegal?"

"I do know a thing or two about guns, Detective. I didn't plan to use it."

"I sincerely wish you hadn't accepted it," I said.

She grimaced, and it was pretty clear that she agreed.

I got up from the table and walked back to the window just to give myself a break. It was snowing again. One inmate licked out her tongue. Initially, I thought it was at me, until I realized her attention was elsewhere. She was trying desperately to catch one of the clusters of snowflakes. Anything to make her forget whatever had landed her here where bars kept freedom out.

"So," I said, shifting away from the woman in the courtyard below, "was that the last time you talked to Janus before hearing about Goodbody's murder?"

"No. He phoned me twice on Saturday, from his Detroit hotel: once before his show, and then again after. So, late that afternoon he called, and it was a pretty short conversation. He just seemed to be feeling me out, asking what I was up to, that sort of thing. Of course, I was working. I was relieved that he seemed to have forgotten about his suggestion that I take Rayford out. Or so I thought. Late that same night he buzzed me again. That time, he was more direct, focusing on his plan, really trying to bully me into carrying it out. I flat out told him no, I'm not a killer."

"So, why didn't you call the police? You might've prevented Rayford's demise, you know—if you had alerted us..."

"Sure, right. That's the *first* thing I thought to do," she said, her voice dripping with sarcasm. Then, after a minute of silence, she acknowledged that she hadn't really taken him seriously. "I figured it was the coke talking. He says and does the weirdest stuff when he's been sniffing powder, only to come back later to say he was just kidding."

"Thin premise, Nina. I don't get why you thought he didn't mean for you to do it. Has he done this before? Was this something he did, pretend to make plans to have someone killed," I asked her, wishing I could cut through the crap and get to the truth.

"I just assumed we could get past it. I wouldn't do it, and Janus' attention would move on to something else. Actually, I was much more concerned that he make it back to Chicago for my most fertile day to try again. It never occurred to me that he would get someone else to do it..." Her voice trailed off.

"You know all this is just your word against his, right?"

"No," she said. "There's proof, if you know where to look. When you went to the house, did you notice the African mask on the wall?"

"Yeah. Nearly scared the shit outta me."

She chuckled. "It has that effect on people. He picked it up during an Afrobeat tour into Niger and Mali. Anyway, it represents a pair of twin gods called the Nummo. Janus loved the idea of there being two of them, since it related to his name and his two-faced nature."

"Okay," I half-growled, not giving a damn about the unnecessary exposition, "So, what about the mask?"

"Well, there are two buzzers that allow access to the house. The first lets guests into the foyer. He likes to leave them there for a minute. If there are two visitors or more, after being startled by the mask, they tend to run their mouths nervously. Well, according to Dogon legend, the mask brings the truth out and will allow a wish to be granted if you whisper into its mouth. Probably more bullshit Janus made up, but he believed it enough to have a voice-activated microphone installed. That was a few years ago."

"Does it still work?"

"Yep. It records to a hard drive on a computer that's gathering dust in a closet upstairs."

"Wow," I couldn't help but exclaim.

"How do you know so much about this piece of equipment," I asked, feigning that I knew nothing of the CPU, while in fact I had already reviewed all the files I could access.

"I set it up for him. I partitioned the hard drive into three different parts—Temple, Side door, and Foyer."

The police computer lab had found all three of the partitions, and the folder names matched the portable hard drive I'd looked at the previous night with Barbosa. The largest folder by far was labeled "Eros" and contained hours of partying and porn. The smaller drive only held a few sessions, but I had recognized each of the "three musketeers", Rayford, Janus, and Nina, in multiple scenes. In the section labeled "Tyche" were recent video files from the gangway door. The last partition, "Echo," presumably held audio files, but it had thus far alluded scrutiny—a click on that file prompted a password request that the others didn't.

"He loves gadgets and, though he's talented at mixing audio files, he doesn't waste his time fooling around with hard frame geeky stuff. He can pay people to do that part, but in this case, it had to be someone he trusted completely, which would be me. Trouble is," Nina said, her tone turning pensive, "upgrading to the latest electronic gadget is one thing, trading in a long-time committed lover for a newer model is grounds for losing that trust." She gave a long sigh, and sat there for a minute, looking down, her messy hair falling partially over her sad face.

"Why do you think he wanted that conversation recorded?" I offered. "I mean, if what you say is true, he obviously talked to you in that place intentionally.

It implicates him. Why would he purposefully create evidence that he conspired to commit murder?"

"You know, I've thought about that, and I can't say it's really that out of character for him. I mean, you know he's a narcissist. Hey, I love him—*loved* him, I mean—and I could easily see it. He is used to being in control and getting what he wants—the usual rules don't apply to him. So, bringing me over there and telling me what to do and how to do it, even handing me the weapon to use...it kind of goes along with his usual psychological gymnastics— wrapping up our shared destiny in order to placate me, something like that. I'm sure it never occurred to him that I would ever refuse—let alone, *betray* him," she said, and a sudden sob escaped her lips.

"And will you?" I prodded, after a moment. I had to catch her before she went inside herself, questioning whether or not her feelings for him had truly passed. Needed to grab her attention before she got distracted and pulled the mental equivalent of catching snowflakes with her figurative tongue. She could join her fellow inmates in that jail-house game after our interview, if she wished.

"Do you have the password to that computer drive?" I asked, watching her.

"I might," she replied, looking up with a crooked smile.

I looked straight at her and smiled back. We held that way for a moment, and I realized that something had changed. There would be no regrets; she was acting with intention.

"He sent me flowers, you know," she began. "Twice".

"Really?"

"Yeah, first in the hospital—a nice spring bouquet, and then I got a dozen red roses here in jail—bet that doesn't happen very often," she snorted, like a laugh.

"So, has he visited you yet?"

"Nope, but he did call. They let me talk to him for a few minutes, but it was all bullshit," she said. "Kept going on and on about what would he do without me, how he was going to get a hotshot lawyer for me, fight this with all his being, so he could have me back—*that* kind of BS. I know what he wanted me to tell him, but he didn't dare say it aloud."

"Which was?" I took the bait.

"The sign-on info for the backup online file storage."

"Online file storage?!" I blurted.

"Yes, um, not for the porn, of course, and not for the side door camera—who would have ever thought that would be important?—No, he liked those sneaky little audio clips of voices, he'd mix them into his productions sometimes, little snippets of someone saying 'The man's a maniac' or 'What the hell?'—both true examples of surreptitiously recorded bits he's used in his work."

"Wait, so what's to stop him from just erasing the recording in question?" My earlier elation had dissipated as I came to understand.

"Oh, I highly doubt he'll be able to access it. You see, for a while, I've been monitoring those files. I had my suspicions that there were others besides Rayford, and I thought I might catch him in the act, or at least, make myself feel better that Janus wasn't triple-timing me. After his last phone call on Saturday night—I don't know why— but I went online and changed the password for the audio-file access. And I know he can't reset it because it's my private email on the account."

My mind did a somersault. "Where is the information written down?"

She looked at me funny-like, and tried to raise her right arm, which was cuffed to the table. "In my head."

"And are you planning to share that information with me?" I asked with a grin.

"Detective, I'm giving it some serious consideration. I've had a few days, lying in the hospital, and then sitting here in jail, to think about how this all went down. I'm not going to go into how PISSED I am, but you can imagine. Cheating on me with that trailer trash and setting me up for murder! No way in *hell* I'm taking the fall for him—for *them*. I'm ready to spill. But first I want to talk to my lawyer. Get my best deal."

"How long are the audio files available?" I asked.

"The system refreshes itself after 30 days, but don't worry, I have a feeling it won't take that long." She gave me the name of the cloud storage company. All I needed now was the username and the password.

I couldn't write very well with my left hand, so I had the deputy come in and write everything down while I dictated. Nina corrected me, and the record a couple of times, and eventually she signed her statement. Once she was done, she seemed more at ease. She'd been led to believe she was just another piece of throwaway tech by the man she had wanted to spend her life with. And now, a jilted lover and an outdated bit of hardware were going to be that man's downfall. I emerged from Cook County Jail with a signed statement implicating Janus in conspiracy to commit murder. Nina wasn't looking to get out of whatever sentence the court threw at her for shooting me, but she wasn't about to go down for murdering poor Goodbody.

While waiting for my ride from the jail, I went into the office and scanned the sworn statement and attached it to an email to my captain with a copy to myself. But rather than sending it right away, I delayed it for a few hours to give myself a chance to get ahead of it.

I'd already reached out to Nina's defense attorney, who was on her way down to the jail to confer with her client. With a lot of luck, I'd have those sign-on credentials by the end of the day.

I had originally planned to swing by the precinct and see Kodjoe and Perry, but I was so exhausted and the pain in my arm was pretty intense, I just needed to get some relief. I hooked up with my ride and sunk into the backseat. With a clumsy left paw, I managed to text Barbosa and ask her to drop by White's Drugstore and also to let Cap and Sarge know that I'd be in touch later.

By the time I walked into my place, it was almost noon. I swallowed two pain pills, nibbled on some cold lasagna straight from the fridge, drank some milk from the carton, and took my ass to bed.

Chapter 11

Ping.
Ping.
Ping, ping.

The noise was like out-of-tune piano keys banged all at once by a wayward child. I imagined that kid to be a little boy, replete with a propeller on a primary colored beanie hat, a slingshot in his back pocket, and a mischievous smirk revealing a missing front tooth. I needed to change that sound. Though it was highly effective at waking me up from even the deadest of slumbers, it was the worst way to regain consciousness in a half-way good mood.

I growled as I rolled over, thankfully to my left.

It dawned on me that I'd been shot and was home recovering. Grateful I hadn't accidentally put my weight on the injury, I noticed that my arm was hurting a little less than earlier.

The irritating pinging was my phone announcing a series of text messages from Barbosa. The manager at White's had been very helpful, had put her in touch with their security company to review the cameras, and had been forthcoming with the name and contact info of the clerk who had worked on Sunday night. Before chasing down those leads, Barbosa verified that, according to the store's receipts, someone had made a cash purchase of a BBT thermometer and a tin of Altoid peppermints at 9:07 pm on the evening in question.

Just then, I got another message. This one was from the Nina's attorney. "UN: nommo1977," the text read, and then my phone repeated the noise. What followed was a long line of arbitrary symbols, numbers, and letters, some capital, others not. There were 20 characters in the password.

Nina had remembered that? She was right: she was a nerd.

Minutes later, I had my computer set up and the credentialing info typed in, (even with my inept left hand) and I was signed into the cloud account on the website. I was presented with a long listing of .wav files, each with a consecutive number.

I started from the top and, with a double click of the mouse, sounds and voices emitted through my earphones. I settled down to listen and take notes. For the next hour or so, I was like a fly on the wall, catching a random series of short activations illustrative of the general rhythms of the household on South Drexel Avenue. Folks coming and going, words being said, a few were people being buzzed in, which would begin with a short conversation... Many were obviously food or package deliveries. Others were business transactions, people coming for work.

Visitors announced themselves. I heard Mrs. Bilandic's voice a couple of times, replying to someone.

Right away, I was able to pick up on Nina's voice. She'd been there five times—twice for work, to pick something up or get something signed for the club, while two of the visits seemed more like dates, based on the nature of her conversation with Janus. The fifth, the most recent, was just the sound of her leaving. There hadn't been any activation when she'd arrived. It wasn't a perfect system.

I'd also isolated what I found to be Rayford Goodbody's voice, which wasn't difficult, but it was eerie. He was there often. Would come in the front door, let himself in with his key and announce himself loudly in song, accompanied with what sounded like dancing or jumping. What an exuberant young man he had been, so full of passion!

Mostly, Janus had been pleasant, sometimes even amorous, and would often spend quite a bit of time talking there in the foyer—knowing, of course, that he was being recorded—and assuming that Goodbody did not. But there were a few interactions when you could tell that the DJ was annoyed at the dancer. Like an alpha dog snarling at a lesser member of the pack, sometimes Janus didn't hold back on letting his irritation show.

Some activations were muffled and nearly silent. Quiet footsteps. No talking. I could only guess these were all Janus, or perhaps someone else who had a key and a reason to be there.

I got up from my chair and went out to the kitchen to get a drink of water and stretch for a bit, before getting right back to it. The next file's date stamp was Friday, February 19th. I took a deep breath, hovering with the cursor for a moment, then clicked.

She hadn't lied about her account of what her boyfriend had asked her to do. He kept sniffling as he laid out the plan and handed over the Saturday night special. At first, it sounded as if he had a cold, and then it occurred to me what Nina had said about him being high. He'd likely just done some lines of cocaine before calling her over. That could've very well been why he didn't consider the microphone recording the incriminating conversation.

I was becoming angry while hearing the talking asshole defecate a plot that would lead to a young man's death that weekend. When my head was clear, I would forward the files to my supervisor and suggest we get a voice analyst to get official verification on Janus. That would do for when this thing went to trial but I didn't need a specialist to identify the Superstar DJ as the conspirator.

Deep breaths, I told myself, inhaling through flared nostrils. *This guy destroyed lives.* I closed my eyes for just a moment. *Out through the mouth.*

When I got my thoughts together, I would have someone from the computer lab be sure Nina hadn't deleted anything that would identify her as the killer. I found other sound bites of food deliveries throughout that fateful weekend, but nothing else of interest. With the Temple being soundproofed, it wasn't a surprise there wasn't a single recording of the killing itself.

In through the nose.

I returned to the file that contained the order. Played it again. One phrase he'd said—and repeated it twice more during the conversation with Nina—"I know you'll come through for me. Baby, I know you love me," reminded me of something I'd heard earlier. I consulted my notes. He'd declared the same thing, word for word, to Rayford Goodbody just a week before he'd had him killed, but at that time, the topic had been changing the choreography for his upcoming concert tour, and not murder.

The sound of his voice grated my nerves into shreds. *And out through the mouth.*

I wanted to copy the file and send it to Cap but my only good hand was quivering so badly, I couldn't get a grip. My breaths were coming too quickly, bordering on hyperventilation. I couldn't see straight, nor could I think. I pushed my computer lid closed and jumped to my feet.

Chapter 12

I felt like I'd been sucker-punched in the snot locker and was seeing the world through a red, watery filter. Head full of steam, I grabbed my car keys and my phone, and bounded down the three flights to my truck, which waited where Jeri had parked it while I was still in the hospital. It didn't matter that the doctor had told me not to drive—I disregarded that order along with Kodjoe's request for an immediate update following my interview with Nina. He'd given explicit instructions that I was still on convalescent leave. My meeting with Nina was an exception, only because he knew she might talk to me—which was a good call.

I didn't disobey an order so much as temporarily sidestep it. The delayed email to Kodjoe with Nneka George's sworn statement was scheduled to send at 4 pm, meaning he would be getting it within the hour. I might still have a chance before that to confront Janus myself.

My arm was really acting up. The pain was excruciating; I let the agony fuel my rage as I put the truck in gear with no clue of where I was heading.

Fortunately, I had Barbosa on speed-dial.

"I need you to do me a favor," I barked into my phone, manhandling it with my left hand, driving with my elbow.

"What favor? And, where are you?" she wanted to know.

"How do you find Janus's whereabouts?"

Her voice was upset now, afraid. "He posts everything

on social media. Fans get constant updates—*why?!*"

"Is he still in town?!"

"Hold on," she said. "He's leaving for Kansas City in the morning. His house is still a crime scene, so he's probably holed up at the club."

Without a thought, I busted a U-turn to head the other way—and dropped my phone. I could hear Jeri yelling but couldn't make out anything she was saying. I hit my brakes at a stoplight and could see it down there on the floorboards between my feet but I couldn't reach it. When the light turned green, I hit the accelerator, causing the phone to slide backward and get stuck somewhere under my seat.

Dammit!

I had already crossed Ashland Street when I remembered I didn't have my piece—not even a holdout in my glove compartment. Figuring the Chevy wouldn't be driven while I was on the mend, Barbosa had moved that weapon back into my apartment. But I didn't have time to go back. I had to get to Duality before Kodjoe got Nina's statement and Jeri figured out what I was doing. Being hopped up on pain meds, maybe I wasn't thinking as clearly as I should have. It didn't occur to me that I might lose my job or get myself killed because, at that point, it no longer mattered. I was experiencing pure, unadulterated rage.

He was like a cancer. Maurice Bolduc's suicide was brought on by Janus's affair with Shauna; Rayford was murdered on his order; and Nina's life was ruined because she followed him blindly. Unlike King Midas, everything the DJ touched—except for music—turned to shit.

Horus answered the door to the club's rear entrance. "Your boss here?" I demanded, trying to push my way past him.

He squared up, blocking me. He was getting paid illegally but, unlike his brother, he didn't have any warrants. It emboldened him and I realized I was about to get into some serious trouble.

I peered over his massive shoulder, bugging my eyes and pointing with a look of surprise. "Aw, HELL nawl!" I hollered, causing him to fall for the oldest trick in the book.

It was just enough. Anybody attacking a human brick wall with the scowl and demeanor of a bulldog had to be out of his damn mind, which I guess I was.

But he didn't play chess and, at most, may have anticipated the punch to come from my right. I reversed my stance, launching my left into motion—the equivalent of an underrated L-shape attack from a knight—and put everything I had into the strike. The jab was quick, connecting to the sweet spot where his jaw met his neck, right below the ear.

I expected a harsh yelp of agony, but I'd underestimated the man named for the falcon-headed god. The bouncer shook it off and frowned in a way that couldn't be meaner. I was wrong to assume that his size would make him slow.

Never that.

His downward hammer strike came from the sky and blasted into my chest like a thunderclap. My knees buckled and I was suddenly a little kid who'd realized the gravity of what he'd gotten into. But it was far too late to take my ball and stomp my way back home.

What goes down must come up and he followed with an uppercut, aiming for my chin. I leaned back just enough to dodge it and felt a *WHOOSH* as his fist sailed toward the heavens. Had he connected, my head would've popped off like it was my sister's baby doll's. But I noticed that it threw him off balance, evoking my early training in Aikido.

There was no way I was going to beat the goon going toe-to-toe, so with my next move, I changed my strategy. No matter how strong an opponent, he can never build up enough muscle to soften a blow to his eyes, his throat, or his testicles. The eyes are the hardest to get because the enemy sees the attack coming. Likewise, the force of a throat punch can be lessened by a simple tucking of the chin.

That left the Land Down Under, aka the Nether Regions, colloquially known as "Deez Nuts." Done right, a light breeze can level even the biggest guy. I chose to use my knee like a gale force wind, ascending with enough thrust to relocate his balls into his chest cavity.

He doubled over and I brought down my good elbow like Thor's mighty hammer to the base of his skull, temporarily disabling the signal between his spine and brain. The result was like the felling of a redwood tree à la Paul Bunyan.

I only had a single pair of cuffs to arrest the DJ, not counting on tangling with anyone else. The chain had the standard three links, so there was no way I was getting both of Horus's hands behind his double-wide back.

Still, I'd be a fool to go up against the dude again at full strength, so I had to do something. I settled on putting one handcuff over his meaty right wrist and securing it to the belt loop behind his back. It would be hard for him to free his right, he could dislocate his shoulder trying, and I might be able to avoid his left.

I grabbed the unconscious bouncer's radio and ear piece, wiping off the latter before putting it to use. I heard nothing and saw no one when I stepped from the outside daylight into the darkened recesses of Duality. It was like a hero's journey to Hades.

* * *

With my heart rate at full tilt, my endorphins kicked into overdrive. That was good for the fact that it took some of the edge off my injured arm, but bad because, with my head beginning to swim, I was overwhelmed with the feeling I would vomit.

I hadn't thought anything out, charging in like a fool, my phone lodged under the car seat, no gun, and no backup. I briefly considered grabbing a bottle from the bar but let that impulse pass. With my arm all jacked up, the bottle could be broken and used against me.

Though Anubis had tried concealing it, I remembered the code to the backstage door from Thursday night and hoped it hadn't been changed. I put my ear to the door and listened. At first there was no sound, and I began to get nervous. Focusing, I could pick up a faint, percussive thump, played in rapid repetition. I wanted Janus to be alone, mixing tracks. With him distracted, maybe I could sneak up on him and...

...*And do WHAT, exactly*? I was already breaking and entering and had assaulted the bouncer in that effort.

My stomach lurched. I was in over my head but had gone too far to turn back. The code worked and the door swung open. I could hear a man's voice coming from the basement. Was he speaking to one of his staff in person or was he on the phone?

The basement door was ajar. The music stopped and I heard Janus curse. Was he working with a singer who wasn't getting the vocals right? Maybe it was an entire group of musicians in the booths and I would be outnumbered.

I gagged, almost going to a knee. Reminded me of my first time in a hot zone, with rounds whizzing past and ricocheting near my head. Letting fear paralyze me would make me a target and that was no good for anyone. I controlled my breathing and stood strong, ignoring the vertigo.

"Hey, Janus," I said, descending the staircase. The tall man was bent over the boards, no doubt working on his next hit. If he didn't cooperate, his next big hit would come from my fist.

"*Who the*—motherfucker, how'd *you* get in here?"

"Who's that," Shauna Bolduc asked.

Janus's hair was an unkempt, half-braided mass and he hadn't shaven in at least a couple days. He wore a tanktop and sweatpants, looking very different from his public persona. Shauna wore a pink matching bra and panties set, her thighs spread on top of a mirrored table. On the glass surface were several white lines sitting just shy of her crotch, waiting to be snorted.

"You ever have cockroaches, baby?"

She looked puzzled, more concerned with what I was going to do than what her lover was rambling about.

"They scurry around, getting into *every damn thang*. Put out traps and they'll avoid them. Spray poison and they eventually become immune to that shit. Try moving to another house and them sons-a-bitches want to go along for the ride. That's what Brandywine is: a goddamn cockroach! What're your nasty little antennas sniffin' out now, boy?"

"You know why I'm here," I informed him.

He ignored me. "Speaking of sniffin' stuff, how about you do some of those lines right there, while I work on these beats? I guarantee the pot o' gold at the end of *that* rainbow is worth the price of admission!"

"Baby," she said in complaint.

"Shut up, bitch! If my man wants to get a whiff o' that sweet thang, you're gonna give it to him, understand?!"

She looked baffled, probably thinking that once she had him to herself, things would be different. Her infidelity prompted her husband's death. She'd left that boring, predictable existence to bet her life and heart on a drug-addled sex fiend who loved no one but himself.

In domestic disputes, most officers tend to focus on the man as the primary aggressor, forgetting how dangerous the woman can be. Not me, and not this woman. She'd jumped up off the table, knocking over her drink; its thick green liquid quickly spread across the table, absorbing the China White.

"Shauna, you stay where you are," I bellowed at her. "Janus, you're coming with me."

"You ain't runnin' shit around here, nigga," he said with disdain. "What, you think that just because you got that bubblegum machine badge, I'm s'posed to be afraid of your ass? Fool, I grew up in the Wild Hundreds *long* before my family settled in Bronzeville!"

I looked about the room to see what potential weapons were available to the two of us. The keyboard, though portable, would be too clumsy for me to pick up and swing with one arm. There were two woodwind instruments: one was a full-size clarinet, propped up on a stand; the other was an old-fashioned wooden piccolo, barely a foot in length. I ignored the little flute and studied the clarinet for a moment, with its smooth, hard frame and the various intricate metallic parts. And finally, sitting on its pedestal in front of the turntable setup, was Shauna's snow globe, it's platinum flakes sparkling.

"James Delbert Porter, Jr., you are under arrest for conspiracy to commit murder. You have the right to remain silent…"

"There you go, using my government name," Janus protested. He had grown agitated, rocking back and forth, his eyes feral in his coked-out state. "And I'll NEVER be silent, muhfuckah," he yelled.

"You have the right to an attorney…"

"Yeah, my lawyer gonna sue you and your candy-ass police department!"

"…one will be provided to you…"

For such a tall man, he moved quickly. Unlike Horus, Janus had a reach and made a lunge for me.

"Get him, baby!" his trailer-park queen shouted.

I blocked his left, weaving to the side, but in doing so, had pivoted into a bad spot. My back was to the soundboard, giving me limited range of movement. I tried kneeing him in his groin as I had the bouncer, but the DJ expected that.

"Faggots always go for the part that fascinates them most," he said with a wicked laugh. "Did you see something the other night that made you wanna come back? Bitch ass!"

I said nothing, realigning myself so I could deliver blows

with my left. He sidestepped the first and was grazed across the cheek with the next.

When he took on a boxer's stance, I knew I was in trouble. His flurry came fast and didn't have my usual stellar reactions. I took a couple of hits to the ribs before he focused in on my injured arm.

Confident and cruel, he bladed his body, loaded, and put his full force behind the punch. The agony manifested in a blinding flash of raw intensity. I howled like a beast and went down on my knees.

He was strong. Both his hands formed a vice around my throat, and he lifted me to my feet, pushing me back up against the mixing table. A maniacal grin graced his face, and one eye squinted with the pleasure of strangling me to death. I could hear Shauna Bolduc in the background, cheering him on.

Through the pain, I tried wrapping my good hand around his wrist, but it did nothing to stop his chokehold. My eyes were bugging out. I wished I would have called Perry or told Barbosa where I was heading. Both of them would have tried to talk me out of doing something this stupid.

It is said that words, as compared to sticks and stones, can never hurt, though I would beg to differ. He clearly had the upper hand—the inability to take in air was weakening me. But it was my would-be murderer voicing his intention of what he wanted to do to me before hearing my death rattle that impacted me most. His attack and her jeering him on, the room spinning, and my eyes feeling as if they would pop out of their sockets were the hurricane. Janus craned his head, assured of his victory, and whispered to me with snarled lips. I had begun to see colorful spots and was fighting to maintain consciousness, but his hot stinking breath in my ear, the droplets of spittle on my cheek were as vivid as his phallic tongue trying to violate my ear canal.

Shauna came closer, wanting to bear witness to the

depravity. She'd already watched her husband's gruesome suicide, so why not this, too?

I felt the knobs of the mixing table digging into my back. His eyes were reddened slits, his grin as wide as the gateway to Hell. He planned to do some digging of his own.

No! *Fuck no, in fact.*

My desire to live was stronger than his ironclad grip.

With my oxygen deprivation, it took tremendous focus for me to stop my legs from flailing and bring my knees to my chest, but I did. Had he figured out what I was about to do, the larger man could have timed it right to pick me up and slam me onto the soundboard.

But he didn't see it coming.

I reeled back and, because leg muscles are always stronger than arms, fired both lower limbs in a succession of kicks, until his grasp weakened. Then I dipped my chin and turned my head to one side, freeing me from the choke. He couldn't hold on.

I was going to roll off the table and put my feet on the floor but he came back too fast, pinning me on the horizontal surface, and proceeding to savagely pound on my wounded arm. This time, I turned onto my side, loaded, and launched the ball of my right foot at an upward angle. There was a hollow, wet implosion and his charge stopped like someone had slammed on the brake. His body crumpled to the floor and his hands went to his throat, attention riveted on his own inability to breathe.

The strike had crushed his windpipe and no air was getting through. For a moment, I marveled at the big man, scissoring his legs and spinning with wide, panicked eyes.

Springing up from the board, I demanded that he hold still, which didn't register with him at all. His face had begun to turn about as blue as his brown skin would allow.

Later on, my written report would reflect that it was necessary to render the subject unconscious, so I could perform a lifesaving maneuver. Using my elbow, I issued a sharp blow, propelling his chin upward, and causing the brain to jar in his oversized head. Janus ceased all movement.

Shauna's barrage of screams and scratches were a surprise, as I'd all but forgotten she was there. I suppose it looked like I'd killed her lover but, in her quest to defend, she was actually keeping me from helping him.

My openhanded palm strike caught both of us off guard. As I'd been trained, the focus of the hit was beyond the target itself, causing her nose to cave in with a soft crunch of cartilage and bone—she now had a red geyser of her own to worry about.

Arms and legs flailing, the scantily clad widow/mistress was out of the equation, and I was able to concentrate on facilitating the DJ's breathing.

Articulation is the name of the game. Sensei Donald's wise countenance popped into my head from way back when I was a freshman in high school. I was getting bullied, and my mom had enrolled me in dojo lessons.

Sensei taught a martial arts hybrid based primarily on Karate. Under the auspices of self-defense, I'd learned the move I was prepared to use on the suffocating celebrity. With Janus lying on his back, throat exposed, I raised my left hand, and intertwined my pointer and middle fingers. In a violent, downward stroke, my fingers penetrated his skin. I dug in, turning to one side, ripping away anything that would hinder his breathing until I felt a soft pop.

With my hand thus encountering the DJ's trachea, I cast about nearby for something to maintain adequate airflow—a drinking straw, a ballpoint pen, even an aquarium hose would work... My gaze slid over to the small musical instrument lying casually on the musical score sheet within reach. As ridiculous as it was, the size was correct. I jammed the tapered mouth end of the wooden pipe into the man's throat and was rewarded with an immediate *pssst!* as patency was established.

From there, he tooted and squeaked with each respiration. Sounded foolish, but damn it, he was alive.

With a bit of duct tape, I was able to jerry rig the makeshift airway. I was glad I could get my right hand to work, along with my teeth, to rip off the tape, but it was agony to do so. I used the rest of the tape to secure his wrists and ankles. Did the same to Shauna.

Completely deflated of energy, I found a spot on the wall that faced the stairway and slid down to the floor. At least I would be able to see anything coming, even if I could no longer fight.

* * *

Turns out, my initial opponent wound up being an asset. When Horus regained consciousness, he took off running toward the nearest service station. A couple of patrolmen spotted the huge, half-cuffed, bulldog-faced linebacker yelling and charging up the street, and decided to investigate. He told them that a crazy pig had raided Duality and was tearing up the place.

I didn't hold it against the bouncer that he'd called me a pig or that he had tried blocking my entrance in the first place. He was just doing his job. I told the responding officers that I'd mistaken him for someone else. I listed the brawly man in my report as a witness instead of a suspect.

Anubis thanked me later when he came to retrieve his brother. "Our mama woulda *killed* us," he exclaimed.

"Get your records clean," I told the twins. "If I ever leave CPD to start my own detective agency, I'd like to hire you two dudes as muscle."

They looked at each other and smiled.

"Paid *above* the table, though," I added, making them frown for a moment before hunching their shoulders in acceptance.

When the smoke had cleared, I got my phone out from under the seat and texted Jeri, who was working a zone too far away for her to come over. She was understandably pissed—but also relieved. I called Perry and told him I would explain everything later on.

Captain Kodjoe was furious when he arrived on scene.

At least he said he was, which meant he had to keep up appearances.

"I'm going to send a car to your house to pick you up tomorrow morning at nine. You can give your statement, then go back home to convalesce and hopefully stay out of trouble." He paused. "One question, though."

"What's that, sir?"

"Did you kick his smug ass?"

"I'm the one talking and he's the one blowing a tune."

"What does *that* mean, Detective?"

I thumbed over my shoulder at the gurney where the strapped-in suspect waited for the paramedics to load him into the ambulance. The head of the stretcher was elevated, and I caught the moment when the renowned DJ saw me standing there. Right away, his erratic breathing sped up— squeaking in and out, in and out, in some kind of off-key melody. One of the EMT's bumped the side of the gurney, and Janus cried out in protest or pain. Sounded like a broken C-minor note.

I could barely stifle a giggle.

Epilogue

The next day, we had a meeting, just the four of us. We spent a lot of time on my actions of the day before, and while the captain was certainly wearing team pride, he also kept up a constant refrain of caution, admonishing me while reminding Perry and Barbosa that I had been lucky this time. He wagged his finger in a paternal gesture and insisted that they never, ever take such stupid risks.

I turned all my information over to my partners, and we agreed to do a weekly check-in on the two related cases while I continued my recovery at home.

There was a knock on the door. With our supervisor's permission, a uniformed officer came in, handed Kodjoe a piece of paper, and dismissed himself. At a glance I recognized the document to be a forensics result.

"Excuse me, detectives. Just a moment."

Barbosa grinned at the subtle mention of her apparent elevation to investigator's status, albeit temporary. Sarge caught it, nodding as he gave me a nudge, as if he knew it was a sign of things to come.

We waited as Kodjoe perused the fine print on the paper, his face impassive.

He looked up and smiled, passing me the doc.

The report was on the smaller vomit spot from the murder scene. It consisted primarily of green leafy vegetable matter, along with pineapple, yogurt and banana. I didn't recall any of those ingredients present in the fridge or in the trash. Which could mean that it was upchuck from the perp.

And then I read further down the form. While the larger puke puddle's DNA had matched the victim's, the genetic findings from the green vomit matched nothing else found around the house. The document stated that the cookie tosser was definitely female. The last line reinforced that this was a preliminary report.

Reading it from over my shoulder, Jeri let out a loud yelp, and I turned to her with a grin.

"You called it, Barbosa!"

"Lemme see that," said Perry, and I handed it over. "You owe me," she said, pointing proudly at me.

To that, I nodded. At this point, she could have anything she wanted without a shred of protest from Yours Truly.

"Good work," Cap added, "Now, ma'am, would you be so kind as to wheelbarrow this cripple home?" He was smiling.

"Gladly."

We all got up, Jeri to get the car and Perry to follow me out.

"I advised Officer Barbosa to stop by Maxwell Street, so you can get that Polish sausage you've been wanting," our boss said. He shelled out several bills from his wallet. "My treat."

I smiled and gingerly shook his hand. Kodjoe was a good man, even if he didn't know about all the places on the South Side that used the same recipe. The actual Maxwell Street district was too far out of the way from where I lived and I didn't want to wait that long.

With several weeks of convalescent leave ahead of me, I was going to do my best to enjoy it. I was heading out of the precinct, people fist-bumping my uninjured left hand. I was no longer the upstart junior detective and had gained the respect of the old heads, of which Perry was the de facto leader.

"I'll walk you down," Sarge insisted.

We got into the elevator and I looked up at him.

He'd gotten rid of the stubbly beard, but kept that furry caterpillar of a mustache. I thought to make some snide remark but decided to go another route. "Man, thanks again for coming by the hospital to check on me. And sorry for you having to come back early from vacation to do it."

"No problem, kid. Just keep your butt outta trouble over the next few weeks. We'll need you in one piece and ready to work as soon as the doctor clears you."

"Why are you escorting me to the car? It's my arm that's injured, not my legs, grunt!"

"There was something I wanted to tell you, but now you caused me to forget, ya piss-pants puddle pirate!"

"That's your maturity kicking in—memory's the first to go."

He scratched his big head. "You're probably right—*oh*, I know what it was." He reached into his shirt pocket and produced a couple of slips of card stock.

"What's this?"

"Read 'em. Or does the sailor have too much water on the brain to figure it out?"

"Eve's Nocturne?"

"Yep. It's a swanky spot up north. They play the music that matters, primarily Smooth Jazz, but they also do Blues, and Classic R&B."

"No Country, though, right?"

He laughed. "We'll save that for another time. I'll get you out for some line dancing at the honky-tonk with me one night."

"Only after you go see Wu Tang with me."

The dumbfounded look on his mug made me smile. "I'm not really into Kung-Fu flicks," he admitted, scratching the stubble on his square chin.

I wasn't even going to try to explain the finer points of the RZA, Meth, or ODB of the Wu Tang Clan—it'd be too much like casting pearls to swine. I ignored his statement, held up the tickets, and asked, "What are these for, anyway?"

"Ummm, let's just call them a get-your-narrow-ass- well-soon present. You and your new lady friend can go out on the town and enjoy."

"But we're not dating," I insisted.

He grinned, knowingly. The names of rappers and Hip Hop groups may have easily flown over his head but Sarge was far from a fool. He knew things I had yet to figure out. "Not yet, but she likes you a lot."

I gave it some thought, considering how Jeri had spent so much time posted up near my hospital bed. That'd been mighty sweet of her. "Who's playing the club?"

"Local outfit: Christopher D'Andre & Friends. He's one of the baddest and best drummers I've ever seen. Plays, tours, and records with some legends, too. You'll dig him."

"Dig? You a hippie, now?"

"Ah, shut your friggin' pie hole. Go home and chill the hell out. Ask Barbosa if she's busy tonight; Take her out on a proper d—"

"She doesn't date coworkers," I interrupted. "...Outing, then. Shit, soiree, if you'd like. Don't call it a date but treat her nicely. Believe me, I know—she has really been there for you. Whether or not it leads to something else, you've got a good friend in her.

"Thanks, Sarge."

"Nothin' to it, kid. Hey, there's your ride," he said, as a police cruiser rolled to a stop. "Got work to do. I'll holler atcha later."

"Detective Brandywine," Jeri said through the open car window.

"Good afternoon, Officer Barbosa." "Heading out to Maxwell Street, right?"

"I know someplace closer that does it up just as well." She glanced at her watch. "Isn't it kind of early for Polish sausage?"

"It's *never* too early."

I climbed into the front seat and, with a bit of effort,

buckled up. The cage between the front and back seats didn't grant much room to extend my long legs, but I would manage.

I didn't initially notice the velvet sack sitting on the middle armrest. She was beaming ear to ear, her eyes darting to the bag, then back to me. I was a bit slow on the uptake. "Something for me?"

Her smile got brighter. I picked it up and pulled out what was inside. It was a hat.

"Now that you're a big-time investigator, you should look the part."

"This is a nice fedora, Jeri." I turned it over in my hand, checking out the colorful feather stuck into the band.

"It's a trilby, actually. Got it in dark gray, so it would match up with most of your suits. See if it'll fit on that oversized head of yours."

I chuckled, dropping the visor so I could see it in the mirror. It did look good on me. Perfect offset for the fact that I preferred wearing high-top sneakers and casual kicks instead of dress shoes. Pulling the narrow brim forward, I dipped the hat rakishly to the right.

"Thanks, partner."

She didn't look in my direction, just put the car in gear. But I could see she was still beaming.

As we drove out of the lot, I gave some thought to leaning across the center console and planting a kiss on her cheek. She might actually turn to me and allow our lips to lock. But it would be unprofessional for two cops to be seen making out in a police unit. As cool as my supervisor could be, I doubt he'd be able to let that slide.

I wanted to regret that we were coworkers instead of lovers but knew I was lucky for the chance to work with and get to know her. She'd held me when I was bleeding and was nursing me back to health. There was no doubt it was more than just a professional friendship brewing between us.

I perused the streets of my hometown as they slid

by the window, the blacktop slick with a chilly March rain. Citizens rushed to and fro, their colorful umbrellas standing out against the dull gray of the sky and the neighborhood's architecture. Warmer weather was on its way and the crime rate was sure to rise with the temperature. Once the doctor declared me fit for full duty, I'd be right back in the shit, high-top sneakers, fedora--no, *trilby*—and all.

I turned and gazed at my driver. For the time being, I would just sit back, listen to the music, and enjoy the ride.

As a kid, I thought that all the songs I heard on the radio were being performed live. In my head, I could see the disc jockey call out the name of the band, then point to them as they fired up their instruments. Of course, by the time I was a teen, that notion was utterly ridiculous. I had become infatuated with girls and was going through all the angst and raging hormones that came with that stage of development. About then, I began to notice that, more often than not, the roulette wheel would spin and land on the soundtrack to my current situation.

The gritty salvo that kicked off the next cut caught my attention and made me sit up in my seat. The Night Tripper's hoodoo-inflected N'awlins Funk was unmistakable from the start. The soaring horns juxtaposed perfectly against a steady groove of bass guitar, drum, and a sizzling cymbal that whispered conspiratorially, like a back-alley home girl about to reveal one of life's freakier little secrets.

Just as I envisioned a younger version of myself ducking off into a gangway to make out with the likes of Barbosa, Dr. John's gravelly, almost cantankerous, baritone began his sermon.

"Shit yeah!" Jeri exclaimed, shaking me from my reverie.

I thought to remind her about her cutting back on the profanity, just to be a smart ass.

"What's up?"

"I friggin' *love* this song," she said gleefully, pointing at the radio.

Why, but of course she did, I thought sarcastically. After all, the selection described my situation almost prophetically.

I dialed back my surging hormones a couple notches.

Jerilyn Barbosa was a law enforcement professional, despite her good looks and my obvious attraction to her. She would likely continue to look after me during my recovery but that's just what partners did. No matter how much I would have enjoyed it, she was not going to show up one night rocking a short-skirted French maid's outfit and bright red lipstick. She was proving to be an excellent cop and a damn good friend—without benefits. With a career to consider, she was not going to risk becoming the subject of petty locker room talk.

I respected her for that.

She was bopping to the rhythm and, though she'd forgotten half the lyrics, she made up for it by singing the ones she remembered loud and off-key. She didn't give a damn what I thought, either.

Her hair was pulled back into a modest bun, which was a styling norm for female officers in uniform. However, one dark brown lock had somehow gotten a mind of its own, falling just below the ear, caressing her cheek. Her forehead had begun to bead with perspiration, and she was lovely.

I considered the song's title: "Right Place, Wrong Time." Though in many ways, it was the story of my love life, I wouldn't even attempt to add my cracked vocals to Jeri's tone-deaf delivery. We would sound like two harmonically impaired alley cats caterwauling at the moon. I would just leave the vocalizing to the good doctor, who couldn't have sung it any better.

THE END

DonMiskel.
wordpress.com

HustleLogic.
video.blog

Lation.org/JaySchleidt

Don Miskel is a writer, blogger, and screenwriter with a military, police, and security background. The first in the Detective Brandywine series, *The Chicago Trilogy* is the author's second published novel, following a horror outing called *Dead Assets*. He has also contributed to several anthologies—*Sins of Time, Darkly Never After,* and multiple *Writers' Anarchy* titles. Don wrote this book as something of a love letter to his hometown. As with his titular character, Don is a native of Chicago. He lives in Virginia, where he is busy working on subsequent Brandywine novels.

Jay Schleidt, multi-faceted artist, created the Brandywine logo as well as the Transition Squared Press logo. Known for his amazing collages, cat artwork, zines, and creative packaging, Jay's diverse body of work spans visual, sound, and performance art. He is a valuable part of the Iowa City local artists community.

Benjamin Mackey has been working as a freelance illustrator for various books, magazines, and films for nearly a decade. He received his Bachelor of Fine Arts in Painting from the University of Iowa. He is the co-creator and illustrator of the comic series, *SAINTS* from Image Comics. He lives in Arizona and enjoys a damn fine cup of coffee.

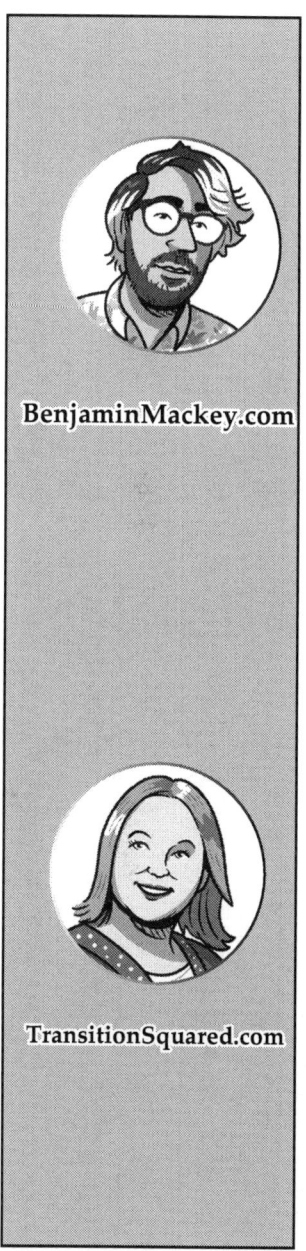

BenjaminMackey.com

After a long career in critical care and emergency nursing, **Pamela Murray** spent many years as an ex-pat trailing spouse in Tokyo and Shanghai. A fiction writer, she taught herself website design and became a certified professional editor. She greatly appreciates Don for trusting her with his precious manuscript for this, the first complete editing, designing, and publishing product of her solo endeavor **Transition Squared Press.**

TransitionSquared.com

Acknowledgements

I remember perusing the liner notes from Sting's first album apart from the Police, *The Dream of the Blue Turtles*. In the acknowledgements section, he revealed that a solo project is anything but; he was right. It takes a host of others, from those taking care of administrative stuff, to the beta readers, to the cheerleaders, to see such a thing to fruition. Though the writing credit to the novel is mine, there is no way I could have done this by myself. First and foremost, I want to thank my book producer, Pamela. She is as phenomenal as she is meticulous—two great attributes for a friend and editor to possess.

A special shout-out goes to Kellz Brandywine, so nicknamed because of her fierce loyalty to the notion of my detective character finally seeing the light of day. Imagine presenting other literary projects to someone who has read most of the things on which you've worked, only for them to continually refer back to a certain unfinished novel. Well, that would be Kellz. Many moons of gratitude for sticking to your guns. I hope the end result is to your liking.

Gracias to Nike and Pat who kept telling me I could and ensuring I did. Thanks to Jeff, Lamont, and Kevin (aka, "Slippy") for technical advice and quality assurance. Thanks also to beta readers Jonah, Joe, and Donald Sr. A bow to Xavier, for allowing his physical likeness to be used for my titular detective. My hat is off to Ben, for his expert artistic rendering, and to Jay, for the wonderful logo design. To each friend, family member, and fan who constantly asked, "So, when's the next book coming out?" your patience is greatly appreciated.

Lastly, I would like to thank each reader of this, the initial run of what will become an ongoing series featuring Brandy and other characters that inhabit his universe.

A storyteller has nothing if not an audience for whom to spin his yarn. My fierce desire is to release a quality product that will leave you wanting more. Feel free to let me know how I did. Share your thoughts by messaging me at: **Info@DonMiskel.com**

Or find me on Facebook at **Don Miskel: Author**

Do you know about the short stories associated with Brandywine's world?

- Don Miskel's "Close Call" is free for the asking. Send Don a note at: Info@DonMiskel.com and put "Close Call" in the subject line.
- "Everyday Heroes", written by Don Miskel and Pamela Murray, was published in the anthology Writer's Anarchy III: Heroes & Villians, and is available for purchase on Amazon.
- Would you like to be notified when we republish "Everyday Heroes" as a stand alone short story? Write to Info@DonMiskel.com with "Everyday Heroes" in the subject line, and follow Don on social media.

©Jay Schleidt

Made in the USA
Lexington, KY
17 November 2019